HOW I LOST THE WAR

FILIPPO BOLOGNA

HOW I LOST THE WAR

Translated from the Italian
by Howard Curtis

PUSHKIN PRESS

English translation © Howard Curtis 2011

First published in Italian in 2009 as
Come ho perso la guerra © Fandango Libri s.r.l

This edition first published in 2011 by
Pushkin Press
12 Chester Terrace
London N1 4ND

British Library Cataloguing in Publication Data:
A catalogue record for this book is available
from the British Library

ISBN 978 1 906548 36 0

Cover Illustration: *Hot Springs in Italy* Roland Gerth
© Roland Gerth Corbis

Frontispiece: *Filippo Bologna*
Courtesy of Fandango

Set in 11 on 14 Monotype Baskerville
and printed in Great Britain on Munken 80 gr
by MPG Book Group

www.pushkinpress.com

Negritude begins at the Ombrone River
Luciano Bianciardi

A DOG HAD ENDED UP INSIDE.

They had heard it barking for days. Weeks. A heart-rending moan, coming from under the ground. A sound so desperate, it made the night all the colder. It sounded like the weeping of a child walled up in a barrel. Gradually, the barking had grown weaker, until it was almost imperceptible, then had ceased altogether. The old men with faces as cracked as old pottery, cigarettes stuck in the sides of their mouths and ties worn only on Sunday, would say *the pit*. And they would say it as if uttering a magic word.

A geologist, a small man no bigger than a sparrow, had hauled himself down into it with ropes. He had got to a certain point, then had come up again and said it was impossible to go any further. So they had thrown in a kind of saffron-coloured sulphur powder used as a reactant. There were those who could have sworn blind that the whole of the following day the water from the Ficoncella and Doccia della Testa springs had come out yellow. But there were also those who could have sworn blind that none of this was true.

To get there, you have to climb a road that was asphalted about twenty years ago, though I remember when it was still just rubble. It winds through the scrub, sometimes in wide curves, sometimes in tight bends, like the hem of a quilt, and keeps climbing steadily, never pausing for breath. Where the slope is at its steepest, near the big water tank that serves the village during periods of drought, it takes a sharp turn to the right. At first, the

9

tank was one of our strategic targets, but then we thought
better of it, because even if we'd tampered with it, the spa
would still have had water, lukewarm water, admittedly,
but water nevertheless. And the only ones to lose out
would have been the poor devils still living down in the
village, with the boilers hissing madly in the cellars like old
people with emphysema. In front of the cabin belonging
to the road- works company, the red one at the side of
the road, there's a small open space where you can leave
your car. Then you can continue on foot. In fact, you
have to. You go along a narrow path full of pools and
puddles that leads into the woods. The path cuts through
a clearing pockmarked with large stones that peek out
from the grass like fragments of a meteorite that shattered
to pieces millions of years ago. You pass what's left of an
old kiln, of which only the outer walls remain, overrun
with brambles. The surface of the path is a bed of dried
leaves that crackle underfoot. The path descends along the
bank of a dried-up stream filled with crushed stones like
the ribs of a fossil. The oak trees crowd in on either side.
The branches of the trees intertwine, reaching up into the
sky in a great weave of wood and leaves that swallows the
light. The juniper bushes give off an intoxicating scent that
seeps into the brain and reawakens lost memories. Every
now and again the undergrowth rustles. A snake or a lizard
slithering behind a rock. Or perhaps a rat. But nothing to
be afraid of. You come to a clearing with a large beech
tree in the middle. It's been there for hundreds of years,
and has a misshapen trunk which even five men forming
a chain would not be able to embrace. It has grown all
twisted on that shelf of land, next to a spring. The roots
are excrescences covered with moss, exposed nerves that
reach down, sinking into the water and the earth. It seems

like the ideal place for a witches' Sabbath. You can almost see the moon high in the sky and the figures of women dancing naked around the beech tree in the flickering light of a bonfire. Halfway along, the path rears up towards the ridge. The tracks of boar and roe deer show you the way. The trunks of the trees are peeled and muddied up to a height of a metre from the ground—the boar roll around in the muddy pools and then clean themselves by rubbing against the bark until it is worn down to the tender sapwood. Once you get to the top of the hill, you can stop and catch your breath. It seems to be a clearing like any other. But it isn't. Not many people know this place. No one knows—and those who do know don't want to— what's beyond it. Where your steps are slowed to a trudge, where even light doesn't penetrate.

All you can do now is make your way between the thorns and nettles that watch over this place like guardians of a ruined temple.

Rocks and loose earth all around. And in the middle, a hole.

You see me the way I am now

Y OU SEE ME the way I am now, but my grandfather whipped the peasants. Although I can't really see it myself. I still have a photograph in my wallet, a photograph of a distant time, long before things started the way they started and ended the way they ended. It's an oval photograph, with the grain of the image fading to green, the green of copper roofs when they oxidise. There he is in his shiny boots and his fustian hunting jacket, with his double-barrelled shotgun over his shoulders, his moustaches and his wide-brimmed hat, mounted on a white mare and looking straight in front of him. Without speaking or moving, his belly held in and his chest out, the air trapped in his lungs, eyes full of pride, like a soldier on parade, and I seem to hear the thoughts buzzing angrily in his head as the photographer takes his time before pressing the shutter—Come on, young man, I haven't got all day.

They called my grandfather Sor Terenzio. I say grandfather, but in reality he was my great-grandfather. They say that, when necessary, he would pull up his sleeves and stir around in the whey to see if his tenant farmer had tried to cheat him by hiding a round of cheese at the bottom of the vat. There never was any, but you never know. My great-grandfather ate priests for breakfast. He ate them up and spat out the cassocks, or rather he cleaned his moustache with the cassocks. It is said that when he was dying, he chased away the priest who wanted to give him the last rites and in a thin voice ad-libbed, *Priests and friars are not forgiving, they praise the dead and swindle the living.* Those were his very words. Or at least I hope so.

You see me the way I am now, but my great-grandfather whipped the peasants. He was a smart character, my great-grandfather. They had a great deal of respect for him in the village, perhaps because of all those whippings. As I've already said, I can't see it. Though I wouldn't be willing to bet that it didn't happen. His initials are still there on a brass plate screwed to the front door—TERENZIO CREMONA. And you have to believe brass plates. The metal, if well polished, withstands the years, unlike men. With the passing of time, that robust, strapping man who went around on horseback and carried a double-barrelled shotgun over his shoulder had given way to an old man with grey drooping moustaches and the sad eyes of a retired champion. On dismounting from his horse, he had lost his proud, masterly bearing, just as he had lost a beautiful wife who had died of peritonitis and a son who, like me, was called Federico Cremona.

Federico had died one summer's day. He had met with a death that was so stupid that only its banality makes it credible. He was coming home in the still light of sunset after spending the afternoon with his friends. He was fifteen years old, slim, with bright blue eyes. He was holding a ball under one arm and with the other was pushing the bicycle by the handlebars. The ball, held against its will between his arm and his side, rebelled against its master and came free of his grip. Federico made an uncoordinated move, the kind of awkward, innocuous move we all make from time to time. He tried to catch it in flight before it rolled down some steep slope, because then it would take hours to find. He lost his balance and fell. The black bicycle, a large man's bicycle which he managed to ride even though

13

he was not yet a man, fell with him. And when he fell, his head hit the pavement hard. He lay there on the ground. He had only a small cut on his temple, and all he felt at first was a little nausea. Then he began to feel bad. They carried him into his big house, which had so many rooms, you could lose yourself in it. They put him in a cool dark room with sheets that smelt of lavender and the curtains drawn and the only sounds filtering in being the voices of the children playing down in the street and the cries of swallows chasing each other frenziedly in the evening air. His mother watched over him night and day, day and night, moistening his lips, changing the cool cloths she placed on his forehead. The doctor came and, smoothing an eyebrow, said that he needed to be bled with leeches. His father was shut up in his study, smoking in silence. He didn't talk to anyone because there was no need to talk, but if he had talked he would have said one word—Why? And Fede's twin, my grandfather Vanni, had already understood. He had understood from his brother's increasingly weak voice as he lay delirious in the dimly lit room, from his mother's weeping, and from his father's silent smoking in the study, surrounded by dusty papers.

From all these things he had understood that he would have two bicycles, two tennis rackets, two rifles, two suits, two horses, two of everything, one too many and one too few. Two destinies and two lives, one of which was not his own.

He had understood that he would continue to feel his brother the way a disabled man still feels his amputated leg, he would continue to see him, the way an old coat of paint can be seen under a new one, to be aware of him, as we are aware of the void left in a room by a piece of furniture that has been moved.

He decided that he would not cry. He did not even cry on the day of the funeral, the day when the village ground to a halt, transfixed by the lugubrious pealing of the bells, and black-clad people came from all over, so many that they could not all get in the church and crowded onto the steps beneath that leaden early afternoon sun. So many people that when the black head of the procession reached the cemetery, the tail was still in the church.

But Vanni decided, or rather vowed, that he would never again talk about Fede. Never. With anyone. And the only thing stronger than a pact between friends is a pact between twins.

Alive and dead

ON THE DAY of the Dead, when I went with my grandmother to visit my family's household gods, while she changed the flowers and prayed under her breath, I would anxiously read the inscription on the tomb, which was too rhetorical to be genuinely touching.

FEDERICO CREMONA 1920–1936

Federico
flower of strength and youth
through a fatal fall
you withered on a hot summer afternoon
when you were still spreading your fragrance of life
you are mourned by your beloved parents
and your brother who could not live if not with you

It made quite an impression on me, seeing that tomb with my name on it in the family chapel. I would try not to look at it, making an effort to lose myself in prayer, barely moving my lips behind my grandmother as she intoned the words of the requiem (*Eternal rest grant them, O lord, and let perpetual light shine on them, may they rest in peace. Amen*) but I couldn't help myself, the tombstone summoned up distant thoughts that overwhelmed me, plunged into me, deep into my throat, like stones down a well. And the biggest one was the thought of seeing myself dead, walled up inside that furnace of ice-cold marble. And yet

I was alive. Even though the stone said I was dead. But I was alive, standing there in front of myself dead. So was I dead or alive? I was both. Alive and dead. Dead and alive.

According to Professor Voinea

A CCORDING TO the work of Professor Voinea of the University of Bucharest, a man who spent his life studying biographical recurrences within generations of the same families, the possibility exists that cases of *inter-generational mesmerism* can occur. It may well be that, because of mysterious forces which work on the bodily fluids, some ancestors can be reincarnated—partially or totally (the literature is divided on this point)—in their descendants. Again according to the theories of Professor Voinea, there are two types of destiny—the dominant and the recessive. Just like character, human destiny, too, may be transmittable genealogically. And this transmission may be regulated by laws that are still unknown but may not be all that dissimilar from the Mendelian laws that govern heredity. The professor's team did tests on a family of traditional peasants in the Carpathians going back six generations and observed some astonishing recurrences of the same biographical situations at a distance of decades. For example, if the grandfather in the family had been cuckolded, it was quite likely that his grandson would also be cuckolded, but not the father, this unfortunate circumstance being a recessive characteristic and therefore likely to skip a generation.

Or again, if one of two brothers was destined to be a failure, and the other a success, it was very likely that their grandchildren would get everything from the former rather than the latter, it being established beyond doubt

18

that a predisposition to failure is dominant compared with a predisposition to success.

I found this article in a scientific magazine of my father's, one of those which are kept in the toilet as a source of inspiration. I've read it many times and thought about it a lot. Professor Voinea is a pioneer in this field, and it may be that this particular case study is too limited to be elevated into a law, but I must say that his theory exerts a certain fascination over me, being as I am the scion of an ancient line. And it isn't just a question of similar names, or tombstones. It's all about blood, not marble. Because sometimes, especially at night, I can feel my ancestors' stale blood slowing my circulation, waking me, and summoning me to great enterprises.

I think it's Federico's unquiet blood, that dead twin's degenerate blood, that boils in my veins, urging me to struggle, motivating me towards rebellion, sarcasm and revelry.

The castle

I HAVE TO SAY IT NOW and get out it of the way. I live in a castle. Or rather, I lived in a castle. With its merlons, its tower jutting proudly over the red roofs, its pigeons, its walls and all the minimum requirements a castle has to have to be called a castle. Living in a castle means living in a state of constant anachronism, which cannot be cured by any temporal remission, and which couldn't help but produce some displacement—however minimal—of my psyche in contrast to the Cartesian axes of history. Being born in a dead place, seeing the light of day in the dark, opening your eyes in an enclosed space, waking up in a sepulchre—that's what living in a castle means. There's nothing magical, nothing princely, in the scowling faces of the ancestors who peer down at you from their soot-darkened portraits. Or in being the only male. The last scion, the repository of a name, a history, a tradition. The tenderest shoot at the tip of the branch, the one most susceptible to the cold—all it takes is an April frost, and it's goodbye harvest. *We're counting on you to perpetuate the race*, my forefathers admonish me severely as I hurry down the dark corridors, past galleries of dirt-blackened portraits, with my head lowered to avoid my kinsmen's inquisitive looks. *Please remember*, the voice of the flesh of your flesh follows you from room to room, *that you have our future in your hands*. Not just in my hands, I have your future in my gonads. So don't count on me.

But how do you get to build a castle in the twentieth century? The century of speed, of the masses, of total war, man walking on the moon and the great leap forward? Only a necrophiliac—or a reactionary—could conceive of a building that was already dead at the dawn of the most modern century in history. Because a castle isn't only a building, it's also a concept. A concept that had been dead and gone for centuries, sunk in the recesses of history along with that absurd chivalric society that once inhabited its rooms. Try for a moment to emerge from the pettiness of your apartment blocks, the dreariness of your terraces, the pretentiousness of your detached houses, and imagine living in a castle. There's nothing romantic, nothing fairy-tale about it, get that out of your heads. It's like living in the dried-up cocoon of a chrysalis. It's horrible. And yet it's sublime. And there's no contradiction at all, because you can't help but feel horror and ecstasy for dying forms. Any painter of still lifes would know what I'm talking about.

I've made the most of it, I swear, the most of the least, I agree, but still the most I possibly could. I'm sure you'll agree with me when I say I could hardly be expected to be a modern man. "You're a nineteenth-century man!" That was what my girlfriends threw at me when they left me (even when I left them). I can well believe it. And that was fine by me. By rights, I should be a fourteenth-century man, or, worse still, a thirteenth-century man. I'm an avant-garde traditionalist, a progressive conservative, a fashionable reactionary. Well, when you come down to it, it could have been worse.

What I still can't understand is what was going through my great-grandfather Terenzio's head when he decided that even if it ruined him he would build a castle. It was he who started the whole thing, who derailed the train of time. And when he had the illusion that he had stopped that train by erecting his castle against the will of history, he of

21

all the passengers was perhaps the most ill at ease. Because a house doesn't belong to the person who builds it but to those who come after him and live in it for generations. Despite the fact that it had been Terenzio who had wanted this house, wanted it with a feverish determination that consumed him and at the same time kept him alive.

Masons, carpenters and artisans came from all over to build the castle, stonecutters from Rapolano, painters from Siena, decorators from Orvieto, architects from Rome, gardeners from Florence. They worked for years. Twenty, thirty. Maybe more. They worked until the money was all gone and my great-grandfather had squandered all his immense fortune. Even the most impatient creditors had to contain their impatience, out of their old respect—or fear, if you like—for our family and for that proud, strong man who whipped his peasants. And they were all paid, down to the last penny. Until the accounts were settled and the money was gone. The last of the artisans was paid with the last of the cash, and all that was left was an empty bank account and a completed castle. Only then did my great-grandfather Terenzio, who had been dead since Fede had died, feel really free to die. You can judge the result for yourselves. I'm certainly not going to quarrel with it. Architecture is a fact. Or rather, it's an object. And you can't quarrel with objects. They either exist or they don't. They're there or they're not. The castle is there, for all to see.

Yes, it's there, but it wasn't always there ... That's what many people say, with a wicked little smile. It's a sensitive, if ultimately futile, question. And it's kept more than one person awake at night, well, me at least.

Because none of the villagers—the peasants, the artisans, the shopkeepers, the professionals, the small landowners, even my close, or comparatively close, relatives—have ever come to terms with the castle. I've thought about that a lot, and have worked out some quite complex theories—too complex, probably, because when you get down to it, it's actually quite simple.

Envy.

Pure envy.

Of the commonest kind.

In fact if you go to my village and pay attention to what people say, the first thing you'll hear is:

"The castle's an imitation."

"I'm sorry?'

"The castle. It isn't a genuine medieval building. It's an imitation."

"Oh … "

"Late nineteenth century … "

"Thanks."

"Don't mention it."

If tourists or strangers arrive, buttonhole some solitary villager who doesn't really want to chat, and have the misfortune to ask him, "Excuse me, is it possible to visit the castle?" the answer will come—"It's an imitation."

If they could, I swear, they'd even have put it on the sign at the entrance to the village:

582 metres above sea level
(THE CASTLE IS AN IMITATION)

So how come that, in all the guides, in all those glossy tourist brochures that are full of mistakes, on every lousy postcard, it's the slender, imposing outline of the tower that dominates? A TV crew comes to shoot one of those travel features that are really only liked by people who have never been to the places they talk about, and, get this, the feature always begins and ends with the tower. They hold a conference, and what do they stick on the cover of the report of proceedings? The castle.

It's odd that all this hatred of the castle should become sublimated in the triumph of its iconography. Because, despite the postcards, that's what it was—hatred. Whenever I was called up to the front of the class, my schoolmistresses would tend to rub it in. *"Monuments of note in our village include an early Christian church of great antiquity, the seventeenth-century palace of the Archpriest, visited by Grand Duke Leopoldo in person, a small chapel with a saddle roof known as the Chapel of the Conception, attributed to Niccolò Circignani, known as Il Pomarancio, and next to the high altar the tomb of Beato Pietro who, according to tradition, died there of cold in February 1638* (so says the latest edition of the guide to the village, revised and corrected by God knows who, though I'd love to know). *Also of interest is a finely crafted font dating from 1596, and a neo-Gothic castle of no historical or artistic significance, which is ... "*

"Cremona, tell me, what is your castle?"

"An imitation, miss!"

"Good. Go back to your seat."

My classmates at the least sign of an argument during a football game, my classmates' mothers as they made me jam sandwiches as a snack, my classmates' friends taking advantage of those rare moments when my mother stepped away from me, leaving me unprotected in the world—in short, everyone, as soon as they had an opportunity, made sure to inform me that the castle in which I lived was *an imitation*. And to think that I did all I could to downplay it as much as possible. The number of times I heard that fatal question addressed to me by an eager tourist—"Excuse me, whose castle is that?" and I, flying high, very high, a superhero in the clear skies of modesty ever since I was little, would lower my eyes and reply, " ... It's private." "But who does it belong to?" the insatiable tourist would insist. "A local family ... " And I would launch my bike at breakneck speed down the slope.

Hardly surprising then, in fact quite understandable, if I had grown up with a complex about this 'imitation castle', a taint I carried with me until I was sixteen or seventeen when, after diligent searching in a dusty, authoritative history book, I read the following—"*The castle is of Lombard origin, and there is evidence that it dates from as far back as the year 1000.*" 1000. One thousand. No more, no less. I can't tell you the relief!

What my great-grandfather had done was a kind of superfetation, in other words, he had built his neo-Gothic castle on a pre-existing complex. A castle for which *there is evidence that it dates from as far back as the year 1000*.

But the definitive confirmation of the castle's authenticity, which helped to dispel any lingering doubts, liberating me for ever from the agonising complex from which I suffered, came a few years later. When my grandfather Vanni, a versatile athlete once legendary as a diver, aviator and sailor, found himself assailed by an incurable disease which transformed him overnight from a decathlete into an old man too weak and proud to drag his tired bones up and down the hundreds of stairs in the castle. The connection between the unacceptable discovery of the disease and the reassuring discovery of the castle's authenticity may be a tenuous one, but it does exist. Because in a very real, tragic sense, it was my grandfather's illness which revealed to me the truth about the castle's origins. No longer able to face the stairs, Vanni, after a meticulous and considered comparison of estimates, finally plumped for a lift. Obviously, the lift would have to be inside the tower. The tower is empty apart from a narrow spiral staircase that climbs all the way to the top until you feel dizzy. Once, on a wild and stormy night, a violent bolt of lightning had struck the top of the structure, gone zigzagging down the stairs and ended its run in the cellar, with a fearful crash that had shut off the current and brought down the bottom of the staircase.

It was from there, at the bottom, where the bolt of lightning had crashed to the ground, that they would have to start in order to install the lift. And it was also there, at the bottom, that confirmation of the castle's authenticity would come. The company hired for the job arrived, carried out a survey and, after a few days, set to work. The first thing they would have to do would be to drill through the walls of the cellars. These were wonderful spaces with barrel vaults, cool in summer and warm in winter, rooms that for hundreds of years had seethed with the fumes of wine and guarded the acrid odour of cheese left to dry in walnut leaves and the heavy smell of hams hanging from the ceiling. The same cellars that contained enormous oak barrels so big that, during the war, when there was a Fascist raid, people hid in them five at a time, the same cellars where they gave Decio, the cellarman—and there are witnesses—fifty-six glasses of wine one after the other, and he didn't collapse but walked out on his own two legs, staggering perhaps, but on his own two legs all the same.

Now that agriculture was dead, weeded out by European Community aid, which paid people not to grow crops, now that the vines had shrivelled and the barrels were empty, the cellars had become little more than a storehouse for various pieces of junk accumulated by men in their daily hustle and bustle. The drill they brought in, however, met with an unexpected obstacle. The wall that had to be breached simply couldn't be breached. It was solid rock reinforced with mortar, and must have been a couple of metres thick. What it was, in fact, was the buttress of the tower. Those medieval architects really knew what they were doing. The drill snorted and hissed, but all to no avail. Finally, after some heart-rending groans, it became blunted and they had to stop the engine twice because they were afraid it would burn up with the effort. "Look, how can you possibly make a hole in this wall?" the worker said, switching off the drill. It's as hard as Verano stone. It must be at least a thousand years old." A thousand years old. One thousand. How sweet that number sounded.

And besides, I was in possession of a secret, one that Grandpa Vanni revealed to me before he died. As far as I remember, it was one of the last times, perhaps even the very last now I come to think about it, when he was still up and about before taking to his bed once and for all and giving in to his illness. I was wandering through the cellars looking for the pump, because my bicycle tyres were flat. All at once, I thought I made out my grandfather's thin, austere figure in the shadows. He was standing in silence in a dark corner, like an animal sensing death.

"Oh, it's you, Grandpa, you gave me a fright … What are you doing here?"

"I know everything about this house, the layout of the rooms, the weight of the doors, the movements of the handles, the squeak of the hinges, the position of the light switches, the numbers of the steps, the edges of the furniture, the borders of the carpets, the frames of the paintings. If I went blind I'd be able to move around the house without anyone's help. You too, as the only male heir, ought to know this house as well as I do."

"But I do know it, Grandpa … "

27

"No, you don't. Come with me."

Grandpa took me by the hand and limped ahead of me until we reached a large barrel, in front of which he stopped as if in front of an altar. Groaning a little he shifted the heavy lid, which resisted at first then yielded to reveal the dark inside of the barrel.

"Come on, don't be afraid."

I summoned my courage and went in after him. At the bottom was a passage, a narrow tunnel, not too low, carved out of the buttress of calcareous rock on which the castle—and, with it, the whole village—was supported. The walls were covered with mould and the floor was sticky. The tunnel sloped sharply downwards. Despite his aching bones, Grandpa advanced without any hesitation. I saw him take something out of his pocket, and a moment later a blue-grey flash lit up our surroundings. He was holding a match with one hand and with the other was shielding the flame from the slight draught that rose from the depths of the tunnel. I followed him, gripping the ribs of his corduroy trousers. All at once, Grandpa came to a halt. The match went out. The darkness echoed with a liquid sound, the kind of sound you might hear in the womb. We were like two strange foetuses waiting to be born.

"Do you hear that?"

"What is it?"

He lit another match, and what I saw in the bluish flash left me speechless. Beneath us was a pit filled with water. From the walls, which were damp with condensation, drops were falling with a dull, regular drip-drip.

"We're under the well in the village square," Grandpa said. "When the castle was under siege, this was how they supplied themselves with water without leaving the castle walls."

I didn't say anything. There are times when there's nothing to say.

I don't know how long we stood there in silence, listening to the drops hammering the surface of the water. Then we went back up again.

So I had the proof. It would have been odd, to say the least, if my grandfather Terenzio—I call him grandfather but, as I said before, he was actually my great-grandfather—had, out of some philological scruple, made those neoclassical architects at the end of the nineteenth century build a tunnel leading from the castle's cellars to a spot underneath the village well in order to supply himself with water when the castle was under siege. Under siege from whom? Oh, of course, those Bolshevik peasants on the first of May. No, joking aside, an anti-siege tunnel would have been a bit of an exaggeration even for a bastion of anti-communism like Grandpa Terenzio.

Oh, if only I could have shown that secret passage to Signora Cannoli, my schoolteacher.

"Excuse me, miss, what is our castle?"

"An imitation, Cremona, an imitation."

"Like hell it is, miss."

That's what I would have said.

As little boys

A S LITTLE BOYS they had scampered about the thousand rooms, chasing each other like puppies, and the end point of these infinite pursuits was always the castle kitchens. Warmth, smoke, cooking smells, the clatter of dishes, the shouting and bustle of women, the cooks watching like vestals over the pots on that eternal fire. The kitchens were the still centre of the castle, the engine room of the great ship on whose decks the lives of dozens of people played themselves out.

As quick as a draught, the twins would rush into the kitchen and slip in between the aprons of the women, who reproached the little masters without much conviction. When the heat and excitement of the chase had died down, Fede and Vanni would seek, indeed demand, the attention of Beppina, Lidia, Adelaide and the others. Beppina had seen them grow since they were babes in arms, and Lidia had even suckled one of them—Signora Clarissa, their mother, had not expected nature to give her twins, nor perhaps had nature expected her to give birth to twins, given that the breasts of the pale Florentine lady who had brought them into the world contained only enough milk for one. That must have been the milk—Vanni was to think much later, one summer afternoon when he was out riding and the scent of broom had assailed his nostrils, reminding him of that grim June—that had given his twin that uninhibited character of his, adding to his veins those promiscuous lower-class traits which fascinated and disturbed him at the same time, so different from the composure and austerity of the rest of the family. Was there something evasive in the profile of Fede's heart? Something hostile to himself and his family, buried somewhere deep in his consciousness? But no, it was only a vague, unmotivated hostility, and he felt a touch of affectionate jealousy towards his fanciful, unapproachable twin. There was no reason to think badly of him. And yet ...

Vanni remembered once waking with a start in the middle of the night, perhaps from a bad dream. He had looked at the room with the eyes of a stranger, finding it difficult to recognise the outlines of things, the way it is when it's foggy. In the confusion of that awakening, his half-closed eyes had searched for the comfort of his brother's presence. But the bed was unmade. And Fede wasn't in it. Vanni felt a pang. A sudden, inexplicable pang. He felt abandoned, as if his brother had left him for ever. And he almost cursed himself for having woken too late. Now the anguish of his dream, of which he could not remember a single thing, was as nothing compared with that of the awakening. He tried to tell himself that perhaps Fede had gone to the bathroom, perhaps he did not feel well, or perhaps he'd simply felt a sudden hunger and had gone down to the kitchen to find some bread and ham. But the thought did not reassure him. He went back under the covers and made an effort to get to sleep again, but to no avail. It was already dawn when Fede came back, breathing heavily. Vanni did not turn round and pretended to be asleep. He heard the heavy boots falling to the floor, and even seemed to feel the relief of those feet finally set free. Then the metallic clatter of the belt buckle falling onto the terracotta tiles and the muffled noise of the body slipping under the blankets.

The following morning, at breakfast, Vanni paid little attention to what his mother was saying, but instead tried to catch some sign that might betray Fede and his vagabond night—a drooping eyelid, a yawn, tired eyes, some clue as to his nocturnal escapade. But there was nothing. Fede looked fine, in fact he seemed rested, had a good appetite, asked for second helpings of everything, minded his own business, and only contributed to the conversation at the right time—in other words, only if asked, because their father was not at all the kind of person who appreciated children interrupting adults when they were talking. At a certain point, Bettina cautiously approached Sor Terenzio, who was sitting solemnly at the head of the table, wiping his grey moustaches with his napkin, and murmured to him:

"Excuse me, sir, Lamberto is outside. He wants to talk to you."

Beyond the door of the dining room, Vanni caught a glimpse of the tall, lean figure of Lamberto, the game-keeper. He stood there hesitantly in his fustian jacket with the ample pockets, holding his hat with both hands at his waist like someone praying.

"He says it's urgent," Beppina added, removing a tray from the table.

"Tell him I'll see him in my study," Sor Terenzio said, his tone neither abrupt nor gentle.

"Yes, sir."

Sor Terenzio rose and quickly stuffed his shirt inside his trousers. Vanni noticed that his boots were shinier than usual today. Or perhaps it was only the light filtering in through the windows and reflecting off the waxed floor that made them look that way. Sor Terenzio was away for about ten minutes. By the time he returned, almond biscuits were being served with sweet wine.

"May I, Mother?"

"Just a sip. You're too young to drink wine … What about you, Vanni? Would you like some?"

"No, thank you, Mother."

Sor Terenzio collapsed heavily onto his chair.

"Is something wrong, dear?"

Fede was dunking a biscuit into the half-finger of sweet wine he had been allowed and Vanni was looking anxiously at his father.

"The gamekeeper says someone broke into the reserve again last night and slaughtered the hares. Lamberto can never catch them. He keeps lying in wait, but ends up spending the night in the open air for nothing. But one night I'll catch them out, and they'll get more than they bargained for. You'll see … "

Fede stopped his dunking and sat there holding his biscuit in mid-air.

This was it, the sign Vanni had been looking for.

Fede was a good shot

F EDE WAS A GOOD SHOT, and whenever he took aim with his double-barrelled shotgun the bell tolled. Ever since he had taken his first shots, as a little boy, it had been clear to everyone that he and the shotgun were as one. That first time he went to the hunting lodge to shoot wood pigeon with his father and the gamekeeper, Fede saw how it was done, and didn't need any further explanations. A wood pigeon passed over the clearing, beating its wings like listless strokes of an oar each time it lost altitude. Fede waited for it along the imaginary line that went from his barrel to infinity. Then he plucked up courage and fired. A grey and white rose blossomed in the air, and as the feathers fell, as light as petals, the body landed in the meadow with a weightless thud.

Vanni also managed well enough. But whenever he pulled the trigger, he would close his eyes, the world around him would tremble for a moment, yellow sparks would swarm in the darkness, and there would be a whistling in his ears. To his father, Vanni was like one of those dogs who might be good but are afraid of gunshots, which means it's a waste of time taking them hunting and they're better off in the garden or perhaps in a basket in front of the fire. And so he stopped taking Vanni hunting, and took only Fede.

It was quite a sight, seeing him shoot. From a distance, he looked like a decapitated trunk, his head flat over the stock of the shotgun, the barrel held straight and firm, at right angles to the body, almost the same length as his whole figure. People would think that it wouldn't take much, a gust of wind, an infinitesimal shift, to tip him forward and bring that fragile human architecture crashing down. You would have sworn that the angry recoil of the double-barrelled twelve-bore shotgun would have knocked the boy's back out of joint. Not a bit of it. His back stayed in place. The shot would rumble through the vineyard and the dog would trot off to recover the pheasant from the middle of the broom.

"Why do you go poaching at night in the reserve?" Vanni asked Fede one evening, just like that, point blank, as they were rubbing down their horses after a ride.

"What do you know about that?"

"You were there again last night."

"That's not true."

"Yes, it is. I saw you and you weren't there."

"I was somewhere else last night, and anyway, how could you have seen me if I wasn't there?"

"You shouldn't steal game," Vanni said, stroking the mane of his magnificent ash-grey Arab mare, La Fiamma.

"I'm not stealing anything. I'm just taking what's mine."

That was Fede's philosophy. Once, when he was a little boy, one of their father's tenant farmers had caught him stealing apricots in the orchard. He had grabbed him by the calf with his rough, hairy hand, determined to make him pay.

"Come down from there and I'll teach you to steal ... "

But when he had recognised his master's son through the branches his expression had changed.

"Look here," Fede had said as he jumped down from the tree. "I was stealing my apricots, not yours ... "

Vanni didn't see things that way at all. He thought rather that the apricots were his father's even when they were the tenant farmer's. That was what he had been accustomed to think. And he was never given a chance to think this might not be the case. Fundamentally, they were both right. It was just that they saw the question from two different sides of the table.

You should have seen the twins when they were little boys

YOU SHOULD HAVE SEEN THE TWINS when they were little boys. In a photograph taken by an American woman photographer in Florence in the 1930s, there they are in their sailor suits, with starched bows, short, slicked-back hair, protruding ears, prominent teeth behind boyish lips, and eyes full of light and life—Fede's with a crafty smile in them like someone who has done something naughty and got away with it, and Vanni's clear and resolute, with the confident expression of someone who knows he'll go far in life.

Winter in Rome, summer and the obligatory feast days in the village. They lived together, but divided. Divided between the affections of their parents, mother and father, Beppina and Lidia, Vanni's white mare La Fiamma and Fede's black horse King. They divided the world by common consent, without any argument, because the world was large, things were plentiful, and tastes differed.

How alike they looked in the uniforms of the Fascist Youth on the day of the rally in the Circus Maximus, with their fezzes pulled down over their heads and their muskets over their shoulders! They were like two peas in a pod. So alike were they that when they were at the Jesuit school, where strokes of the cane were as common as prayers, and the time came for the third-year exams but Fede was sick in bed on the day of the oral—scarlet fever! the doctor said, removing the stethoscope while

37

the boy put his clothes back on over his thin ribs—Vanni did the exam for him. And when his mother came to the door to fetch him for the second time, she who would have recognised them even in the dark, from the smell, from the shape of the ears, the line of the hair, and from the different intensity of light in their clear eyes, let slip, "Let's go, Vanni," and was immediately pulled up by the teacher—"But signora, even you don't recognise them and you're their mother … " "You're right, you're right, what a scatterbrain I am … " she said, clutching Vanni's hand, while the boy's heart pounded with the effort of keeping the secret. "Come on now, let's go, Fede … " And she hurried off, pulling her skirt after her. Because they were not like twins in books or fairy tales, where one has a scar, a mole, or some kind of birthmark that the other does not have. They had nothing like that, and people couldn't tell which was one and which the other. One was the other, and the other was one. And yet death had recognised them. Death, which is like a mother who waits up for you, a dog that smells you in the dark, a midwife that pulls you out with forceps, a sniper who never misses. Death would never mistake one for the other. Death knew which one it had taken away and which it had left. And perhaps, just perhaps, it also knew why.

As riders, they were in the vanguard

A S RIDERS, they were in the vanguard. In Rome during
the winter they trained in the Piazza di Siena, and the
horses were still with them even when they dismounted. If
either of them had already made love with a woman, his
own body and his horse's would have seemed to him like two
bodies locked in a single, timeless embrace. But they were
both still virgins, and there were some things they could not
know.

But they knew how to control a horse's trembling muscles,
how to predict its ill-considered swerves, how to second-
guess its cowardly psychology. Because they had been born
on horseback, because they were the best of their class.

Then there were the huge rallies, the uniforms, the
pennants, the parades, the competitions, and the Fascist
youth camps—Vanni believed in all that, but Fede didn't.
Vanni worked hard to keep his uniform neat and tidy,
pored over the Duce's words, and even went to mass.

In competitions, the instructor would always pick Fede
up on something—the collar of his jacket was undone,
his black shirt was badly buttoned, his boots were covered
in dust. But when he mounted his horse, when you saw
him jumping hurdle after hurdle with as much naturalness
and grace as if he were riding a fawn, how could you ever
say anything to him? He would launch the horse into
the air, and the animal would vault over the hurdle and
land noiselessly on the other side, as if landing in snow.
Vanni was good, too, he had an excellent command of

the animal, impeccable style, and never made a mistake. But he wasn't like Fede. Fede managed to abolish gravity, to tame the horse's taut muscularity and translate it into speed, ease and lightness.

Roman salutes

THE NEWS that the Fascist bigwig Fortunato Augusto Becagli would be visiting our village created quite a stir. The community, mostly made up of peasants and artisans, had always been averse to Fascism. The landowners, merchants and professionals, frightened by the threat of a possible Bolshevik revolution which would decree the collectivisation of the land and the confiscation of property, had joined the movement more out of self-interest than conviction. On the other side, it was obvious that those who had nothing to collectivise or confiscate had nothing to fear. Which meant that they had no reason to be Fascists. In addition, Fascism had at first ridden a certain anti-bourgeois wave, frightening even future supporters of the regime. Then, when even Mussolini had grasped that in order to rule he needed the blessing of the Church and the support of the bourgeoisie, even the least intelligent of the local worthies had realised that there was nothing to fear from Fascism. If anything, there was something to gain. The poor, on the other hand, had realised that there was only something to lose. But by the time they had realised this, it was too late. Because everything happened in Rome, and only distant echoes reached us, like cannon fire from ships on the high seas.

In the village, life had remained as it had always been, and relations were still based on a notion of civility and age-old class divisions, even after the March on Rome. Since Mussolini had come to power, the only thing different was that although there was nobody who could claim to be a real Fascist, nor was there anybody who could claim to be a real anti-Fascist. At least in public. Where you did start to see a few blackshirts. The blackest of all belonged to Ubaldo Bellomo, a tank soldier with a criminal record as long as a sung novena who had become an estate manager for the Cremona family. His authority, already formidable given his position, had grown even stronger since he had returned covered in medals from the war in Africa, grim-faced and sporting the fearful nickname Negus, which he had gained in the field. A mere word from him was enough to bring disgrace to a family.

Any Fascist Party official carried more weight now than a marshal of the *carabinieri*, and the prefects and police commissioners turned a blind eye, or even two, to Fascist abuse and violence. In preparation for the rally for Becagli, there were a number of preventive arrests, as well as other shameful acts of intimidation, planned and executed with great zeal. A couple of workers from a local kiln were made to swallow castor oil, a few peasants were placed under lock and key, and the village was spruced up and carefully inspected to make sure there was nothing and nobody that might spoil the rally or undermine the good name of the community in Becagli's eyes. Now they just had to wait for the bigwig to arrive, with all due solemnity. Becagli has been a union organiser, a hero of Fiume, an undersecretary to the Ministry for the Liberated Lands—a department almost immediately abolished because of a lack of raw materials—and now occupied a high office in the Fascist Party.

In a half-day of work beneath the weak March sun, the carpenters, urged on by the indefatigable Negus, erected a magnificent wooden platform in the village square.

The Marchese Rocco Barbetti Martorelli, an old brother-in-arms of Sor Terenzio, was now Fascist mayor of the village. In preparation for the arrival of the bigwig, he had given precise instructions to ensure that everything went smoothly. With the anti-Fascists in the cooler, his one worry was the village urchins. These ragged young hotheads had organised themselves into gangs who went around in short trousers all year long, with catapults in their back pockets—they were experts in the art of guerrilla warfare, skilled at throwing stones and then making tactical retreats. Barbetti Martorelli was very worried that these rascals might spoil the celebrations with some new trick of their own. His reputation and career were on the line. He had to prevent disorder at all costs, with every means at his disposal, good or bad. As it was well known to everyone that, thanks to his undeniable charisma, Federico Cremona often took command of the urchins' military operations, the Mayor had decided to go to the Cremonas' castle, on the pretext of a social call, to deliver a none-too-veiled warning—this time, no insubordination of any kind would be tolerated, and the family crest could not be used to cover up Fede's misdeeds. The rally was particularly important for the fate of the village's thermal economy. Given the way the Duce had supported Chianciano, the most influential people in the area had brought a great deal of pressure to bear to ensure that our village, too, might enjoy the prestige accruing to a modern thermal spa. The rally for Becagli was to focus precisely on this point, and it was expected to lead to a firm revival of the spa project, with even some special consideration from the Duce himself.

Mayor Rocco Barbetti Martorelli, his boots polished and his belt nice and tight beneath his black coat, rubbed his

43

hands because of the bitter cold, and rang the service bell at the Cremona house.

The door was opened by Beppina.

"I'd like to see Sor Terenzio."

"Sor Terenzio is resting and doesn't want to be disturbed."

"Sor Terenzio can rest another time. I need to talk to him."

"Wait here. I'll see what I can do."

Beppina disappeared into the shadows beyond the door. After a very long wait, during which the Mayor adjusted his belt and went over in his mind the speech he would make, Sor Terenzio appeared in the crack of the door, with the surly expression of someone who has been woken suddenly. Sor Terenzio, my great-grandfather, a veteran of the Great War, had always been a lukewarm Fascist. He was a dynamic character who had no truck with democracy, in fact he was the prototype of the perfect Fascist, but he had always refused public office and avoided overt manifestations of loyalty to the regime. His resistance was, above all, an aristocratic reflex. Being of a solid feudal mentality, he found it hard to tolerate the boldness shown by those merchants or petits bourgeois who, all done up in their black shirts, now allowed themselves a familiarity and an appropriation of powers he found equally distasteful.

"Good day to you, Sor Terenzio, how are you?"

"I'd have been better off in bed," he said in a low voice.

"I beg your pardon?"

"Come in."

Sor Terenzio led the Marchese into a damp, narrow hall, where two huge but harmless crossed halberds, neither of which had ever vibrated in combat, hung above a stone architrave. The Marchese came from a nobler house than the Cremona family, which he knew to be of modest origins, even Jewish in the distant past. To be more precise, the Marchese came from an extremely old and now decayed family whose surviving properties were easy to spot amid others because of their neglected and ruined condition. It was natural, therefore, that the poor Marchese had a complex about his fallen state and did not feel at all comfortable in the presence of the Cremonas.

Sor Terenzio, instead of taking the Mayor into the good drawing room where the fire always blazed until the end of May, led him into a frozen, cramped little study where he usually received unwelcome visitors, a room with walls overrun by bookshelves full of teetering volumes whose presence in the house was like that of stowaways in the hold of a ship, along with old hunting prints and sinister relics of journeys to remote places. Sor Terenzio sat down behind a dark desk which looked like a sarcophagus and motioned the Mayor to an inquisitor's leather chair. Outside, even though it was the end of March and the lime trees in the avenue that led to the baths displayed a few timid shoots, it was still cold. And within the inhospitable silence of these walls, the cold was so intense that it would have strangled any conversation at birth. The men looked at each other in silence, then, when they began to speak, the words emerged from their mouths thick with the steam of their breaths, like animals in their winter stables.

"I hear you're going to have a good crop this year. With all the rain there's been … "

"It's too early to say. You should never trust a month with an r in it."

"With an r?"

45

"January, February, March, April ... "

" ... September, October, November, December."

"Precisely."

"Good Lord, but then half the year is unreliable!" the Mayor said, laughing as if it were a good joke.

Terenzio cut him short. "I'm sure you haven't come here to talk about my crops. Say what you have to say."

"It's about your son."

"Which one?" Terenzio asked, even though he already knew the answer.

"That's a good one. Federico, who else?"

"What has he done?"

"Nothing yet."

"Well, then?"

"It's what he might do that worries me."

"We tamed East Africa. I wouldn't worry about something like that."

"You weren't even worried when he set fire to the Christmas crib. You know the rally for Becagli is tomorrow."

"Who doesn't?"

"I hope to see you in the front row."

"I might have some important business to attend to."

"A good Fascist never fails to attend a Fascist rally."

"I agree."

"Well, then?"

"I'll see if I can get away."

"You'd do better to see that your son stays at home. I don't want trouble this time, or you can forget about the building permit."

"Is there anything else?"

"No."

"Good."

"Good."

Much indisposed by the cold, the Marchese rose and walked to the door. Reaching it, he stopped.

"Take care this time. If Federico gets up to one of his tricks during the rally, you can summon up all the contacts you have, but even the Duce himself won't be able to save your son. He'll leave for the Horn of Africa, as God is my witness. You have the word of the Marchese Barbetti Martorelli."

"Talking of words given, didn't I hear something about a gambling debt incurred over Christmas at the pharmacist's house?"

"I don't recall."

The Marchese clicked his heels and gave a Roman salute. Sor Terenzio closed the door behind him and went back to bed.

Either you eat your soup

T HE PUNISHMENT, like all punishments, was unjust and hateful. But this one more than the others, because there was no reason for it. However hard he tried, he couldn't find a shred of justification. He was quite used to punishment. His father may have been a good man deep down, but he could be grumpy, a fact that was well known to everyone. But this time, he found it particularly hard to swallow. Rather like the soup that had triggered this diplomatic incident. They all knew that he didn't like soup, he hadn't liked it since he was a baby, with all those bubbles of yellow and red grease swimming against the light, but they were always making him eat it. At dinner that evening, his father had insisted that he finish his soup. A silence had descended over the table, a silence as grim as the bottom of the plate. Vanni had hastened to finish his own soup, then offered to eat Fede's as well. Their mother had smiled, a sweet but determined smile that meant he should keep out of it. Vanni had shrugged his shoulders and wiped his mouth with his napkin. Eat it. No, I'm not going to. I said eat it. I said no. I said yes. And I said no. In the meantime, the soup had got cold. And if it was not very inviting when it was still steaming hot, you can imagine how it was when it was cold. Fede had risen abruptly, had taken an ember from the fireplace—the fire had gone out—and thrown it in the dish, causing a veil of ashes as light as the first snow to settle on the white tablecloth. With an expression that resembled a storm, Sor Terenzio had looked at Fede, and without saying a word had grabbed him by the ear and led him out. His punishment was to be locked in the Chiappini sisters' room.

The Chiappini sisters had been two old aunts on their mother's side. They had been deaf from birth because of an attack of measles, and were both spinsters. They had always lived in Florence, and always together, until Sor Terenzio, under pressure from his wife, had reluctantly agreed to have them come and live in one of the many empty quarters in the castle. The sisters spent their time painting mannered paintings, mostly baskets of blue and white flowers and blond cherubs with pink cheeks. While they were alive, Vanni and Fede, who were children at the time, had gone to see them every now and again in the rooms they occupied on the top floor, where the servants also lived, little attic rooms that were hot in summer and cold in winter. The Chiappini sisters would stroke them with their bony old hands and emit guttural sounds in an effort to speak. Vanni would remain silent—he was too scared of the sisters to say a word—but Fede would put on an angelic expression and move his lips like an actor in a silent film, and the Chiappini sisters would press their ear trumpets further into their ears in an attempt to hear him. Vanni would continue to keep silent, while Fede would continue with his sadistic game. The sister who spoke the better of the two would say, "'at a 'ovely 'ittle 'oy, 'at a 'ity 'e 'an't understand ... " and they would hand him a brass bowl that stood on an embroidered doily in the middle of the table and let him pick the sweets he wanted.

The Chiappini sisters' rooms were now empty. Since they had both passed away in their sleep, on the same night and in the same bed, dying together just as they had always lived together, everything had remained as it was. The doctor who saw them lying curled up in bed said that it looked rather like a case of simultaneous suicide but there was such an Olympian serenity on their faces, their eyes gently closed, that the idea of a double suicide remained merely a macabre conjecture. There was still a half-finished canvas on the easel, left over from that night—all it showed was the soft white wings and pink cheeks of a legless cherub.

The soup with the ash was placed on the little table, where the sweet bowl still stood. "Don't leave until you eat it" were the only words his father said to him before he pulled the door of the room to and the lock snapped shut with unarguable finality.

Now that Fede thought of it, the punishment of the soup might have some connection with a suspicious visit from the Mayor, Barbetti Martorelli, whom he had seen entering the house through the mullioned window that looked out on the little square. He would miss the rally and the fanfare in honour of Becagli. He would also miss those pancakes he loved, made with a mysterious ancient mixture the old people called *ambiosina*, a word which probably meant nothing but which they uttered as though it were something sacred. Usually, they were made only for carnival, but in honour of Becagli's coming the Mayor had given permission to depart from tradition. He would miss going to the rally with Achille's gang, which was still the most feared even though it had been decimated by the pre-emptive punishments their parents had inflicted under pressure from the Fascists. Achille, his lieutenants, and all the rest of the gang were sure to need him, his inventiveness, his tactical and military abilities. Because even though they had studied the situation at great length, no one had come up with a satisfactory plan to disrupt the rally, which on paper seemed armour-plated and showed every sign of being the success predicted by Barbetti Martorelli. That bastard. Damn him.

It'll be like the day of judgement

I T'LL BE LIKE THE DAY OF JUDGEMENT, someone had joked, referring to the rally, but no one had paid much attention. The previous day had been gloriously sunny, even though at intervals an icy wind rose, abruptly lowering the temperature by several degrees and making people say that they didn't know what clothes to wear.

It was the evening before the rally. The platform was ready. Banners with sayings of the Duce on them, personally selected from his speeches by the Mayor, who was sure they would please Becagli, had been hung in full view—REALITY IS ALWAYS CONSISTENT. I HAVE REFUSED TO DESTROY. WE MUST DRAMATISE LIFE. Only a few hours to the rally, and everything seemed to be under control. What worried the 'general staff' was not so much the political situation as the meteorological one.

Sunset had revealed a worrying prospect. Threatening black clouds were massing on the horizon like waves breaking on a distant shore. The temperature had fallen abruptly, as happens in March, and there was a foreboding stillness in the air. Out of this pregnant silence, something like a remote tremor arose, perhaps the echo of an abortive hailstorm somewhere beyond the brown ridges of the low hills. In the chiaroscuro of the last light, the mountain tops on the horizon were shrouded in cloud.

Mayor Barbetti Martorelli, both elbows resting on the big wall, with Negus at his side, and surrounded by a knot

51

of blackshirts waiting for an oracle, was looking through his binoculars towards where the red was fading to black.

There followed an anxious silence.

"What do you say, Mayor?" Spazzavento said.

The Mayor did not reply.

"When Mount Amiata puts his hat on," an old peasant behind them said, "go back home and get your umbrella."

"Silence!" Negus roared.

"That's what the proverb says … " the peasant said in his defence.

"Jinx!" one of the comrades said. "Mind your own hat!" And with a clip on the ear, he knocked the peasant's cap off his head. Muttering an incomprehensible oath between his teeth, the peasant ran off in pursuit of it.

In frustration, the Mayor abandoned his meteorological post, and consoled himself with contemplating the finished work—the platform was well placed, between an acacia and an iron antenna, in the most sheltered corner of the square, where a recess between the houses formed a natural plateau and the walls would be like a bass drum, amplifying the resonance of the speaker's words. He could not help but feel content—everything had been studied down to the last detail. In so far as details could be studied.

March snow

I T HAD BEEN A LONG SILENT NIGHT for Fede. Too silent. It wasn't the sunlight filtering through the slats of the shutters that woke Fede as he lay fully dressed on the sofa. It was the silence. Fede rushed to the windows, opened the panes, and flung wide the shutters. And what he saw was not the reason for all that silence, but silence itself.

White. All white. Snow. Lots of snow.

The snow had fallen lightly but inexorably through the night, obliterating the village. In its place there was what looked like a vast cloud that had come to rest amid the streets and the houses. Above all this whiteness, the sky glowed a deep blue.

The snow was not far short of a metre high, which was exceptional for March. And even though the temperature was not too harsh and everything might well melt in a few hours—because, as Lidia always said, March snow lasts only from the evening until the next morning—it was still a formidable sight. The chimney pots no longer stood out on the roofs, but were hidden like animals crouching in their lairs, their presence only recognisable from the thin tongues of grey smoke blowing up into the sky. The steps of the church had become a gentle ramp. The eaves were like ropes of snow connecting the buildings one to another, tying the whole village together. In the corner of the square, where the north wind blew, the heaps of snow were as high as sheaves. The flakes that detached themselves from the tiles, cornices and window sills, large flakes borne on the wind, whirled in the air like swarms of insects on heat. The lines and forms that rose and fell met at an indefinite point halfway between everything and nothing, and the houses looked as if they had dripped from an enormous candle. There were very few prints on the immaculate white blanket. The only readable track was the deep one that led from the sacristy to the door of the town hall. Further down, on the side nearest the square, where the platform had been erected, cries and the scraping of shovels could be heard.

The Fascists were struggling to liberate the village from the snow as they would not have done against an invader. They had looked everywhere for helping hands to clear the square and the streets. They had taken people from their houses, dragged out reluctant old men who dug in their heels at the doors of their houses like stubborn mules, pulled from their beds startled young men who had been enjoying the sweet sleep of a Fascist Saturday, organised the tramps and layabouts, threatened the undecided and urged on the zealots. They had conscripted men and women, young and old—anyone who could hold a shovel in their hands was put to work. The square had been almost cleared by the teams of diggers who were working without pause under Negus' direction. High white cones rose like funeral pyres on either side of a corridor of snow leading from the *carabinieri* barracks to the platform. Even though the wind had turned to a sirocco and was becoming milder, all that snow made the air crisp, and if you stood still you certainly felt the cold. That was why the band had gone into a garage to rehearse some of the more difficult passages of a certain little march and some of the blackshirts were engaging in gymnastic exercises, hopping and jumping to overcome the cold rather than to display their athletic exuberance. Some reports said that the main road was passable—a couple of hundred metres further down, towards the plain, what for us was snow had been nothing but rain. Telephone calls between the various local sections of the Fascist Party confirmed that Becagli was on his way, and cablegrams bounced from section to section said that his arrival was imminent. It was now eleven in the morning—only an hour until the start of the rally.

In the little square below Fede's house—Fede still being locked in the Chiappini sisters' rooms, without the slightest intention of eating that ash soup—the shovellers were hard at work. The entrance to the town hall, the big door with the travertine cornice, had been cleared of snow. The steps of the church had regained their usual jagged shape. Fede was determined not to miss the rally. Before sleep overcame him, he had considered a number of options, inspected the room and all the objects in it, examined the lock, which seemed impregnable, and the door, which had no obvious weak spots. Hoping for help from Vanni was pure illusion—at that hour, his beloved twin—Fede imagined—was already offering his arm to their father who, wrapped in his greatcoat, would say, "When I'm old, you'll be my walking stick … " and together, arm in arm, father and son would walk down to the square like figures in a devotional painting.

Sor Terenzio had not chosen at random. He knew it wasn't easy to escape from that domestic prison. But there was one thing he had not predicted, in as much as it could be included in a list of unpredictable things.

The snow had reformulated not only proportions and shapes, but spaces and distances. The shovellers were shovelling, and without thinking twice they were piling all the snow against the wall. The wall beneath the window of the Chiappini sisters' room. Where a gentle ramp a couple of metres high had been formed. In normal conditions of gravity, that first-floor window was no more than five metres above the ground. With that heaped snow beneath it, if you took away from the height the metre or so of his body hanging from the window ledge, it would only be about a couple of metres. The soft snow would easily cushion his fall. With a bit of courage, it could be done.

Beelzebub

F EDE HAD FOUND HIM one October morning as he was scouring the scrub for mushrooms. Suddenly a thick, milky fog had descended on the world, making it vanish as if by magic. He could no longer even see his own hands. Even though he knew that stretch of wood well, it was impossible to keep a sense of direction, because rather than moving you felt as if you were swimming in endless mire. You had to walk with your arms out in front of you like a sleepwalker if you didn't want to bump into a tree or end up in a spinach patch. It was impossible to advance, and Fede crouched at the foot of a tree and waiting for the curtain of fog to clear a little. Suddenly he heard barking—two short barks and one long one. It wasn't baying, and it wasn't howling. It was almost like a signal. The barking was coming closer. But Fede couldn't pinpoint where it was coming from. He got to his feet and listened. He heard the barking again—resolute, but not threatening. It had changed direction, and now seemed to be coming from behind him. He turned and listened again, and again there came that same unmistakable barking. This time, though, it came from the side. He turned to look first one way, then the other, and at that moment he heard the galloping of a quadruped on a trail of leaves. He twisted round to avoid being attacked from the rear. But he was too late. A black hairy creature came rushing out of the fog, jumped on him and threw him to the ground. In a flash, the animal was at his throat. And began to lick him.

He called him Beelzebub. Perhaps because he had emerged from the foggy heath like a creature of the underworld. A true mongrel, but intelligent, Beelzebub was a cross between a hunting dog and some unspecified breed. Unlike a devil, though, Beelzebub did not have a tail. Not that it had been cut off. Fede had inspected him carefully and had come to the conclusion that he had never had one.

It was not clear if Beelzebub was a truffle dog, a guard dog or a gun dog, but the fact was that from the start he and Fede were made for each other. Fede never did find out where he had come from, who his previous master had been, or for what obscure reason he had been abandoned. Like a man who marries a woman of the streets, he was content to love him and not ask questions about his past. And Beelzebub repaid his master's discretion with affection and gratitude. By day, he would come and eat out of Fede's hands, wagging his imaginary tail in the air. The boy had also tried to make him an improvised basket by nailing together planks from a few fruit crates. When he had finished it, he lined it with old blankets. But Beelzebub did not take to it. He preferred the open air. At night, he would disappear, and only the woods knew where he went to sleep. But he was not a stray. He was Fede's dog.

Right from their first days together, Fede had discovered that the dog had two peculiarities. The first was that he could not stand bells. Every time the bell tower in the church shook its enormous clappers with ecclesiastical fury, Beelzebub would start howling in pain, as if the sound were hammering his skull. He would yelp and whine and roll on the ground, then start to bark and growl with rage in the direction of the church until the metallic echoes evaporated into the sky, leaving the village deafened.

Worst of all was vespers. At the hour when the artisans stood in the doorways of their workshops, enjoying the last cigarette of a long day's work, and the peasants were returning home exhausted from the fields, the sacristan, even though he looked as if he was at death's door, gathered his strength and grasped hold of the bell rope like a man possessed.

Not to such an extent as the dog, but Fede, whose room looked out on the church square, also found the pealing of the bells hateful. Now that, with money from the parishioners, they had relieved the gaunt sacristan of his task and installed in the bell tower a diabolical electric motor with a timer, the bells had started ringing at night, too, marking the hours and even, to make matters worse, the half-hours. Fede's ear had become accustomed to the bells and generally ignored them, but when, for some reason, he could not sleep, he would hear that zealous nightwatchman tolling the hours and half-hours, replacing the sovereign time of night with a time domesticated by man. The night was longer or shorter depending on whether the voice of the bell was louder than sleep or less loud, the eve of a parting more painful, the eve of an exam more oppressive. Everything depended on that damned bell.

Beelzebub's second peculiarity, so to speak, was that he barked at priests and Fascists. Perhaps it was only a simple association of the effect—the bells—and the possible cause—the priest—or perhaps, who knows, there was something else besides an intolerance of ecclesiastics. Perhaps it was an aversion to the colour, since every time he saw a black robe fluttering in the wind as it passed through the streets of the village, he couldn't look at it and began to grind his teeth and snarl threateningly at the curate. Because of the analogy of colour, Beelzebub also hated blackshirts. This was a serious problem because they were much more belligerent than the old parish priest.

Or you jump out of the window

T HE VILLAGE WAS DESERTED and silent. The sun had climbed high in the sky. The snow was starting to melt and the water was flowing in the eaves and gurgling in the drains.

Fede opened the window just as the band struck up its opening fanfare, indicating that things were getting under way. He leant over the ledge, turned so that he faced backwards, and held tight to the frame of the window until his hands grasped the travertine cornice. He hung in the void for a moment, closed his eyes, and let go.

He felt a hot breath and something rough and wet rasping the snow off his face. He rubbed his snow-powdered eyes and saw Beelzebub's black muzzle above him. He took the dog's head in his hands and scratched him under the chin. The animal lowered his eyes as a sign of gratitude. Fede shook the snow off his clothes and, with Beelzebub beside him, set off for the square.

White and black were the dominant colours that day. The white of the clouds, the snow, and Fede's teeth. The black of the Fascists, the coats and Beelzebub. The band came to the end of a painful little march, the final wrong notes drowned out by applause.

It was difficult at first to get through the crowd. A forest of heads and hair blocked his view. He forced his way through, his dog squeezing into the human path opened by his master with much shoving and treading on toes, until both dog and boy reached the side of the square. Fede took off his belt and used it to tie Beelzebub to a bench at the foot of an acacia. "Stay," he said. The dog crouched under the bench.

Then Fede heaved himself up onto the trunk and sat down astride the fork of a branch. Because of his weight, some of the snow that was still on the tree dropped, and a few people raised their hands to their hats and looked up at the sky uncomprehendingly. Becagli was on the platform. He was a short man, with virile moustaches, and a bald skull as smooth as a pebble in a river. Proceedings were coming to a close, and the crowd were waiting anxiously for the pièce de résistance of his speech. In the front row, in the middle of the usual worthies, sat Sor Terenzio and Vanni. Becagli cleared his throat.

"As for the baths … "

Applause from the crowd.

Becagli made a downward movement with his palm, as if to say wait, wait.

" … As for your—our—beloved baths, which were Etruscan and then Roman, I can assure you they will be … "

Fede looked down. Beelzebub was gone.

" … Fascist!"

A roar went up from the crowd.

"The damage caused by too much freedom is clear for all to see. Law and order are returning in triumph from their long exile. We will sweep away the inertia of previous administrations with the broom of action, we will strangle laxity with the gloves of resolve … Never again will the waters—which have gushed abundantly in these pleasant lands for millennia, be lukewarm—and nor will our hearts. They will boil and steam, heated by the ardour and passion of Fascism."

More applause.

"The Duce himself wishes you to know … "

A quiver went through the crowd.

" … wishes you to know … "

The black figure of Beelzebub appeared for a second close to the platform, then was immediately hidden again by the legs of the crowd.

" … that your noble baths, where the wife of the emperor Octavius Augustus bathed chastely, will be restored to their former, Roman splendour!"

Here, Becagli was expecting the square to erupt in triumphant applause.

Instead, there was a moment of stunned silence, followed by an outburst of coarse laughter.

It took Becagli a moment to realise what was happening. He felt something damp on his calves and looked down. At his feet, he saw a wretched black beast standing on three legs with its fourth leg up in the air. When the last drops had fallen, it set itself back on its four legs.

They took him. They put him inside a bag and beat him mercilessly. Two men dressed in black put the bag over their shoulders and went into the wood. They walked past a kiln and across a clearing strewn with large stones. They made their way through the thorn bushes with that bag, from which emerged an ever-fainter whining and which kept inflating and deflating slightly as if it were a dying lung. The men looked at each other and opened the bag.

"Go to hell," one of them said.

And they threw the dog into the hole.

Beelzebub, the devil's dog, fell into the darkness with a whine like a distant siren.

He was going, or perhaps returning, to his master.

He couldn't get over it

FEDE COULDN'T GET OVER IT. They had told him that the dog was dead, but he could find no rest. At night, as if in a nightmare, he had the impression that he could hear him. He would hear a moan that was like the crying of a baby trapped in a cider barrel, then that unmistakable call of his, two short barks and one long one, which seemed to come from somewhere under the ground. He was sure it was Beelzebub—or his ghost—calling for help to his young master on earth. One night, he woke with a start, that heart-rending appeal in his ears. He was sure of it. From somewhere down below, Beelzebub was calling him. Get me out, he was saying, get me out of here. He heard a yelping that made his flesh creep, as if the animal were being pursued by unnameable creatures. Although unsure whether that call came from the world of the living or that of the dead, Fede left the house in his pyjamas, and like a water diviner set off in search of the source of the moaning. He followed it, taking care not to lose it, listening carefully to isolate it from the funereal chanting of the owls and the sinister chorus of night noises.

The intermittent yelping took him out of the village. He had the feeling that the sound came from the centre of the earth. It was like the beating of a buried heart. And the beating was now stronger, now weaker. Fede followed it, beyond the houses, beyond the bridge, beyond the avenue of trees. If anyone had seen him walking in the night dressed as he was, barefoot, in his woollen underpants and nightshirt, they would have taken him for a werewolf. The sound was imperceptible now. He heard it only with the ear of the soul. The call took him as far as the great wrought-iron gate of the thermal baths. Then the signal disappeared.

Vanni had grown up without Fede

VANNI HAD GROWN UP without Fede. But every time he walked along the dark corridors of his house, he was aware that someone else had moved through that space before him. And he also sensed mysterious presences in those rooms and felt as though he were being watched by unseen eyes.

There were moments when he felt as though Fede were behind him, he could see him out of the back of his head, feel an icy breath on his neck, and turn abruptly, as if playing a children's game. But it wasn't Fede. No. It wasn't anybody. It was just an impression. That was all.

Since that terrible day when the screws had taken root in the living wood and Fede's coffin had been placed in the family chapel, he had had everything. The best schools, foreign governesses, summers at Santa Marinella, excursions on sailing boats, the sailing boats themselves, English shoes, the Gilera Otto Bulloni and the Alfa Romeo sports car with the white number plates and the embossed words on the chassis and the press cuttings of the races it had won. Even things he never asked for, he got. As if these were reparations his old father was paying life in order to maintain a modicum of peace. Or perhaps all that unasked-for giving was as good a way as any of expiating a grave sin, one that Sor Terenzio had not even committed but for which he nevertheless felt responsible.

At first, genetics had matched the twins well, a diligent champion trotter and a thoroughbred that needed taming.

Grandfather Terenzio—I call him grandfather but he was of course my great-grandfather—had secretly decided that, once tamed, it would be Federico who would climb onto the bridge and steer the family in the right direction, managing the hundreds of hectares which in summer blazed golden with wheat and in winter became harsh and bare when the north wind blew. As for Vanni, he was sure to become an engineer or an architect—it was impossible not to notice that he had an eye for distances and proportions, and an innate aptitude for mathematics, for making effortless split-second mental calculations. And his father, and his grandfather, that is, my great-grandfather, the one who whipped the peasants, had indeed noticed it. But Fede's death had shuffled the deck, wrecking the game of life which my grandfather thought he was playing. So, instead of studying engineering, Vanni had had to plump for agriculture. There was no room for negotiation—family pragmatism ruled out any kind of individual impulse from the start.

Without putting up a fight, Vanni had found himself alone in a padded suite in the best hotel in the small provincial town where they had sent him to study. Coming back from the Christmas vacation, he would look out through the wide windows of the suite at the high street and watch the hats, furs and overcoats pass by at that falsely busy pace into which provincials force themselves in order to feel like city dwellers. The botany textbook lay open at a random page, and the street lights took heart and came on as the streets themselves grew emptier. It seemed to him that he did not have much to think about. And he awaited dinner with a sense of anxiety. Now that the holidays were over, and the last Christmas guests had left, the hotel was sinking into that desolate interregnum between Christmas and Easter, months as bare as the branches of the elms drooping in the park, absurdly long, idle days when there was nothing to do but wait for the spring thaw, signalled by the appearance of tourists and students again sitting on the steps of the church with cigarettes in their mouths and their faces turned to the sun. But the spring was still a long way away, and for the moment he would once again find himself dramatically alone in the hotel's large dining room, with his personal waiter, in livery, standing to attention, watching over his table for the entire duration of the meal. Would he survive another evening surrounded by the metallic clatter of cutlery on plates, the glacial tinkling of crystal glasses, the sommelier's white gloves, the pauses between one course and the next? Would he resist the temptation to wipe his mouth on the waiter's sleeve when that immaculate arm passed in front of him? And, above all, would he manage to avoid the eyes of those guests, all strangers to him, who were always looking for company? Would he be able to politely ward off the unrequested confidences of the travelling salesmen? Would he succeed in evading the stale desires of the elderly ladies who frequented the hotel? Yes. He would. Not for much longer. But at least for another evening.

After dinner, he might perhaps play a few games in the billiard room, without even the satisfaction of smoking a cigarette in peace—a habit he had tried to take up, but to no avail.

And before going up to his room, he would exchange a few words with some of the other guests about the weather and decline, with a neutral "No thank you", the polite proposal of a game of bridge by the hotel manager, who called him "young sir" even though he had grown a goatee and had even bought himself a pipe.

He had to make up his mind to talk to his father. He couldn't stand it there much longer.

Vanni had had time

V ANNI HAD HAD TIME to forget the solitude of that hotel. He had had time to lose a war, gain a degree, get married, have a son, and become a graduate, husband and father. And when Sor Terenzio had died, Vanni had found himself in charge of a huge estate, with fields to be cultivated, the sunny ones or the shady ones, depending on whether the fields faced south or north, as the peasants pointed out with astral precision, and hectares and hectares of woods as far as the eye could see, as the old estate manager would say to express, in his own way, the concept of infinity. And farm after farm, and olive grove after olive grove, and vines on the steep hillsides, and smooth fallows, and gullies so deep you could fall and break your neck, and dunes of golden corn.

And a mountain of debts. Because Sor Terenzio, my great-grandfather, had left him a bitter legacy. The castle had cost a lot, but Terenzio had signed cheques and dispensed banknotes with a subdued pain—he wouldn't have been able to say where it came from, but it was from somewhere inside. The man was old. He had built a castle, had two sons, lost one of them. Had he paid everyone? No one was owed a single lira. But there was still one last creditor, as Terenzio put it, the most troublesome of all, the one who, when he came to cash in, would present him with a bill for his whole life. That creditor was death. Not that he minded, not at all—perhaps he would meet Fede again, perhaps they could go hunting together. But in the end it was only the thought of that reunion that stirred his tired heart, because it had been some time since Terenzio had last believed either in paradise or in the sermons of priests. Like a dog who eats grass in spring, the old man was looking for a natural way to cleanse his soul in preparation for death, or rebirth.

While Terenzio was looking at the world with lightless eyes, and Vanni was at war, the estate manager had got through what was left of that huge inheritance. So when Vanni had returned, looking older than his years, he had barely had time to watch the last shovelful of earth fall on his father's coffin, and already there was no time to weep. The following day, for the first time without his father, he had gone down into the study and sat down at his desk. He had sat down the way his father had sat down, and had immediately felt the way his father must have felt—that he was on the bridge of a ship. A ship that was sinking.

Behind the majestic walnut desk, which did indeed seem like the deck of a ship, he would receive the estate manager, the tenant farmers, the creditors. There would be a hot, bitter coffee brought to his bed in the morning by the housekeeper, his daily shave, knotting his tie without looking at the mirror—child's play for someone who'd been in the navy—and then he would go down into the study to meet the people. He would go down, and the people would come up, not the other way round, because the Cremona house had been built like that, at the highest point of the village. Every bloody day, Vanni would go down. First he would go through the invoices, the bills, the account books, interrupted by a few telephone calls to which he would reply curtly, giving as little as possible away. All things considered, he was a good boss, and apart from the fact that he *was* the boss, people had no reason to complain.

The years had passed, and so had the season of regrets. Not much expenditure, and a lot of thrift. And the debt had been settled.

In the meantime Vanni had taken a wife, a beautiful child bride fifteen years his junior. She had lost her father, and had found a new one in Vanni, a self-made man who still had in his eyes the memory of the patrol boats steaming across the Straits of Sicily. She, on the other hand, still had in her soul her sadness for that father who had died young and in her nose the smell of the refectory in the convent school where they had put her while the bombs fell outside.

Together, he and she had had children. They had raised them, with the help of nursemaids. With every child, life, like a fire sweeping through the undergrowth, moves forward, the war becomes ever more remote, and the difficult years of peasant unrest, and life becomes ever more distant from life.

It wasn't an easy matter, running the estate. It took nerve, but nerve was something Vanni had. Once, when he was in the garden, gazing out from the great terrace that overlooked the valley at his estate stretching as far as the corn-covered hills, he saw, down in the valley, in the middle of the fields, that a combine harvester had stopped because of an argument between the worker who was operating it and another who was towing the forage wagon, a good man but a hothead. Every minute that the harvester was still meant five minutes for the tractor with the forage wagon loading and unloading the corn, and ten for the trucks that were going to and from the cooperative while there was still light. Each minute was an eternity for Vanni.

From the distance, Vanni had seen the harvester parked on the hump of the fallow like an old man who has paused to catch his breath. He had immediately understood. He took his car, and parked above the road. With long, uninterrupted strides, he had cut through the field, cursing the bristly stubble. He reached the harvester. The workers, who had been arguing heatedly, fell silent at his approach.

"What's happening? Why have you stopped?"

"It's Anselmo."

Vanni looked Anselmo straight in the eyes.

"No, it's him. He—"

"I don't care who it was. I asked why you've stopped."

"Sir, this is the second time he's turned in the wrong place and made me wait, and we're dying of the heat—"

"It's not true. I didn't turn in the wrong place. I know this field, and I now that's the right place, otherwise you risk overturning … "

Vanni had looked from one to the other of the two workers. Then he had gripped the steps of the harvester and with a thrust like a diver had climbed up and in a moment had slipped into the cabin leaving behind him a whiff of aftershave. The workers stood looking at him. Vanni started the engine and set off with the cutter bar raised. With a grinding of gears, the harvester moved like a red ladybird across the vast yellow field. Very slowly, it advanced into the already threshed corner. Reaching the end of the field near the ridge, where the slope became hazardous and the sea of corn broke against a patch of earth beyond which there was only air, the combine harvester slowed, seemed to roll on its side like a ship that was overladen, then fearlessly threw itself down the slope. The men, standing motionless in the sun, shielded their eyes with their hands and held their breaths. Down there, at the end of the field, with a magisterial turn, the harvester straightened up and reversed direction. It lowered the cutter bar and advanced in a cloud of dust. Perhaps the field seemed bigger, or the harvester was going more slowly, but to the men standing in the sun those minutes were like hours. When the machine reached them, facing in the opposite direction from which it had started, Vanni switched off the engine. In the sun, in the middle of the corn, even time stood still. The only sound was the chirping of the cicadas.

A name and a destiny

HOW WELL I UNDERSTOOD FEDE. His restlessness, his vocation for freedom. And how well I understood Vanni. His composure, his certainties which had become uncertainties when his brother died. All at once, he was faced with that sense of unpreparedness all second sons feel when they lose their elder brothers. The need to come out of the trench and launch an attack without covering fire. The abrupt sensation of finding yourself in the front-line, without anyone covering your back. The reluctance to assume all your responsibilities, to meet all the expectations people have of you. His parents, the family, the dynasty, the course of history, everything was suddenly loaded on his young shoulders. I don't have this from hearsay, I know how pheasant is eaten in the Cremona household—two bites of the breast and the rest to the dogs. I've also felt their cruel condemnation. I'm the only male in the whole family, I feel the weight of centuries on my back. You have no idea how much of myself I saw in that story which wasn't even mine. How could I not know that one day those two twins, those two characters, those two destinies, one combative and the other prudent, one passionate and the other rational, one victorious and the other defeated, those two stories, one open-ended and one closed, would finally be reconciled and brought together again in my destiny, in my character, in my story? As to how Fede had ended up inside me, I can only hypothesise. And the most convincing hypothesis is that after Fede's death, it was as if Vanni had swallowed his

73

departed twin, as if he carried him inside like a screw in a bone, invisible but always present, and painful when there's a change in the weather. Fede's character had moved from the grandfather into the father's genotype without manifesting itself, to then reappear in me after skipping a generation, just as Mendel teaches.

I felt that it was Fede in particular who lived again in me, Fede mitigated by Vanni. And I knew it wouldn't be easy for me to assume the dead twin's bleak destiny. But I was certain that somehow I had to do it, it was up to me, that's all. I wasn't usurping anything because there was that name—Federico—that name was in my life and in his life, it was in his death and it would be in mine. And it made me the legitimate replacement for the departed twin. And even though I was inside that name and that destiny twice, like being in a shapeless old coat which wasn't my size and didn't suit me, I was in it. What could I do? I had inherited it. It wouldn't have been right to refuse it. A name and a destiny. They were all I had when I came into the world.

Well, we wanted development

WELL, WE WANTED development. That's what they said in the village. Here it is. Now you have it. It's all yours. So don't come and tell me you're not happy. While I wait for the coffee, which is taking ages to boil, Lea is out getting firewood, and the boys have been away since this morning and haven't come back yet (let's hope nothing has happened to them), it seems to me I can see it as if it was now. Yes. Development. Whatever it was, it clearly got off on the wrong foot here.

It was an ordinary weekday. A Mercedes with an NA registration had pulled up at the lay-by on the main road and deposited three Nigerian women with scarred faces, before setting off again in a screech of tyres, black diesel smoke burning the piston rings. The three black women— no black people had been seen in these parts since the German retreat, apart from the Rwandan priest they had sent to the evangelical frontier, a remote parish of the municipality, the which reverend during the usual Easter time round of home visits had heard someone answer him from behind a door, *Thanks, we don't want anything!*—the three black women, as I was saying, had certainly not passed unnoticed. The news spread quickly, and randy pensioners went up and down the main road like swarms of bees, uncertain what to do. In the square, small knots of people had spontaneously formed, discussing the situation, and trying to choose someone to be their ambassador. The wisest among them suggested ways of keeping this unexpected resource from the eyes of wives and bigots. Unfortunately for them, they spent too long debating the matter. All it took was one telephone call—no one is sure who made it—and the three African Aphrodites were picked up by the *carabinieri*. The grim-faced old men resumed their card games—whose hand was it?—commenting laconically— Well, they wanted development.

When I'm in the tent at night, unable to get to sleep and listening spellbound to an owl marking time like a metronome, that sentence echoes in my head like a broken record.

Water has been the real curse. And what a curse! Better not to have had any. Or rather no, that's too much, it sounds like blasphemy. Better to have had some. But not too much of it, and cold. That's it. It was all that hot water that made us anxious. My God, what are going to do with it? people thought. It's a divine blessing, manna from heaven, it would be a damned pity not to use it, we should give thanks to the Lord. But the water, although hot, isn't boiling hot, at the source it doesn't even reach forty degrees, if you just can't wait you can go to Petriolo to scald your bellies, or to Terme dei Papi, where citizens of Viterbo in their furs, with their bosomy wives and their already obese children, immerse themselves. Or if you're German and like eating overcooked pasta, then go to Ischia. What do you want with us?

The good thing is, it doesn't stink. In fact, it doesn't have any smell at all. Our water isn't like the water in Saturnia, which is white and sulphurous and leaves the unmistakable odour of rotten eggs on your skin for a day or two. There must be iron in our water. I deduce that from the red seaweed and from the rusty aftertaste which wouldn't escape the nose of any connoisseur bather or qualified sommelier who opened his nostrils wide and took a deep breath … Tell me, what is this water good for? the tourist from the Po valley asks anxiously. Is it good for the skin? For the liver? What about the eyes? And what can you tell me about the mud baths? What do you want me to say, signora? If you like, I can tell you that it's good for the liver, the skin and the eyes, that if you drink a little glass of it as soon as you wake up in the morning you'll see it's good for the bladder, not to mention your skin, shrivelled as it is by your considerable age, too much lighting and the miasmas of the city, so come on, smear mud all over yourself and your blocked pores will sweat like they used to … No, I'm sorry, I retract everything, I'm not telling you what you want me to tell you. I'll tell you the truth, the whole truth, and nothing but the truth. It's water, signora. You know, H_2O. Thermal water. Running water. Water plain and simple. It doesn't do you any good and it doesn't do you any harm. It doesn't do anything. Anything at all. Having said that, it's a free country, so go and spend your money at a beauty farm, go and have mud shovelled on to you while you wear those ridiculous paper knickers, go and don't be afraid of showing a stranger rolls of fat, a wrinkled neck, wattles, drooping breasts, and whatever remains of a body after life has used it for sixty years or so. I repeat, you have the sacrosanct right to be massaged by a guru who asks you if you have cervical problems as he smears your body with essential oils (essential to whom? Maybe to the masseur?) and products which have been cynically tested, yes, you did read that correctly, I said 'cynically', which will make your skin as glossy and oily as a gladiator's. And when, wearing your paper birthday suit, you find yourself in a somewhat discreditable position in which no one, not even your husband, has dared to put you for years, don't tell me I didn't warn you. You should be happy.

It might have been enough to enjoy this divine blessing of hot water and leave it at that without doing you know what, and in my opinion God Almighty—for those who believe in Him—would have been even happier. Instead of which, they got all worked up about development. They were afraid of losing ground, of being left behind. They had to do something. Everyone was obsessed with doing something. Something, anything. And now that they've done it, or rather, now that they've caused it to be done, why aren't they even good people, now that they've spoilt it all and everything's gone to the dogs, what to do, what to do, tell me, what to do?

And that name was Ottone Gattai

I'LL NEVER FORGET THAT DAY.

THEATRE OF THE FRIENDS OF THE LAND 6.00 PM.
All inhabitants of the municipality are invited to the meeting
Thermalism and Development—the Future at Our Feet
Speaker—Ottone Gattai, Managing Director of Aquatrade and
President of the New Consortium for Thermal Development.
Followed by refreshments courtesy of the Cantinori pastry shop.
Everyone welcome.

Posters and leaflets in every format and colour plastered the village. The municipal theatre was crowded. The auditorium was packed, the stalls and gallery filled to the brim. In the dress circle, you could see the stooped back of the notary, Perugini, who, it was said, had killed a peasant when, as a young man, he had been a pacemaker for the Mille Miglia, the monocle of Doctor Solfanelli with his bejewelled wife, the thin moustache of Marshal Tacconi, the ruddy cheeks of Don Vitaliano, known as Don Perignon or Don Byron because of his devotion to alcohol. When he was particularly tipsy, Don Perignon would lose the thread of his sermons, and sometimes at Mass he'd go off the rails completely in ways that were far from orthodox. Immediately behind these worthies, Rita, in her cardigan that smelt of mothballs. Rita was a spinster who had never married because she had never found the right man, according to her, or because she was as ugly as

79

the cemetery gate, according to us. Just behind her, Bice, a widow who, since her husband, who had beaten her, had died, had experienced a rebirth—when she dolled herself up to go to the cemetery to put flowers on his grave, there were some who said that she wasn't bad and might even be worth a discreet screw. And there was Giustina with her Poldelio, her adopted son who had had polio as a child and at the age of twenty had become the principal soloist in the parish choir, which was satisfaction enough for her. In other words, the same line-up that usually presided in the front row in church were all there, ready and correct, in the theatre. Down in the stalls, on the left wing, the Bertocchis and the Pagninis, large communist families who together, united in the sacred bond of the hammer and sickle, what with all their many relatives, raked in more than a hundred safe votes for the Party, and then, in rows, further back but on the right, liberals and moderates, which was an elegant way of saying reactionaries and Fascists, with some of my relatives and other landowners prudently occupying the back rows, worried that the changing of the guard that had been rumoured for months might somehow undermine their age-old privileges. Leaning against the wall (he never sat down, as a mark of protest against the establishment), Oronzo Giancane, an unemployed teacher of anarchist leanings, who had been sent from Bitonto as a supply teacher and, as also happened with that Camorrista sent to the village for a period of obligatory residence, had never left. I, too, was at the back, in the coolness of a corner, filling my lungs with the smell of fresh paint which had hung over the theatre ever since they had taken down the scaffolding in a hurry and finished the renovations in record time. I looked at the cream-coloured walls, the second-rate decorations in dull hues which ran all the way round the hall along the cornice.

And I looked at another product of that unholy restoration, the fish bolts with which the seats had been fixed for ever to the floor, wiping out with a turn of a bolt a glorious past as a dance floor. No one would ever again dance on that floor where so many feet had intertwined, sought each other, stepped on each other at winter carnival dances and at evening dances in spring, which had produced many children who weren't even aware of the fact.

It's pointless for me to repeat it—that day in the Municipal Theatre, formerly the Theatre of the Friends of the Land, the people who always appeared on important occasions were all there. And also there, and just as eager, were the councillors and the Mayor. Red and sweaty, his tie tightly knotted, looking as unnatural as a peasant imprisoned in his Sunday best, with a microphone in front of him, the Mayor was waiting for something, I don't know what, to break the embarrassingly long silence which precedes all public announcements. The long rectangular table at the foot of the platform was laid with a beautiful white tablecloth which hung to the floor. On the table, slices of pizza, appetisers (also kindly supplied by the Cantinori pastry shop), wild boar sausages, a round of cheese from Piacenza, a tray with chicken livers on toast (the kind you can buy in a supermarket), an array of bottles of wine—only ten years earlier there would have been a simple demijohn with a plastic tube which you sucked and then plugged with your thumb the same way you got petrol for your moped. But this time, no, this time they had done things in style.

For years, the baths had been languishing in a semi-comatose state, and the council seemed finally to have found a buyer interested in reviving them. What was needed was a personality who could be relied on, an authoritative name. And that name was Ottone Gattai.

Ottone Gattai, a textile manufacturer from Pistoia, born 1936, ignorant but intelligent, a self-made man. Someone of few words, with a rough-and-ready philosophy, good leadership skills, and plenty of common sense. Tall, sturdy, unusually abstemious for a Tuscan, didn't drink, didn't smoke cigarettes, only short, mature cigars, a high forehead, a hard, direct look, a resolute chin, white crew-cut hair and thick eyebrows, the bearing of an estate manager. Ottone Gattai had already taken over other small thermal spas which were little more than pools for washing clothes and had transformed them into genuine, well-managed resorts, with mud baths, massage, health spas, beauty farms and all the rest of that body-care claptrap that gives meaning to the lives of ladies of a certain age with rich husbands and grown-up children. After Saturnia, his company, Aquatrade Limited, had acquired, one after the other, Monsummano, Bagno Vignoni, Chianciano, Sant'Albino and Petriolo, wresting control from impromptu, high-risk managements and shaky thermal consortiums. Every spurt, splash, gully and rivulet of thermal water was the property of Ottone Gattai and Aquatrade.

And now here was Ottone Gattai, sitting there rumpled and disdainful, with his elbows on the table, to the right of the Mayor, who in the meantime had provoked some catcalls by his clumsy handling of the microphone. Once the technical problems had been resolved, our first citizen made his requisite opening remarks, serving Ottone Gattai up to us on a silver platter. And I'll never forget that speech of his, because, if we are where we are now, it's as a consequence of the calamitous words that were said on that even more calamitous occasion.

The Mayor took the plunge and opened his mouth. "Com … citizens … there has been a great deal of talk lately about our baths … after the recent false steps … "

"You're a scandal!" came a hostile voice from the stalls.

" … we did in fact look at the possibility of district heating for a while … anyway, after years of false steps, with the way the wind is blowing, we can't allow ourselves the luxury of keeping the baths closed. If we fail again this time, the prestige of our village will be set back twenty years. But we won't fail."

A subdued buzz went through the hall.

"And it's in order not to fail that we have backed a thoroughbred, a leader in the field. Give a big hand to the man who has bought the Thermal Consortium, the sultan of hot water—OTTONE GATTAI!"

Slowly and solemnly, Gattai took his everlasting cigar from his lips, looked as if he was about to spit, and began speaking in a low, firm voice.

"My name is Ottone Gattai. I've never been given anything by anyone. I was born in Quarrata, in the province of Pistoia. My father was a ragman, who lived poor and died poor. When I was a child, my two brothers and I had one pair of shoes between us. Whoever woke up first got to put them on. I was always the one who woke up first. Any questions?"

"Simone Rubbieri, *Il Corriere di Siena*—Signor Gattai, why have you decided to buy our village baths?"

"Because the Mayor went down on his knees and begged me, and because I got them for almost nothing."

"Marzio Mazzoni, *La Nazione*. I have two questions. You began your business career running a firm that unblocked cesspits. My first question is how do you answer those malicious people who say you made your money from shit, the second—"

"Let them try not to shit, if they can."

That silenced the stalls, apart from a few outbreaks of coughing. Finally a hand was raised.

"Signor Gattai, Diulio Beltarme, from the Mountain Territorial Association. In Saturnia, you built a hotel which looks like an aircraft carrier. We've seen the plans, and, well, the fact is, with all that concrete, we're a little bit worried about the environmental impact … "

"If I were you, I'd be more worried if your baths stayed the way they are … and besides, if there's a lot of concrete, then all the better—it means they'll last."

The Mayor interrupted the barrage of questions to Gattai. "I must say that the project proposed by Signor Gattai and Aquatrade is not just about concrete buildings. It also addresses other issues relating to leisure time, such as golf courses, tennis courts, five-a-side football fields, a riding school with adjoining racetracks, open-air parks and reserved areas, swimming pools, restaurants, boutiques, jobs, lots of jobs, and above all—something which is particularly dear to us—the image of our village."

"Signor Gattai, I'm Carlo Benelli, chairman of the Tourist Promotion Board. As far as I understand, your perspective, for good or ill, is a purely commercial one, which doesn't do justice to the thermal phenomenon as a whole. The baths are not only an economic resource, they're above all part of our cultural heritage, and have been in this area as long as human settlement. Just think of the use the Etruscans made of the baths—"

"I don't give a fuck for the Etruscans. I'm bringing in the Russians, not the Etruscans."

And that's how it all started.

That's why we'll win

S INCE THE CONSTRUCTION SITE for the spa had started working at full steam, the village had been repopulated. Not with tourists but with workers. Almost all of them—bricklayers, labourers, painters, plumbers—were from the south, lean young men with wild faces and black hair, who by day got sunstroke or scraped their fingers on the icebound site and by night drank bottle after bottle of Moretti in the village bars. And it could hardly be said that the impact of a large concentration of adult males in a village historically lacking in women—and many of the few there were were hardly fanciable, unless you had a ravenous appetite and were very adaptable—was a negligible problem. At first, the young workers' sexual drive expressed itself in bold, testosterone-fuelled glances directed towards the few women of child-bearing age in the area. And as is well known, no glance, once cast, fails to reach its target. Even when it doesn't seem like it.

All the same, winter in our area made its presence felt not only in the rigour of those six hundred metres exposed to the wind that howled through the alleys of the village, slapping the doors and puffing like a green lizard through the window frames, or in the snow which, like a beloved guest, paid us at least a couple of visits a year. No, not only in that. The winter also made its presence felt below the waist. If those young men felt cold being such a long way from the southern sun, they felt even colder being separated from their wives and girlfriends for months on end. While the great thermal catafalque grew day by day, with dizzying speed, while the scaffolding rose into the sky, while the great earth-moving machines excavated without pause, devouring fruit trees, fields and olive groves—a wrong move by a bulldozer had swallowed up the age-old Ficoncella spring, diverting it God knows where—so the desires and boldness of those alert young men with their street-urchin eyes and tanned necks also grew. Sitting with their beers outside the bars, or standing in the sun during breaks, with their cigarettes behind their ears and their mortadella panini in their hands, the workers took heart and moved from glances to comments. An excessive amount of lipstick, a shorter skirt, a more daring hairdo—it wasn't difficult for an attentive observer to note in the local women small, flirtatious variations on the theme of everyday negligence. Variations which demonstrated that those impertinent glances had indeed hit their target, because a woman, even when she does not look, always knows she is being looked at. The very fact of knowing, of sensing a man's eyes on her, makes her consciously more beautiful and more mischievous. And so the ugly ones became passable, and the passable ones almost pretty. The miracle of making these resigned wives feel like women again had occurred without their stupid husbands noticing a thing. In a few months, almost a dozen marriages ended. Hasty, uncommunicative, resigned marriages, marked by weariness or lack of initiative, marriages which, perhaps through some curious principle of conjugal dynamics, would have lasted to the end if external factors had not intervened to disturb their civil status. I was not at all surprised when young married women left husbands, work and children for young bricklayers and carpenters with dark eyebrows and incomprehensible ways of speaking, precipitating the village into a storm of scandals, with mothers-in-law again becoming mothers, husbands sons, and daughters-in-law sluts and, as such, enemies of the community. I wasn't surprised because I knew what those marriages were like, and I knew how and where those engagements had turned into marriages. Engagements that had begun as adolescent flings and soon turned into serious relationships, like customs that become laws. Pizza on a Saturday night, although only during the first few months of the engagement, occasional visits to the cinema, maybe at Christmas time, Sunday afternoons in the car, parked in the square, listening to the matches. They were together five, ten years. Then, just like when you fall asleep on the bus and wake up at the terminal, some suddenly realised where they were. When that happened, there were only two solutions—get married or break up. I remember one couple, both about thirty, who, after a ten-year engagement that was almost a marriage, found themselves one autumn afternoon sitting on a bench, silently watching the cars raise the leaves as they sped past on the main road. "Why don't we get married?" she ventured. "Why don't we break up?" he replied. "All right," she said. And they broke up, right there on the bench, without a word.

Lazy husbands who systematically neglected their wives. Never a pizza, never a compliment or a pair of earrings. Never anything. And after a while the husbands, returning exhausted from work, even stopped desiring their wives. It was inevitable that the first man to remind these young women that they were women, to unearth that buried femininity, would hit the jackpot without too much effort. But there was another reason I wasn't surprised.

It was because I believed in the theory of historical recurrence. I was convinced not only that destinies were

87

transmittable, as Professor Voinea believed, but also that certain situations repeated themselves with impressive fidelity, provided the same anthropological conditions were in place.

Something similar had happened in the Seventies, when telecommunications workers had come to the area to lay high-tension cables, my village being on the route of the Florence-Rome power line. Then, too, a number of marriages had broken up, and the only reason others had resisted was not because there was such a strong bond between the spouses but because we were so unemancipated. It had taken those telecommunications workers to bring us the sexual revolution ten years late, because in this area 1968 had made no impression, except for a few workers who came back from the city at weekends with longer hair, shirts with huge collars and a longing to pick a quarrel. Take Sante, who during the week sweated for his pay in a factory in Florence, risking his knuckles on the lathe, and on Fridays returned to the village with a wonderfully insolent student-protestor attitude. This infuriated Milo the petrol station attendant, who, entering the bar and finding Sante lying on the billiard table studying the cushion and lining up a shot, walked behind him and hissed, "Cut your hair, you queer!" Sante's response was to stand up on the billiard table and raise a clenched left hand in the air. Then Corinto, the barkeeper, walked up with a billiard cue in his hand and brought it down angrily on Sante's boots. "Get down! Get down, damn it!" That was what the generation gap amounted to in our village.

But it was the upheaval caused by the telecommunications workers that gave even some of the few villagers an excuse to be more daring. One of them, named Corticelli, had fallen in love with a Sardinian girl who did the cleaning for a retired general who lived with his old mother. Encouraged by the success of the workers, Corticelli summoned up courage and phoned the Sardinian girl. The telephone calls became more frequent, and an encounter was on the cards. To avoid his friends' endless ribbing (Haven't you asked her yet? Are you going to pop the question on bonded paper?), Corticelli would answer non-committally and then, taking a long way round, go and telephone from the public booth at the far end of the square, hoping for a little privacy. What the poor man didn't know was that, with the help of an accommodating telecommunications worker, his friends were connected to a branch line which went from the cabin to the exchange just outside the walls, and listened to all his phone calls. From the innocent, awkward conversation between the Sardinian girl and Corticelli, it didn't take them long to realise that nothing that wasn't platonic had happened between the two of them. They decided to play a practical joke. One evening the telephone rang in the Corticelli house and he picked up the receiver. From the other end came a man's voice with a strong Sardinian accent and a threatening tone. "I know all about it. Gigliola told me everything. You've shamed my daughter. You must assume your responsibilities." "I will, I will!" Corticelli blurted in a thin voice, even though he had not even consummated their relationship.

For me, just like him, there's no turning back, and I assume all my responsibilities. The responsibility not to stand and watch while they take your land away from under your feet, the responsibility to tell the story of what happened, the responsibility to defend what is mine and drive out the invader. That's what we're fighting for. That's why we'll win. We hope.

Petrol is still too cheap

A WINTER EVENING, a sky filled with stars, the kind of clear sky you never see in a city, swept by the north wind which makes the air sharp and the stars bright. The usual stroll after the usual dinner of grilled meat and red wine. The usual itinerary, from the square to the bridge to the crossroads to the medieval gate to the square. Hands in pockets, cigarettes in mouths, the smoke mingling with the steam of our breaths, the same chatter as ever, women, laughter, familiar anecdotes constantly retold with infinite variations, like a game of chess. My friends, we talked crap in front of the fire, we spewed out words in the night, always in expectation of something that was going to happen. But what was going to happen none of us knew for certain. Could that something have been development? Who knows, perhaps it was. What's certain is that that evening, something, or rather someone, happened. Nothing to do with Nigerian whores this time. No, this time it was worse.

Wrapped in our *vitelloni* coats, we passed the restaurant in the square, and saw a few figures moving about behind the big French windows, in the warm light of the interior. The kind of light that evokes warm, welcoming rooms, pastel shades and wooden seats upholstered in straw, Tuscan crostini, ravioli with pigeon, and a highly respectable wine cellar. We had actually been talking about wine that winter evening in which it seems to me I can now glimpse the beginning of the end. Anyway, there we are strolling and talking about wine, debating whether Guadaltasso was superior to Tignanello, and we start to get heated, and before long someone is bound to say that the Fonterutoli you can buy from Esselunga for ten euros is better than the Badia in Passignano and it'll end in a fight, I'm sure. So to divert attention and calm things down a bit, I come out with the well-worn opinion that nobody wanted Morellino, not even if it was Bordeaux ... and then Garrone tells the story we all know about the Americans who went to buy Morellino at Scansano, driving to a farm and stopping in the farmyard where there's a little old man sleeping in the shade. And the Americans wake him and he's pissed off that they've woken him and he doesn't want to sell to them, and the Americans insist and he curses but in the end yields and says to them, in dialect, "Reverse!" gesturing to them to drive their car backwards towards the cellar and the Americans look at him in bewilderment and he doesn't give a damn whether or not they understand him and keeps saying, "Reverse! If you want wine, reverse, if not, clear off ... " And of course he's right. Even though we all know the story, we all say "Go on, Garrone tell it!" And Garrone tells the story, and we're all screaming with laughter just as we pass the door of the restaurant, which we're surprised to see closed, although admittedly it's quite cold, and we look inside casually just to see who's there. And we see a table with two red-faced men with big bellies and two tall blonde girls sitting at it. On the table, there's an array of bottles of wine, and these two heavy, half-bald guys are smoking their cigars and fondling these beautiful young girls just like two gangsters. But we don't give a damn, let them do what they want, and we're about to carry on walking except that one of them starts to stare at us and then to shout something in a language we don't understand. Then he says "*Italianskyyyyy* … " and belches, and his companion shakes with laughter. Conti says, "They're drunk!" And Garrone, who's quick to take offence, says, "What are these guys doing here?" And we say, "Come on, let's go, what do you care, they're just a couple of drunks, let's walk a bit and then go to bed." But the man inside the restaurant keeps pointing at us and laughing and Garrone stamps his feet like a donkey. "I want to know what the hell those bastards are laughing about … " And he goes straight to the entrance of the restaurant. Then one of the two stops laughing (the other hasn't noticed a thing and continues laughing) and becomes serious, grips his chair as if to get up, and quickly puts his hand under his jacket. At that moment, one of the girls leaps to her feet and runs to the door and stands with her arm across the doorway, stopping Garrone from going in. She's about twenty, and very beautiful. She has clear eyes and shoulder-length blonde hair and a dress with a plunging neckline, and must be feeling quite cold standing there in the doorway.

"Please," she says in English, "go, go, go! Go away, please."

"What?"

"Please."

English sounds so dramatic in that beautiful Russian mouth of hers. "Please," she said. And now she repeats it in a tone which is almost a supplication. She's so beautiful, she could disarm me with one look. Garrone lowers his eyes, turns and, without saying a word, walks off. We, too, resume our stroll. In silence. I turn and see that the girl is still there, and I have the impression she's looking at me. That is, that she's looking *specifically* at me. *Only* me. We walk quickly and now she's little more than a patch against the light in the illumined doorway of the restaurant.

For a while, we all remain silent. We walk in the night. Then Tito asks, "What did she say to you?" No one answers him, no one ever answers Tito. And as we walk without talking, we hear a rumble like an approaching storm, and we barely have time to realise that a ball of light is coming round the bend at a crazy speed. We throw ourselves to the side of the street to avoid being run over. An enormous black SUV turns the corner at high speed, and the tyres screech on the asphalt like a dog being kicked in the ribs. As it speeds past me, I see out of the corner of my eye behind the wheel the two big-bellied guys from before, sprawled in their leather seats and laughing, they nearly ran us over, and they're laughing, those bastards. They're laughing. Even though no sound emerges from that darkened driving compartment, I seem to hear their coarse laughter, just as I feel on me those fingers gripping their cigars and fondling the girls in the restaurant. Here they are, here are the girls, in the back seats, but I catch only a glimpse of them, or rather, one of them, the one who said *please*. The one who looked at me. Once again I have the impression that she's looking at me, and it seems to me that this time she's sad, this time she's trying to say *sorry, sorry*.

The car disappears into the distance, its powerful headlights devouring the darkness. We get up again, feel ourselves, and look at each other the way I imagine survivors look at each other. Nothing broken. We're all fine. Garrone shakes out his coat and says, "Petrol is still too cheap … "

"But who were they?" Conti asks.

Everyone shrugs, as if to say, who knows?

Then Tito, who's kept silent so far because no one ever asks him anything, says, "They were Russians."

"Russians?"

"Yes, Russians."

"How do you know?"

"I know."

"But how do you know?"

"They're staying at the Hotel Terme."

"And what are they doing here?"

"Apparently Gattai invited them. He's looking for partners for his spa."

It was a piece of luck

WE SHOULD ALWAYS THINK TWICE before leaving a woman, before changing our car, before giving a felt sweater to charity. In future, the past could come in useful. It was a piece of luck that my grandfather had hidden at the bottom of the well in the cellar the old Mauser he'd stolen from a commando. Obviously, it's always been kept dry, inside a watertight case. A Mauser Kar 48, a Kar Karabiner, made in Germany and issued to the diehards of the Italian Social Republic. Last shot fired at Salò. 7.62 calibre, locked with a bolt—it's the prince of breechblocks—there's no hunting rifle or carbine that doesn't have one. It's my weapon. It's not all that accurate but it's my security, it would never leave me in the lurch.

Of course it's not like the machine pistol that belongs to Antoine, the Communist sommelier and expert on wine, neo-realism and guerrilla tactics sent to us by our comrades in the Bordeaux section. They, too, had taken to the hills to fight the American multinational which has bought all the vineyards with the intention of eradicating almost all Cabernet Francs and Sauvignons and replacing them with a Californian York-Madeira that's resistant to phylloxera. But our French comrades will pay dearly. The machine pistol, as I was saying, now that's a weapon, made by Schmeisser and Heinrich Wagner in 1938, a remarkable year for submachine guns and champagne—according to Antoine, that year the vines clinging to the cliffs at Rheims bent beneath the weight of bunches of grapes as big as wigs. A patented weapon with a shortened spring, made of pressed metal, with a folding tubular stock, and a casing and cheekpieces of Bakelite. Almost five hundred shots a minute, velocity at the muzzle three hundred and sixty-five metres a second. It's simple, light, and never jams. Antoine says he stole it from a Wehrmacht corporal who had propped it against an oak tree while he went behind a hedge to have a shit.

Tito, on the other hand, has a .72 calibre Garand automatic rifle that can pick off a pool attendant at the spa at half a kilometre. They hire another and Tito calmly picks him off again. Since September, he has blown away nine pool attendants. *Pow, pow*, he never misses. He usually crouches behind the broken wall of the farmhouse above the road which enjoys a privileged view. To the west, the broad shoulders of the Amiata and the ridges of the Val d'Orcia, to the north, the gentle outline of the Cetona and in the middle, unmistakable, the spa.

The Aquatrade Resort

THE AQUATRADE RESORT rises at the foot of the hills. It dominates the middle of the valley, with its pharaonic central body over which flutters a large flag with a blue clawed serpent on a white background, the hated emblem of the even more hated Aquatrade. From the central building, the two huge side wings fan out, built on what remains of the old Medicean portico. At first glance, the effect is that of a huge pink foreign body in the middle of the verdant valley. The colour was imposed by the Academy of Fine Arts, a magic fig leaf intended by those patented geniuses at the regional board in Siena to reduce the environmental impact of a few million cubic metres of reinforced concrete. Embedded in the concrete are hundreds, thousands of windows, like the portholes of an ocean liner. Behind every window, a room, all those rooms, all the same, furnished by a gay designer with pink shades and apricot curtains. And then the terraces looking out on the golf course, a view granted only to a dozen imperial suites reserved for Mafiosi and other rich and powerful men from around the world when they come to soak their balls at the spa. All around, hundreds of metres of electrified fence, barbed wire and watchtowers, with Gattai's private police force watching over every crack, every square centimetre.

There it is, the Aquatrade Resort, the largest and most expensive spa resort in the world. There it is, as still as a sphinx. Thirty-six swimming pools, two of them Olympic, an Ayurvedic pool, an authentic wood-heated Finnish sauna—an absurdity that last year consumed at least a hectare of forest—and one for pets (the only one in the world, as far as I know), twelve gyms, two golf courses, three normal-sized football fields, five tennis courts, fifty boutiques, nine restaurants and three hairdressing salons. Including one for dogs.

With the Russian-made binoculars I bought from the Poles on the main road, I can see the swimming pool, the beach umbrellas, the cascades, even the splashes when the divers go in and the bathers' tattoos.

And to think that for years they led us up the garden path, promising us a *social spa*. Baths for everyone, they wanted. Now the cheapest rooms are 1,500 euros per night. But it wasn't always like this. Far from it.

We're coming to get you

F OR THOUSANDS OF YEARS we had been very lucky. No one had ever done anything. There were some who were fine with that, they had no interest in doing anything because they thought it would just be worse than before, and those who weren't fine with it but were too poor or too disorganised to do anything. No one moved. From the Etruscans to the Fascists, by way of the grand dukes and the Piedmontese, if you want to see ultraconservatism in action, or inaction, there it is.

There had always been water. And people used it the way people use water. The women washed clothes in it, the men watered their kitchen gardens, the boys bathed in it, because in those days there was no one to venture the opinion that water would be the oil of the future, that new wars would be fought to secure the planet's water resources. The Medicis had built a fine, elegant portico for their baths, a row of slender travertine columns, and two centuries later the grand dukes had simply tidied the baths up a bit and surrounded them with a lovely Italian garden.

When, without fuss, the grand dukes went on their way, the Piedmontese arrived, and they had so many problems to deal with, they certainly weren't going to waste their time on hot water. In the years following unification, not a single pipe was laid. The baths became a wagon shed, then a storeroom for household belongings, until, at the beginning of the twentieth century, when bourgeois families began taking holidays in the country, the decision was taken to restore them to their former use. With a couple of coats of whitewash and a little work, the baths reopened their doors. When, years later, the Duce came along and turned Chianciano into a modern thermal spa and a tourist spot *à la page*, or even *à la mode*, the Fascist mayor, in the hope that Mussolini would come to visit our village, had had the idea of building at the entrance to the baths a small triumphal arch of red bricks, on the front of which he had had engraved in Roman characters SALVS PER AQVAM. But the Duce never passed beneath that arch. In fact, he never came to this area at all. Which was just as well, because at the very least he would have got a few raspberries, as people here have always been Communists. At the end of the war, no one is quite sure by what route, three adventurers arrived from Libya. Scenting danger and the first stirrings of colonial defeat, they had wound up the little they had in Tripolitania and got out before King Idris kicked them out. Their names were Rossi, Poretti and Morelli, and they took charge of the baths, paying rent to the municipality. At least that's what I was told by a retired stonecutter who seems able to answer any question you ask him. But their thermal adventure didn't last long. Sensing the possibility of a good deal, they palmed off their white elephant on a certain Count Ranieri della Staffa. But it was difficult to square the accounts, even for a count, and so, when Ranieri realised that, along with the baths, he had also inherited a small mountain of debts, even though he had made a commitment to the Mayor to resolve the ruinous financial situation, he packed his bags one morning and quietly left the Locanda del Ponte in his dressing gown and slippers. Sometimes, men not only forget things, they also forget the reasons behind those things. So it was that the baths were completely neglected. From time to time, a peasant's plough would hit a stone which then turned out to be an Etruscan urn or a broken column, but after all the Etruscans and the Romans had been here at one time, so it was hardly remarkable if they had left a bit of a mess behind them.

Then came the years of agrarian reform. The focus was on modernisation and increasing productivity rather than an equal redistribution of the land, and attempted to promote both small peasant holdings and large capitalist-style agricultural estates. A failed, half-hearted, typically Italian kind of reform, but a reform all the same. A measure by virtue of which the peasants came to an ultimate realisation of the atavistic, universal law that says that the more things change, the more they stay the same, and claimed their centuries-old rights, and the big landowners, like us, dreamt of selling everything and running off, to Brazil, for example. In fact, a friend of Vanni's, a Calabrian prince, Rodolfo Donnabruna, a handsome man with a constant tan, muscular arms, a boatswain's neck and an adventurer's chin, didn't think twice. He packed up everything and bought himself an estate the size of Calabria in the Mato Grosso, one of the few civilised places remaining in the world where you could still whip the peasants undisturbed. For Donnabruna, no more exhausting disputes with the peasants, no more attacks of colour blindness at the sight of the red flag, no more spitting bile on the 1st of May (in Mato Grosso a normal day between the 30th of April and the 2nd of May), so my faction envied him quite a bit. Lucky him, said that those who had decided to stay.

As a matter of fact, the first of May was a genuinely ominous day for my family, as ominous for us as it was glorious for the local peasants. To my blood relatives, it was like being under curfew, because of the rally held in the town square, beneath the large windows on the first floor of the Cremona house, and the peasants, all Communists, who were worked up and eager to commit outrageous, unmentionable acts against both heritage and individuals, not just singing 'Bandiera Rossa' in unison, but something much more outrageous and unmentionable. Once it had been ascertained that there were no children listening, the story was told, in a thin voice, of an effigy of a little child with the words TERENZIO CREMONA WE'RE COMING TO GET YOU written on it tossed into the flames on the 1st of May when my father was a year old—my father who, in obedience to family nomenclature, just as I bear with pride the name of that dead twin, bore that of my legendary grandfather who whipped the peasants—Terenzio.

In those days the countryside was still populated, the farms inhabited, the village lively, with the shops open, the taverns noisy and the streets echoing to the metallic shuffle of hobnailed boots. Of course, the distinction between villagers and peasants was starting to be felt, with the former more evolved and better disposed to novelty and change, and the latter less sociable, more distrustful, but nothing that couldn't be overcome with a few glasses of wine during a wake. But, as time passed, the villagers never missed an opportunity to show off their village-ness to the peasants, who felt increasingly uncomfortable, especially since asphalt had spread like an oil slick as far as the gates of the village, completely rewriting the history and geography of the distances between places. The peasants, for their part, hunkered down in their stubborn isolation, making an effort to come to the village as seldom as possible, only when it was strictly necessary, to buy what the farms could no longer supply for themselves. The most hardcore of the country children, those who truly resisted becoming urbanised, were nevertheless forced to come to the village to attend school. On foot, seeing as there was no school bus until the end of the Sixties. When you come down to it—and stretching things a bit for the sake of argument—the Fifties weren't all that bad. The revolution didn't happen, there was no bloodbath, no pogrom, the land was redistributed, but with moderation, and everything went smoothly, or almost everything. Those who had remained had their revenge on those who had left, like poor old Donnabruna, trapped down there in the Mato Grosso, who according to the latest news had contracted malaria and had only one leg—it was said that the other had been amputated due to gangrene brought on by a snake bite. The first half of the Sixties was very similar to the Fifties, except that you saw a few more sideburns and a few more cars in the village. And—a detail not to be lightly dismissed—no one really starved. However terrible hunger can be in the countryside, it is never as bad as hunger in a city, because there's always an egg, a bit of cheese, a quart of wine, a tomato to spread on your bread, always something to chew on. At the end of the Sixties, the farms and lands gradually emptied, the sons of the peasants having realised that with the manual skills they possessed they might as well become factory workers or bricklayers in the city. And so they left for Florence, Rome, or somewhere else *up north*, as they said, accompanying the words with an allusive upward movement of the head.

A lot of people left in those days. To name but one, a certain Gianfranco Nerozzi had attempted a sortie to the capital. The son of Gottardo Nerozzi, who was famous in the area for lifting a mule on his back for a bet, and grandson of the late Germano Nerozzi, who could bend a ten-lira coin between his thumb and forefinger, Gianfranco Nerozzi was a large, stout man with a past (never denied) as a blackshirt, much appreciated for his famous imitation of Laurel and Hardy, feared for his marked penchant for fighting—apparently, a slap had once cost him a million in compensation—and renowned for boasting about remote, complicated ties of kinship, displaying an inappropriate, if not completely excessive, familiarity towards perfect strangers, especially when he needed a favour. "What do you mean, who am I?" he would answer his mistrustful interlocutor. "Don't you recognise me? I carried you in my arms! I bathed you naked, damn it!" But not everyone was ready to be convinced that they had been bathed naked by Nerozzi, especially if they were older than he was.

No one knows exactly how, but overnight Nerozzi became a refrigerator salesman and, rather like those sawbones in the Wild West, went off in search of his fortune far from home. *Far* meant Rome, though it wasn't even two hundred kilometres away. "Excuse me. Nerozzi's the name, ice is the game," he would announce in a martial rhythm, introducing himself to his unlikely customers. In the hope of offloading a few refrigerators, he would play the gallant with women and the gentleman with men. Unfortunately, in Rome there was no one he had bathed naked. As a result, he had started to skip meals with increasing frequency. In the end, he had had to leave his room in a boarding house and moved to a building under construction, where a bricklayer, whom he had convinced was a distant relative of his, was charitable enough to let him sleep on the scaffolding. He could keep his few personal effects in the tool shed, as long as he wasn't discovered by the site supervisor.

Among his few belongings, the one he most treasured was a good suit he had had made to measure soon after his departure, selling a pocket watch that had been left to him—this time it was true—by a distant relative of his. And it was that suit which gave Nerozzi the idea for an ingenious method of making ends meet. During the week he mostly stayed in bed, with only a cappuccino in his stomach, tightening his belt and making do with nothing. On Saturday and Sunday he would carefully shave, put on his good suit and look at himself in a few shop windows— yes, he was still a good-looking man. Then he would get on particular buses that plied far-flung routes on the outskirts of the city. He had started frequenting working-class restaurants beyond the walls, which, he had discovered, were always being used at weekends for christenings and weddings. Thanks to his verve and his undeniably impressive bearing, he would casually gatecrash the party. First of all he would kiss the bride and then warmly shake hands with the groom, accompanying all this with a hailstorm of compliments and congratulations which shot up like fireworks from his deep voice. Exploiting, last but not least, his proverbial party piece—his imitation of Laurel and Hardy—he won the goodwill of many of the guests. When they sat down to dinner, he preferred to place himself strategically at a distance, often close to the children, who did not ask too many questions and left a lot of leftovers on their plates. He would raise his glass for every toast, and join in all the songs he knew in his fine deep baritone voice, respond to smiles with smiles and glances with glances, and not get up from table until he had repeated the last of the innumerable courses. Only then would he break away from the table and display all his surprising abilities as a dancer. Despite his bulk, he navigated his way with uncommon grace through waltzes and mazurkas, sweeping along with him large, bored ladies who seemed, in his arms, to regain an agility they had lost—or perhaps had never had. Thank to this wedding scam, he had managed not only to survive but even to wangle a few casual fucks with a number of ladies who were—let's be clear about this—no longer in the first flush of youth. When it was time to go home, by which time he was bloated with food and drink, he would say goodbye without insisting too much, and leave. At which point, the groom's relatives would say to the bride's relatives—"Nice man, that friend of yours, what's his name?" "Who do you mean?" "You know, that big guy!" And the bride's relatives would say to the groom's relatives—"What do you mean, *our* friend? We thought he was a friend of *yours* ... "

But by then Nerozzi was already on his way home.

The scale model is in the town hall

NEROZZI MAY HAVE LEFT, but others had stayed. And some had revived the old subject of the baths. The baths were closed, no pools, no mud, no cures. But Corinto, the owner of one of the two village bars, had been either enterprising or foolhardy enough to transform the Casina del Bosso, a small brick factory with a little tower that was part of the baths complex, into a kind of summer bar-dance hall. At first, it was the voice of Renato Carosone coming from the jukebox that shattered the silence of the pine wood around the baths, while the young men played billiards under the arbour and the old men peered at each other over their cards, trying to guess who had a good hand. Then it was the turn of a small band which livened up a makeshift dance floor put together from long, nailed-down planks and a great longing to dance. In the early Sixties, the mopeds parked three deep along the avenue leading to the baths testified to the fact that Corinto's initiative had been quite successful. The young men who worked hard all week as mechanics or apprentices were happy to kill the endless summer Sundays at the Casina del Bosso. The jukebox had been replaced by a band called the Gringos, a ramshackle but eager local band with a drummer who thrashed the snare drum as if it were a flail for beating grain in the farmyard. On those gentle summer evenings, the least shy among the men, inspired by the scent of jasmine, would make laconic approaches to the opposite sex.

"Want to dance?"

"No, I don't trust you in a slow dance, in case you want to do the shake afterwards … "

On the dance floor of the Casino del Bosso, promising young newcomers had their baptism of fire, and more experienced dancers, such as Nerozzi, received their ultimate accolades.

The summers passed to the aggressive rhythm of beat music, but soon even those innocent dance evenings at the Casina del Bosso waned. Corinto started saying that he had been losing money recently and that his children had no desire to do the job, in short, that he no longer felt up to it. The Casina del Bosso closed its doors, and they stayed closed until a man named Matteucci arrived from Rome. He was an impatient man with an offhand manner, as if in a hurry to put something behind him. This Matteucci offered to reopen the hotel, the bar and the swimming pool. Given that Matteucci was paying for the reconstruction work out of his own pocket, the council did not ask too many questions and gave their consent. Matteucci was a short, thickset man, with a cheap cigarette always dangling from his lips and some rough and ready methods—to announce to the absent-minded customers in the swimming pool that lunch was served, he would first have the Abyssinian, his dark-skinned, down-at-heel attendant and jack of all trades, sound the bugle, and then for the second call would fire a revolver twice into the air. The ravioli didn't often get cold … At night, Matteucci would personally patrol the gardens. On one occasion, he heard noises coming from the swimming pool. It didn't take him long to realise that some louts from the village had climbed the perimeter fence to scrounge a bathe. The columns of water raised by the shots from his .22 calibre were very persuasive and the young men—miraculously unharmed—took to flight. The *carabinieri* were informed of what had happened and Matteucci was advised by the marshal to moderate his use of firearms.

But even Matteucci ended up going through the motions, and eventually left, hounded by his own anxiety, for some other unlikely entrepreneurial mirage. In the Seventies, the Party—in our area, there is only one, and you don't have to be more specific—which controlled the municipality decided to put the baths into temporary receivership and instituted a kind of thermal Soviet, an inter-territorial consortium which was supposed to move the village smoothly towards a thermal dictatorship of the proletariat. Soon, batteries of aerosols were set up, the swimming pool was equipped with a large number of small, spartan but democratic prefabricated changing rooms, and a policy of containing the prices was instituted. For a while, it seemed to work, partly through the method of compulsory bathing, which meant that on the orders of the Party many members were taken to the swimming pool, some against their will. At the end of the Seventies, in this climate of real socialism, it was agreed that the old and graceful grand ducal baths with their Medicean portico was too obvious an expression of bourgeois concepts of architecture and, as such, was an enemy of the people. It was therefore decided to proceed with the construction of a new, modern, functional spa, which would meet the criteria of a true working-class aesthetic. Several plans were examined, and the one finally chosen was by the communal surveyor, whose design was inspired by a Czechoslovakian hospital to which he had been admitted just in time for a renal colic during a trip organised by the local savings bank. After six months, the scaffolding was taken down, despite the fact that the work was not finished, because an important figure in the Party at a national level was coming to our area and absolutely needed to cut the ribbon for the baths of the people. So, next to the old grand ducal baths with their Medicean portico, there now stood an enormous grey phalanstery with whole areas left in a rough, unfinished state. And thus they remained, because the money for the work ran out soon afterwards and everything stayed as it was. Even in the more orthodox Party circles, now that the Eighties were imminent, there were those who started to utter under their breath words like *investment, capital, entrepreneurs*. After a number of meetings, it was decided that it was necessary to open up a little to the market, in moderation, of course, but necessary all the same. These were prodigious years. The Mayor, through the intermediary of a music teacher who had married a local woman, arranged a meeting with some Sicilian entrepreneurs, including a distant relative of his, who, it was said, had made his fortune in America and had returned with capital to invest. They landed their little two-seater Piper in an abandoned quarry, raising a cloud of astonishment. The architect Della Pecora and his partner, Signor Lepanto, were given accommodation in the one tavern in the village, with all due honours.

Every morning, the Mayor would personally go and pick them up from the inn for a daily walk to discover the most agreeable spots in the area. The sports facilities having been inaugurated, it was only a matter of putting the finishing touches to the spa and you could already go in with your slippers and bathrobe. The most influential Party functionaries fought over the guests like dogs over a bone, and cracked the whip over their wives from the first light of dawn, forcing them to bend over pastry boards, rolling kilometres of thick spaghetti, and to sweat over pots, stirring complicated sauces. During these lunches, the deference of the hosts turned to the most brazen servility, while Lepanto and Della Pecora, like old card-playing partners, exchanged knowing glances accompanied by strange signs incomprehensible to anyone apart from themselves. During a meeting at the town hall, they asked permission to get up, and whispered together for some time under the large window at the far end of the room, keeping the rest of those present, who were anxious to clinch the deal, in suspense. After this mysterious consultation, they said that everything was fine, that the deal was done. Before the contract had even been signed, the Mayor wrote a letter to *La Nazione* announcing the happy event. At last our village was emerging from its isolationism and opening up to investment. The future was just around the corner. In any case, the most critical comrades were reassured—a company would be set up, jointly owned—fifty-fifty—by the municipality and the Sicilians. Della Pecora and Lepanto pointed out that they had a few difficult questions to resolve with a number of Swiss banks, and that as soon as they had the ready cash their practice would let them have the project and they would start work. A couple of months passed, and not even one brick had been laid. The aircraft was towed into the garden of the music teacher's cottage, because, they said, it could no longer stay in the quarry. The invitations to lunch became increasingly rare and the list of expenses incurred by the two Sicilian entrepreneurs grew ever longer. The Mayor decided to take matters in hand. One evening, he invited the two men to dinner at a restaurant, which was an infallible way to get an audience with them, and in the middle of the meal, his voice cracking with emotion, he said that, not so much for his own sake, since he knew that the Swiss were pernickety and that certain matters took time, as for the

111

sake of the more sceptical among the villagers, it was time to demonstrate that they were not playing games with the water, yes, indeed, it was time to strike a blow, what was needed was a gesture, a sign, something tangible.

"That's a low blow, Mayor," Della Pecora interrupted him, breaking off from noisily sucking a snail from its shell. "Are you having doubts, by any chance?"

"No, no, not at all, but you know how it is … The federation in Siena are putting pressure on me and—"

"Our practice sent us the plans just today. Within two or three weeks—just put the snails down there, signorina— yes, within two, or three weeks at the most—we've checked with Switzerland—the banks will let us have the cash we need."

The Mayor's eyes shone like an owl's in the dark. The following day, in the foyer of the town hall, there was a solemn ceremony at which Lepanto and Della Pecora lifted a sheet and uncovered an impressive scale model of the village. Astonishment hung for a few seconds in the room, then the voice of an old man was heard from the back.

"What is that, a crib?"

The corpulent architect Della Pecora explained the titanic project with a stick, while Lepanto simply nodded behind his usual sunglasses and the Mayor grovelled now to one, now to the other, visibly excited.

"The campsite will be here, and this is the new swimming pool, this small square adjoining the village will be a heliport, and this area in the immediate vicinity is the runway for the hovercraft, which will take tourists from the village to the spa and then from the spa back to the village."

"The runway for what?" a little boy in the front row asked, to be met by an immediate slap from his father.

"Shut up and listen to the architect."

"No, no, let him speak, it's all right … The hovercraft, young man, the hovercraft, the transport of the future. One day you'll understand."

The party leaders were beside themselves with excitement, and even the Mayor's father, a former partisan, the kind who still kept his rifle under his bed, was moved to a few tears.

Della Pecora and Lepanto said they had to leave. They were going to withdraw the money from Switzerland personally, because it was a delicate matter—fifty billion after all—"How much?" the Mayor asked with a start—*fifty*. It was better to withdraw it in person. In the meantime, they could start to lay the first stone, as they would be back from Zurich within a few days. The two men left the Piper, which needed maintenance, in the music teacher's garden (in fact, while they were in Zurich, they would also try to find replacement parts) and the ominous scale model in the foyer of the town hall. They packed their bags and, waved on their way by a procession, were taken to the station by the one taxi driver in the village.

A few people dared to express a degree of wariness about the project, and about the reliability of Lepanto and Della Pecora in general, and were immediately branded as ultraconservative, retrograde, bourgeois, enemies of progress, and fools. But even the most trusting had a few vague doubts.

"Will they really do all these things?"

"Are you joking? The scale model is in the town hall … You think they'd make a scale model like that, and then? … "

The Piper is still in the schoolmaster's garden. Dingo, an old German shepherd dog with leishmaniasis, sleeps in it. I have no idea what happened to the scale model.

The wind is blowing hot and humid

THE WIND IS BLOWING hot and humid on this autumn evening. I'm full of aches and pains, because of living in the scrub I believe, where the damp gets into your bones and stays inside you like a bad habit. How long is it since I last slept properly in a bed? One day it rains, and the next the sun comes out and everything brightens up. But the land, this black land, seems to keep humidity trapped under a carpet of leaves that never gets dry. Never. It has stopped raining and the last drops are carried away by the hot, humid sirocco wind. I know this wind, and it doesn't bode well. It's a wind that comes from the desert and brings only sand and tears. When it goes away, it leaves behind it a strange post-atomic light—and a coating of sand on your car. It's now been two days since the boys left on a mission, and I'm starting to get really worried. Last night, I saw a flash of light in the depths of the scrub a couple of kilometres from here, just outside enemy territory. I thought it might be the boys, and was almost on the point of sending up a Bengal light to signal my position, but then it occurred to me that it might be a trap set by that crafty devil Unterwasser. It's very unlikely, in fact, that the boys would do something so careless as to strike a light outside the enclosure. Unterwasser's riflemen, those damned mercenaries with their ice-cold eyes and steady hands, who Ottone Gattai paid good money to bring from Baden Baden, would have been overjoyed. No, maybe it was a will-o'-the-wisp or something like that. I'll wait until dawn and then go and look for them. I'll wait until dawn next to the embers of this extinguished fire, just so as not to die of solitude. No, there's no danger of being seen here, there's enough fog to mask the smoke, which drifts off into the branches. This morning, to kill time, I cut some firewood, then tried, unsuccessfully, to repair the radio and again made an inventory of our arsenal—a couple of crates of ammunition, a dozen grenades, three anti-personnel mines and seven bullets for the PIAT, that's all that's left, after a year of guerrilla warfare. We're almost out of resources, we've used up the little we managed, through an intermediary, to buy from that Russian mafioso who was a guest of Gattai's. If only he knew that the arms we're fighting with were sold to us by one of his best customers, he'd be spitting bile. What a beautiful sight that would be! But I can't spoil my chances with such a valuable contact just for a bit of personal satisfaction. It's final victory that we want, even though my conviction and my morale have been weakening for some time now. I stayed in camp because the boys say they can't run the risk of my falling into enemy hands. They might torture me, make me say things I would regret, like when I quarrel with Lea, and compromise the outcome of the war. They say they're still in contact, they haven't abandoned hope that reinforcements will arrive, they say it's best not to risk it, that it's pointless everyone going. So here I am, eating my heart out, sitting by a silent radio which ought to be giving me good news about the other thermal fronts, but, apart from a small counter-offensive from Colonel Marengo to slow down the advance of an armoured convoy of Austrian tourists along the main road to Saturnia, the news is not reassuring. The other formations at war with Aquatrade are almost scattered, without provisions or supplies, and with their communications half cut off, while Gattai's mercenaries are holding on to their positions, the baths are full, the hotels have no vacancies and the overall capacity of thermal water doesn't seem to be affected by the breaches we've managed to make in the pipes in the last few months. When we, too, have fallen, it will be child's play for Unterwasser to mop up the last pockets of resistance. And Lea is also outside with the boys. My Lea.

The first time I saw her

T HE FIRST TIME I SAW HER, I had arrived on time, for some inexplicable reason. The professor had begun his semiotics lecture by recounting the strange story of a man who had been caught filing away a corner of the pyramid of Kheops. Caught and arrested, he had explained to the police that for four years he had been working hard on a series of complex trigonometrical calculations which would demonstrate 'once and for all' that the pyramids, being in perfect astral alignment with the constellation of the Pleiades, were the work of aliens from outer space. Unfortunately, the calculations were out by just a few degrees. So he had had the idea of solving the equations with a file.

Lea, too, is a bit like that man. If reality doesn't correspond to her ideas, she prefers to change reality rather than her ideas. Anyway, the handle of the door at the back of the hall turned slowly, the door opened, and two eyes appeared, of an unprecedented blue, a heavenly blue, an impregnable blue, which was not for us humans. Those eyes quickly looked around and came to rest on me. Lea entered that room by chance, the way a butterfly enters a house through an open window, comes to rest and slowly opens its wings, so that you can admire it in all its beauty. Lea did the same, crossed the room with resolute steps, her chest out like the figurehead of a ship, her boots shiny, her stride martial, without looking at anyone but knowing that she was being looked at by everyone. She wore a white jacket pulled in at the waist, and her hair was loose and her cheeks red. There were plenty of empty seats at the back, but she came directly towards me.

"May I?" she asked, after she had sat down. I was too tongue-tied to answer her. That same evening, we went together to a concert. At the end of the concert, when everyone had left, she and I stayed there looking at each other, as if we wanted to say something without quite knowing what. The technicians had started to dismantle the stage, and on the empty square waste paper and cigarette butts whirled in a sudden wind that seemed to presage a storm. We looked at each other for a long time and, just as I was cursing myself for not having the courage to kiss her, Lea kissed me.

"You have very white teeth," she said.

And that impressed me, because usually people talk about eyes, lips, hair, but not about teeth.

"Teeth are important. You should clean them often. I could never kiss a guy with bad teeth."

Those were her very words. And then she kissed me again.

Since that kiss, we have always been together. And even in the armed struggle Lea has remained by my side, and has never betrayed me. At least as far as I know.

But look, there's a light down there. It's the signal! Three long flashes, three short ones and three long, the opposite of an SOS. It's not especially original as a signal, but Unterwasser's German Landsknechts are as ignorant as jackasses. They're coming back, yes, it's them! I can't see them but it's as if I can. I see them descending a steep slope alongside a barbed-wire fence, running across the bare clearing and plunging back into the depths of the undergrowth for cover. They must already be climbing the hill with the breath choked in their lungs. If I close my eyes, I can hear their hearts beating like drums in the night. At their head, Lea setting the pace, her slender, muscular horsewoman's legs forcing her combat boots up the path, her eyes glittering in the darkness like those of a bird of prey, then Antoine, with his bristly beard and long hair, his strong French accent and his heavy, confident poacher's steps; a bit further back I imagine Conti, thin and humorous, with his elegant gait, his handkerchief tied with a sailor's knot round his neck, and then Garrone the argumentative, cursing the too many cigarettes that are burning now in his chest and grumbling about his aching feet, and, bringing up the rear, Tito, light-footed, a ghost gliding through the night, as silent and obedient as a good soldier needs to be. It's them, my men, my men and my woman, they're all I have.

Young man, don't do what I did

The president of the Thermal Consortium, in accordance with the municipal decree issued the 10th of November of the current year, has, due to flagrant violations of the water regulations in force, ordered the confiscation of all sewage waters contained on the agricultural estate known as L'Olmaia, situated in the municipality of *** and belonging to the Counts Barbetti Martorelli. The estate consists of thirty-six holdings, with a sowable area of about four hundred hectares, a total of two irrigation tanks, a stream for fishing containing barbel and chub, both small and medium size, a swimming pool with a diving board and equipped with a tarpaulin, and a small inflatable pool for children.

Henceforth, the income and waters of the estate will benefit the Thermal Consortium. The confiscation has been carried out as prescribed by law and in the presence of Marshall Oreste Tacconi, commander of the carabinieri station of ***.

This was the text of the municipal ordinance fixed with scotch tape to the counter in the bar. I read it and reread it with growing apprehension. So what I had heard about the renting of the waters and the exceptional measures put in place to control and ration them was true.

Gattai had not wasted his time. After the presentation in the theatre of his lavish project to revive the baths, he had signed an outrageous contract with the municipality, which granted him the use, abuse, exploitation and usufruct of all the thermal waters present in the territory of the munici-pality for a period of thirty-five years. By blackmailing the unions and parties with the promise of hundreds of jobs, flattering the ambitions of local politicians and civil servants frustrated by years of systematic failures, pandering to the dreams of financial gain entertained by local merchants who saw the spa as the goose that laid the golden egg, Gattai had immediately gained the upper hand. And for a ridiculous price, he had won the whole kitty, like a casino croupier who, after an unlucky round of betting, rakes in the chips while the players look on, powerless to do anything. Apart from the baths, Gattai had also secured for himself the commercial exploitation of all the thermal waters present in the territory. Except that in that clause of the contract, the word 'thermal' had been deliberately omitted. What was mentioned was water in general. So that theoretically, and very soon practically, he had become the owner of the waters. All of them. He would have been able to present himself at your house in his bathrobe, with his shampoo in his hand, and demand to take a shower in your bathroom, or to requisition your cisterns in the name of the law. One year, during the harvest, a man named Arrigo had told me about a breakdown in the water pipes in a village close to mine. The village had been divided into two sections, one with water and the other without. The days passed and the breakdown had still not been repaired. The citizens protested to the Mayor, who, as the experienced politician that he was, countered the criticisms with formulas such as 'as soon as possible', 'temporary inconvenience', 'we're doing our best', and other phrases of that kind which mean that nobody is doing anything. I think they were taking their time because the Mayor's house was in the part of the village that had water. One day, a cousin of Arrigo's who wasn't as patient as he was turned up in dressing gown and slippers at the Mayor's door, with his comb and shampoo.

121

"Yes?"

"Signora, is your husband at home?"

"Who wants him?"

"Pierino from Casamatta."

"One moment."

"Mayor?"

"What is it?"

"Do you have water here?"

"Yes, why?"

"Open the door then, I've come to take a shower … "

I don't know how, but in drawing up the contract, Ottone Gattai had managed to have included within the grounds of the spa the Chiesina, a small, bare parish church, early Christian in origin, with, at the back, a fig tree that produced very sweet, fleshy black figs at the end of September, and, at the front, an arcaded loggia where as children we parked our bicycles or took shelter and waited for the rain to stop when we were caught in a storm on a lazy summer afternoon. Now the little church is used as a weapons store for the armed men commanded by Gattai's right-hand man, that damned Kraut Unterwasser. *Polizei, privat polizei.* As soon as he opened the spa, Gattai had immediately realised that in order to control the territory and defend the resort, he needed a specially selected and very loyal private police force. While the establishment was still being run in, Gattai offered packages and complete treatments to a restricted circle of powerful people—politicians, generals, television presenters, businessmen—which made for a lot of free publicity that would keep the powerful thermal machine boiling. He must have thought it was a good thing to ingratiate himself, because you never know how it might help in future. One of the people he invited was a rich German industrialist from the Ruhr, who brought with him a friend, a man named Unterwasser who claimed to have been the personal secretary to the Elector of Saxony. I don't know if he really had been the secretary to the Elector of Saxony, what is certain is that Unterwasser was a former SS officer, supreme commander of the canine unit of the Third Reich, who had somehow evaded Nuremburg and half the world's intelligence services. Bald, one eye a pale grey almost devoid of pigmentation, the other of glass—lost in battle according to him, a badly treated stye according to information in my possession. Unterwassser is a bony old man, thin and angular, almost as if his body were the psychosomatic result of an evil temperament slowly eroding a physique too thin to offer any resistance. It was he who was given the task of forming a vigilante force entrusted with the security of the entire resort complex. Under cover of putting together an innocent team of nightwatchmen, Unterwasser recruited dozens of retired Swiss Guards, pool attendants from Baden Baden, sons of Nazis, and cut-throats and mercenaries with years of experience in Rhodesia, the Congo, Liberia and other hotspots. The rumours that had been circulating for a while concerning Gattai's legendary despotism and Mussolinian methods were taking a sinister form.

The confiscation of the Barbetti Martorellis' estate was a fact, a worrying fact. But how could it have been allowed? I wanted to submit the question to a lawyer friend of mine, who had given me an appointment, but unfortunately, as I was heading towards the square, I was stopped in front of the church steps by none other than Count Barbetti Martorelli himself. Our house, a Renaissance building communicating with the castle, had two large matching doors which look out onto the church square. This central location meant that it was impossible to escape without running into someone you would have preferred not to run into. The most difficult time was the end of Mass. You had to be very careful not to leave home at exactly the same time as the stream of worshippers, or else you were screwed. Vague relatives, pensioners in sad grey overcoats, provincial petits bourgeois in mothballs, spiteful bigots, lubricious Christian Democrats, virtuous citizens, devout Communists, deaf old people. A camphor embrace, a touch of mangy fur, an overly vigorous handshake, an unsolicited maxim, an inappropriate quip, a slobbering kiss with a smudge of lipstick, a whiff of stale perfume— everyone had something to give you on their way out of Mass. But to get back to old Count Barbetti Martorelli, he caught me at a delicate point of tangency between my late awakening and his precocious exit from the Mass. He took me by the arm, which was an awful habit of his, and, nodding towards an attractive working-class girl descending the church steps with a nice pair of tits jiggling up and down under her sober black dress, said, "Young man, you're still young, don't do what I did. I wasted so many opportunities because of stupid class prejudices … "

The count didn't have time to say anything more because his wife came out of the church at that moment and took him in hand. I gave up the idea of asking him for further details about the confiscation of his estate. "I'll be sure to, count," I said, loosening myself from his hateful grip, and returned home.

To avoid more encounters of this kind, I decided it would be simpler to phone my friend the lawyer. So I called him and told him what was happening, and asked him how it was possible that all that could happen within the law. I wanted to know if the fears I was harbouring for my family were in any way founded. We, too, had our piece of land in the sun, with farmhouses, three of them miraculously served by hot water which—like a gift from God, my grandmother would say—gushed copiously on our estate. Water which for thousands of years had served the tomatoes or the animals, natural pools that gushed amid old, abandoned Fiat 500s turned into hen houses, piles of logs, cellophane dust sheets, plastic buckets and rusty tools. The peasants had never thought of using the water for hedonistic purposes, which was why, at best, the springs had been intubated and blocked with a siphon or a tap, but more often than not had just been left in the open, as God—or someone on his behalf—had created them.

Only my grandfather Vanni, the son of the man who whipped the peasants, a lean, handsome, elegant man with melancholy green eyes who, because of the fact that his dead twin's destiny had been contracted out to him, had found himself with the mind of an engineer trapped in the profession of an agronomist, had had the idea of channelling into a pool all that water which every day for thousands of years had lost its way amid grassy ditches and the croaking of frogs. And so, following his own particular conception of spartan, rational architecture, Grandfather Vanni had built two communicating, reinforced-concrete basins, prettifying them a little by placing stones found in the fields and old sun-yellowed terracotta bricks round the edges. Then the floodgates had been opened and the water, channelled through a large underground plastic pipe, had started docilely to fill the basins.

"Good, good," I remember my grandfather saying, watching that little cascade slowly fill the pool like a child watching rapt as the water level rises in a bathtub. That basin—which had come out very well, at least according to my uncle who immediately undressed to give it a try, even though it wasn't yet full—had been followed by two others, the design of which had gradually become less spartan.

"Yes, yes," my grandfather said one evening, as I was sitting on his knees in the garden under the branches of the cedar.

"Yes what, Grandpa?" I asked distractedly.

"I've just thought how I'm going to do the second swimming pool."

"Ah," I said, the way adults did, even though I didn't understand. My grandfather went up to his study to get a pen and paper and came back under the shade of the old cedar, whose long branches stretched towards the sun like arms held out to a man who has fallen into the sea. Vanni sat down at the corner of the stone table and after about ten minutes came up with a design for the basin—a perfect rectangle with two half moons at the ends. And in fact that is exactly how the great swimming pool was built, adjacent to, but more beautiful and deeper than, the first one.

"Yes, it's beautiful but … how to put this, less cosy, less intimate," commented my uncle, who had got a taste for it and refused to come out of the water—for some time now, he had been in the habit of having the newspaper brought to him at the edge of the basin and of being served meals in the little forty-degree pool, emerging only from time to time to light a cigarette when there was no one in the vicinity who could pass it to him already lit. "This is the life!" my uncle would say, inhaling voluptuous mouthfuls of smoke and stretching his neck out of the water like a little tortoise trying to reach a lettuce leaf. The second basin had been followed by a third, a larger, circular one, in the last of the holdings blessed by hot water. And so my grandfather, whom my grandmother idolised, had left us three wonderful swimming pools as an inheritance.

My friend the lawyer phoned me back a few days later. He had studied the situation carefully, examining all the clauses of the contract Gattai had drawn up when he rented the baths. It was a Machiavellian masterstroke—the company had been set up as a profit-sharing partnership, initially fifty-one per cent to Gattai and forty-nine to be shared between the municipality and the province, but a well-camouflaged clause anticipated that the municipality would gradually reduce its quota until it disappeared almost completely and they were left with a negligible one per cent. The laws which governed the exploitation of thermal waters were the same as those that regulated mining concessions. The contract provided for an exclusive concession—Ottone Gattai was the one true, indisputable owner of the waters. There wasn't much we could do, Gattai was on the side of the law, or rather, the law was on the side of Gattai. In the light of that, the confiscation of the Barbetti Martorellis' water became a truly worrying precedent. Something like that could easily happen to us, too, at any moment.

For Epiphany, we would play Monopoly

F OR EPIPHANY, we would play Monopoly. At the Cremona house, we gathered together all our closest relatives and assembled in one of the many rooms built by grandfather Terenzio, the one who whipped the peasants. A room which was closed almost the whole year except for Epiphany and visits by acquaintances of my grand-parents', the Gherardis, reason enough to call this room 'the Gherardi Room'. The Gherardi Room was one of the few rooms in the castle that had no frescoes. It had high ceilings, plain white walls and a floor of baked herring-bone clay which, after decades of wax polishing, was now a dark red, almost amber colour. There was also a com-fortable refectory table with a dozen penitential chairs and a loggia that housed a library which could be reached by a narrow wooden staircase. There was nothing special about the room. The only thing I had really liked about it ever since I was little was an authentic Garibaldian mus-ket transformed into a night lamp, with the lampshade mounted on the bayonet and the switch where the trigger had been.

It was in this room that we played Monopoly. But not the classic Monopoly that all families play. No, our Monopoly was a special one. The names of the houses and buildings had been replaced with the names of properties belonging to the Cremona family, which had been meticulously written out by my grandmother and stuck one by one on the folding board, in accordance with their colour, value, and the original location. 'Park of Victory' became 'Villa Alibrandi'. 'Narrow Lane' was transformed into 'La Paiccia Farm', 'Water Company' was changed into 'Combine Harvester Warehouse'. And the things that could happen during the game had also been modified with an enviably childlike imagination. *Go to jail and miss a turn* became *The workers ask for a wage rise. Go back two squares* became *The European Union suspend grants for organic farming* ...

As my grandmother, with maniacal patience, updated the Monopoly board every year to take account of any new disposal or acquisition of property, it ended up being the one reliable record of the state of the Cremona family's assets. During one of these games of Monopoly, as the dice were rolling on the table, I decided to broach the subject.

"Did you hear about the Barbetti Martorellis?" I asked.

"Your turn," my grandmother said, handing me the dice.

I took it and squeezed it in the palm of my hand. "Did you hear how they confiscated one of his holdings because of the water?"

My grandmother looked up from the collection of chips and stopped counting. "The Barbetti Martorellis deserved it."

"What did they do to deserve it?"

"They know what they did," she replied, with an ambiguous smile on her face.

I felt the eyes of the whole family on me. "You seem almost happy, all of you ... "

"What do you mean, happy?" my grandmother said. "You know, those who do evil have evil done to them in return ... "

Over the years my grandmother had developed this subtle, radical version of Christian philosophy. She maintained that it is in evil that we see people's true characters, and that a knowledge of evil is necessary for our neighbour to finally resolve to do good. It all seemed a bit convoluted to me.

"What evil have the Barbetti Martorellis ever done? But the point is, aren't you afraid that what happened to them could happen to us? We also have farms with hot water. What if one morning the *carabinieri* turn up with a plumber and close the taps and sequestrate everything? What do we do then?"

"Oh, no, that mustn't happen," said my uncle, who had been silent until then.

"It won't happen," my grandmother said.

"How can you be so sure?" I insisted.

"We've had guarantees from Signor Gattai," my grandmother replied, as if she were replying for everyone.

"You're holding up the game," my cousin said in an irritable tone that still annoys me when I think about it.

I threw the dice.

One-two-three-four and five. *The caterpillar tractor's cardan joint is broken. Miss a turn for maintenance.*

Peasants were worse than their masters

SEPTEMBER ARRIVED, the days grew shorter, the air turned transparent, and the light over the woods and the bare ridges was radiant. This was the moment Gattai choose for his fateful announcement. More than three months in advance he decided to show his hand and fix the date for the inauguration of the spa—the thirty-first of December. The invitations were sent out, written in beautiful swirling writing on headed stationery which had been printed a good three months earlier. And as usual, those who had been invited missed no opportunity to tell those who hadn't been invited. The disagreements and gossip triggered by the imminent 'exclusive' party being thrown by Ottone Gattai got the whole village worked up. I remember that I was at the barber's, and Abele, a villager who had his hair cut every two weeks, commented on the 'selective' invitations.

"I hear they invited you," he said, referring to my family, "which means the Ricciardis and the Guidis will definitely be there … "

I closed my eyes while the barber brushed my face, and shrugged as if to say that I really didn't give a damn.

"I also heard," Abele continued, "that they invited my cousin, Capoduro's daughter, who somehow managed to graduate in the end, God knows how, but everybody knows she's having an affair with the deputy mayor, and now that she's having an affair with the deputy mayor, it just so happens they've hired her for the spa … "

Then he paused for a moment, his protruding ears glowing in the mirror.

"Now that she's graduated and can say two or three words of English, she thinks she's God knows who. I heard she insisted that I shouldn't be invited. I heard that now she feels she's somebody, she's ashamed of the time when she was nobody. I was always told that when they got power, peasants were worse than their masters, but I never wanted to believe it. For God's sake, she can graduate, she can learn English, she can have an affair with the deputy mayor, and she can even get herself invited to Gattai's party, but to me she'll always be Capoduro's daughter."

I didn't know what to say. I paid and left.

Paul Newman

IT'S VERY HOT TODAY. Nobody can breathe. Even the war has turned sluggish because of the excessive heat. We are all sprawled in the shade of a chestnut tree. Some take off their shoes and some light cigarettes. Antoine lies down, arranges his rucksack as if it were a cushion and lays his head on it, extracts the flask of Rémy Martin from his pocket and sighs as he sips his cognac.

"*Mon Dieu … qu'il fait chaud, putain! L'année prochaine je me tire en Suède!*"

"What does he want?" Sante asks.

"He says it's damn hot and if it continues like this he'll go to Sweden next year."

"Why should he go to Sweden?" Garrone says. "They don't even drink wine there."

Lea goes into the tent. Then she has second thoughts and comes out again. She takes me by the hand as if she wanted to make love with me. Inside the tent, it's as hot as a greenhouse. I look at Lea, but she doesn't look at me. It's clear that she didn't bring me into the tent to make love but to tell me something important.

"Well?"

"Sixty minutes."

"It wasn't just sixty minutes, you were out for two days. I was very worried. You still haven't given me your report."

"How strict you are. We took a long way round. Unter-wasser's pigs were everywhere. A reconnaissance patrol. They narrowly missed us."

"Did you find anything?"

"Forget about the south. Apart from the entrance that's the most heavily guarded side, the fences are all electrified, and there's no way through. There are two watchtowers. Two guards in each tower, who change every six hours. And searchlights that sweep the perimeter. I timed them—two minutes to do a complete sweep."

"What about the east? Did you look where I told you to look?"

"Yes, but you can forget about that, too. The wall of the swimming pool is reinforced concrete, with steel railings at the top. It's a fortress, you can't get through that way. I've never seen such a tough wall."

"That wall's so tough because they built the swimming pool back to front, with the containing wall that should have faced the hill facing the road and vice versa ... Who knows, maybe some surveyor who couldn't tell his right hand from his left followed Lepanto and Della Pecora's old plans to the letter."

"Whose plans?"

"Nothing, an old story, before I met you. What do the boys say?"

"What can they say? They're tired. What does the radio say?"

"Nothing."

"And the reinforcements that were supposed to be coming from Bagno Vignoni?"

"Nothing yet."

"So we've been left to fight alone?"

"Seems that way."

"Tell me the truth. What chance is there that we can win this war?"

"I don't know, Lea, I don't know."

"Tell me the truth."

"I don't think we have much chance."

Lea touches one of her breasts, with a gesture so natural that it makes me uncomfortable, because I'd like to be the only one to enjoy the privilege and right now I'm jealous even of her hands that are wandering into her cleavage. I'd like to kiss her, I'd like to make love to her now, with the heroic smell of physical effort on her. I slip behind her and put my arms around her, then touch her breasts, but she tries to wriggle away. I try to kiss her on the neck.

"Stop it! The others are outside, now's not the time."

It hasn't been the time for quite a while. She pirouettes like a skater and runs out. I go after her, so as not to be left alone with her rejection, which hurts me like a punch in the ribs. I leave the tent and see the boys sprawling as I had left them.

Antoine is dozing. Garrone is carving something with his pocket knife. Palombo is trying to light a cigarette with the help of the sun and a magnifying glass. It seems a lost battle to me, like everything else. Palombo is a new recruit, he's from the sea and was the last person to join the brigade. He used to watch over the yachts in Port'Ercole. His father before him watched over the yachts in Port'Ercole. Even his grandfather watched over the yachts in Port'Ercole. One day he turned up here, like a beached dolphin. He said, "I know everything. I'm ready." In my opinion, he wasn't. But he is now.

Palombo sighs.

"What is it?" I ask.

"Nothing."

"It must be something. No one sighs just for the hell of it."

"It's just that nothing's happening here. It's just that we've been fighting for months, and now it's pointless to pretend, we're cut off from reinforcements, no one has the courage to say it, but the war is lost."

"*Garçon, ne parle pas avec cette légèreté.*"

Antoine has woken with a start from a torpor he might never have known before in his life, and looks at Palombo in a way that makes me glad I'm not in Palombo's shoes.

"*On ne combat pas pour gagner, mais pour combattre.*"

Then he goes back to sleep.

"I never understand what that one says."

"Show Antoine some respect," Garrone says, raising his eyes from his pocket knife and looking straight and hard at Palombo. "What do you want with us? What are you doing in this war? We're land people, you're a man of the sea, what possessed you to come to us?"

"Do you want to know?" Palombo says. "Do you really want to know? I'll tell you. I was out on my boat, fishing and looking at the sea, my sea. It was a good day for fishing, I'd already caught a bream and an amberjack with a head like a two-year-old child. After a while, I see this liner coming, like a big white iron, it's endless, all its windows are dark, there doesn't seem to be anyone on board, apart from the women on deck who were steering it, giving each other instructions through walkie-talkies, guiding it into dock. The boat is coming straight towards me, now I can see that there's also a short man with white hair on board, he's with two bimbos, one dark and one blonde, who don't look real. And I feel as if I know him, I have the impression I've seen him before, except there's no time to think where, because the ship is coming straight towards me. I can already see myself in the water, when the ship turns suddenly at the last moment, spitting out sea water from its engines and splashing me in the face. Then this huge white ship moves away, heading for port. I have to steady myself not to end up in the water, the boat rears up like a horse being held by ropes. The rods and the fish are thrown out and fall in the water, and I'm still there like an idiot sitting at the bottom of the boat, and all at once I remember who that little man is with the two bimbos and where I saw him."

"Where?"

"In films."

"Who is he?"

"Por Niuma."

"Who?"

"Por Niuma." That's exactly how he says it—*Por Niuma*.

"You mean Paul Newman?"

"That's right, what did I say? Por Niuma."

"And what has Paul Newman got to do with our cause?"

"A lot. If a man of seventy can turn up like that in the shallows where I've been fishing since I was little, but not just any man of seventy, a man of seventy who happens to be Por Niuma with a seventeen-metre yacht and these topless bimbos whose combined ages are less than seventy, I think it's a sign. It's a sign that the world is going in one direction, and I don't like the direction the world is going in. They say this direction I don't like is called globalisation. Call it what you like, I tell you it's a sign that we need to start fighting, that's all. I'm never going to knock at the door of Por Niuma's house. I'm never going to take three whores from the Argentario and go to Hollywood and throw Por Niuma off his air bed as he sunbathes by the swimming pool. When I heard from a friend in Saturnia about you, and your village, and what was happening,

Gattai, the Russians, I told myself—Gattai is to you what Por Niuma is to me. I didn't think twice and I left. That's what Por Niuma has got to do with this."

"Maybe. But in my opinion Paul Newman hasn't got a damned thing to do with it."

All of them except us

E ARLY ONE MORNING, I saw him coming out through the
imposing gates of the Aquatrade resort, clean-shaven
and self-confident in his partridge-coloured gabardine.
There was a beggar in front of the entrance to the hotel. He
looked imploringly at Ottone Gattai.

"I'm hungry," he said in a low, calm voice.

"That's a good sign," Ottone Gattai said, slapping him
on the back.

The man scared me. Since that confiscation of the
Barbetti Martorellis' pools, I hadn't been feeling too
secure. My family continued to flaunt their certainty that
everything was fine.

"They won't touch a hair on our heads," they would say.

"But how can you be so sure? What makes you so certain
he'll keep his word?"

"Because your grandfather up there"—eyes cast towards
heaven, the eyeballs almost turning back in their sockets,
and a sign of the cross embroidered in the air with one
finger—"is watching over us. I already told you, we've had
guarantees, trust me."

As far as the guarantees about land were concerned, my
grandmother was referring to an informal meeting she had
had with Gattai, who had been trying to get his hands on a
large olive grove we owned adjoining the Aquatrade Resort.
As far as the supernatural source of her sense of certainty
was concerned, directly connected with my late lamented
grandfather Vanni, I had some doubts. My doubts centred

on the fact that my grandfather, like my great grandfather, had not been a great lover of priests. Not that he had been born anti-clerical, but he had certainly become so. He had told me about his mounting hatred of priests during his time at a Jesuit college in Rome, where even on Sunday they had to assist at morning mass on pain of being taken off the register. We could sum it up by saying that my grandfather had been born a believer and died an atheist. Then, once he had left the scene, he had had to suffer a posthumous beatification promoted by my grandmother, who had kept quiet about her true inclinations all her life. Since my grandfather had died, she had freed herself from any lingering sense of discomfort and had exhumed that slumbering Catholicism which for years had survived like a spore under the ground and had made it germinate. But nothing can take from me my doubts that my grandfather was wholeheartedly sponsoring that conversion from up in heaven.

The reason for this unthinking confidence, I was only later to discover, was that there had been a kind of gentleman's agreement between Gattai and the most influential families in the village. We had a fine olive grove, just adjacent to the area of the resort marked out for construction, which was of considerable interest to the King Midas of the waters. In exchange for a transfer of the land, Gattai and the Mayor undertook not to be too strict over the question of the exclusive rights to the thermal waters. For the moment, my uncle's ablutions were saved.

But I wasn't convinced by this supposed non-aggression pact. The Mayor taking Gattai's intolerable Doberman out early in the morning to do his business, the arrival in the village of Ottone Gattai's son Otello, with his slicked-back hair and arrogant manner, speeding through the built-up area in his black Alfa Romeo Spider, going right past the *carabinieri* barracks with tyres screeching, heedless of any pensioners and children who might be crossing the street—these things had to mean something. If nothing else, it meant someone was turning a blind eye, giving in without a fight, and that certainly wasn't a good omen.

In the meantime, Gattai had installed himself in a semi-permanent way in the town hall, in those cool rooms with their coffered ceilings, transforming the most beautiful room in the building, the Gonfalone Hall, into his personal office. The spa was now a reality, and after years of failure and heartbreak, even the biggest sceptics and the most fervent Communists, or the biggest sceptics among the Communists, had had to change their minds. It was clear that it had taken a private individual to get things back on their feet. Now the great work was almost finished and the thermal machine simply needed a little fine tuning. Tests were carried out to prepare for the inauguration, which was now only a month away. The personnel managers were working at a frenetic rhythm, one interview after another to arrive at a shortlist of employees. The Party were overjoyed because for the first time there was full employment. There was not a single family which did not have at least one member working for or in the Aquatrade Resort, a building as large as a battleship and as imposing as a ziggurat, a virtual fortress completely sufficient unto itself. Gattai had entrusted the task of training the top management and selecting the 'crew' to his right hand man, Field Marshal Unterwasser, whose true character as a Nazi villain we would soon get to know all too well. Aquatrade had given the go-ahead to hire pool attendants, masseurs, mud therapists, gym instructors, barbers, chefs, cooks, waiters, cleaning women, journalists, doctors, clerks and secretaries. They did not seem to have limited themselves to the number of people that concrete monster could actually absorb.

"What does your husband do?"

"He works at the spa."

"How about yours?"

"He works at the spa."

"And your daughter?"

"The same."

"And what about you, what do you do?"

"I work at the spa."

They all worked at the spa. There were people who had left secure jobs, jobs they had done for decades, just to be part of the great Aquatrade family. There were those who assembled kitchens in the factories along the Cassia who had suddenly become warehousemen at the spa, local surveyors and accountants who had joined specialised departments in the spa administration, pensioners transformed into gardeners, housewives into manicurists, paramedics who had discovered talents as dietitians, shop assistants transmuted into beauticians. Once they had entered the warm womb of the spa, they would all have their tasks to perform, they just shouldn't be in a hurry. To assist with the hiring, a political commission had been set up which judged the suitability of the candidates case by case according to certain relevant parameters—loyalty to the Party, devotion to the cause, willingness to serve. The commissioners cross-matched the profiles and hired on behalf of Aquatrade. Gattai hired and swelled his tanned chest, his shirt unbuttoned over his manly white skin in the middle of which glittered a massive chain. He hired and strutted across the square in his khaki safari trousers, carrying a leather briefcase packed with papers. He hired and walked up and down the steps of the town hall. He hired and stroked his dog. He hired and chomped his cigar. The politicians who had warmly supported Gattai's consortium were over the moon at having unexpectedly—for once in their lives—kept the promises about employment they had made during the election campaign. The young were happy because there was work at last, the old were happy partly because the young were happy and partly because they were proud at seeing our little municipality stand out among the other villages in the area.

Even friends and acquaintances, even the idlers who you would say would never work, all settled down to work at the spa. All of them. Except us.

Garrone was looking for a job, or so he said, but making sure he didn't find one because he had promised his girlfriend that they would marry as soon as he did. Conti was holding on tight to his job as an assistant in a tie shop in Florence and only came to the village at weekends or on a weekday if there was a dinner and we gave him a bit of advance notice. And Tito, who was still working at the Pensione Bardassi ('work' is saying a lot, a doctor once advised absolute rest—two weeks' uninterrupted work without a day off). Then there was Lea. Who of course was continuing with her university studies, devoting herself to her powerful political-science thesis on hidden motives and conspiracies behind the official version of 9/11, entitled *No Aeroplane Crashed into the Towers—What the Americans Have Never Told Us.*

And finally there was me. Fresh from my studies, torn between my perfunctory knowledge of science and technology and my vaguely humanistic erudition, I was made of compliant dough, which meant that I would work without needing to. I was looking for a serious job but hoped I wouldn't find it, because if I had found it I would have had the feeling I was taking it away from someone who was sure to need it more than me. And there were plenty of those.

Like eels

L IKE EELS IN THE SARGASSO SEA, come rain or come shine, towards midday on Saturday, without needing to pre-arrange anything, we all met in the square. Some from Florence, Siena, Rome, some who had never left the village, some who had never even left the square, and you found them dressed in the same clothes, sitting on the same bench and even in the same position in which you had left them the previous week—the fact remains that at midday we were all present at roll call, newspapers in our hands, the lingering taste of coffee in our mouths, a few lit cigarettes here and there.

And we hung around the square talking about nothing until around lunchtime, when the first of us who heeded the complaints of his stomach would break off at the stroke of the bell and say, "Bye, I'll see you for the aperitif." Leaning on the parapet, huddled in our overcoats with the fur collars raised and our half-full glasses now beyond the orbit of the tables outside the bar, at the very least you would have found me, Garrone, Tito, Sante and Conti looking at the vast beehive of the new thermal complex and the red sun crouching obediently behind the brown spurs of Castell'Azzara, already dotted with the first lights of the street lamps.

The new village had grown since we had spent afternoons playing football in those deserted streets between one construction site and the other, using iron rods left on the sites to make goalposts and the white-and-red tapes around the buildings under construction to mark the boundary of the pitch.

The first house built outside the historical centre had been that large white house overlooking the bend in the road just after the bridge, a massive, sober house, with brown window frames and a sloping roof with a little dormer window in the middle. Then, like people suddenly turning up for a picnic, that house situated in open country was joined by others. All that working-class housing in the Sixties had been built without any regular plan or any architectural idea, almost as if cocking a snook at the beauty of the places it was going to disfigure, as if its very ugliness was a revolutionary ideal, a social leveller, a subtle form of aesthetic revenge meant to please everyone. The new neighbourhoods had grown without direction or logic, except the logic of bad taste. They faced each other at a distance of a few metres, displaying the most disparate styles—four-square barrack-like brick and concrete buildings glared at absurd semi-detached houses in bush-hammered grey concrete, ugly apartment blocks with Turkish frames and anodised aluminium trimming survived next to unfinished buildings left in a rough state. Via Galileo Galilei—so named by the comrades on the council—and Via Roma, the new village's two main thoroughfares, had soon become too heavy with traffic for us to hold our little matches there. Just as our fathers had had to move the pitch from the crossroads on the main road to a safer place because of the increase in traffic, so we had had to withdraw, abandoning a field expropriated by the relentless advance of construction which was redrawing places and streets.

What would you say to a cordial

S OMETIMES I PASSED THE SKELETON of the Pensione
Famiglia, all that remained of the dream of a hotel-
ier from Emilia Romagna named Ferranti, who had had
the bright idea of selling a prosperous hotel in Riccione
and building one in my village, which was the equivalent
of diving head-first into an empty swimming pool. He
had taken that dive, but did not realise where and how
he would land until two years later, when, on the verge
of bankruptcy, in a cold rainy October, he found himself
the last soldier presiding over the monument to the fallen.
The monument was his hotel, with only one guest still on
the register. This guest was an elderly lawyer from Rome, a
pedant fascinated with old coins whom everyone avoided
like the plague because he was so boring. He had been ill
for days, confined to bed by a persistent fever and whoop-
ing cough. Finally Ferranti, at the insistence of his guest,
increasingly weak after a fearful nocturnal coughing fit,
reluctantly decided to call the emergency services. A thin,
young doctor who looked older than his years arrived,
wearing a sinister loden coat and carrying an imitation-
leather bag, his face giving all the signs that he had been
sleeping fully clothed on a cot in the outpatients department. He took his stethoscope from the bag and listened
to the lawyer's chest in religious silence, hushing him each
time he tried to open his mouth. Then he shook his head.

"What is it?" the lawyer kept asking impatiently. "Is it
serious, doctor? Tell me!"

146

Ferranti took the doctor by the arm and, whispering in his ear, slowly dragged him out of the room.

"He's caught pneumonia," the doctor said, putting his stethoscope back in his bag. "He should be in hospital, otherwise … "

"Otherwise?"

"Given how damp it is here … it's quite possible that—"

"What?"

"That he'll go—"

"No, he can't go! He said he was staying all month!"

"I don't think you understand … If he's not taken to hospital, he'll end up in the cemetery."

To Ferretti, the hospitalisation of his one paying customer would mean the tragic closure of his hotel. Even death was better than hospitalisation.

"No! … What would you say to a cordial, doctor?" Ferretti said, in attempt to downplay the situation. But all to no avail. No cordial. The lawyer was taken to hospital just in time to be saved from pleurisy. After a while, they put him in a private room because even in hospital he wouldn't stop talking, and they couldn't stand it any more. Ferrerri closed the hotel, went back to Riccione, and was never heard of again. Neither was the lawyer.

We've done so much for you

MY MOTHER LOOKED GREAT that New Year's Eve when they inaugurated the Aquatrade Resort. Elegant in her blue-green satin dress, revealing enough to hint at the fact that she had been a beautiful woman and sober enough to make it clear that she wasn't one any more. A woman who dresses like a Gypsy and in restaurants asks if the fish is fresh, with the strength of a peasant woman from the steppes and the elegance of a Parisian grande dame. Father looked impressive in all his darkly dressed bulk, carrying an enormous black umbrella that made him look like a character straight out of the Alinari gallery. No, Dad has never had much style. He's a good, honest, intelligent man with such a great sense of duty and family—and every time I remind him of this his eyes light up—that he would never have acted like that other relative of mine about whom someone said at the bar, *If he had been born poor he would have had a lot of trouble just getting by.* My father, by contrast, has always worked hard. He's a cowboy stranded beyond the frontier, a nineteenth-century man, a hunter, a doctor, a florid poet. However hard he tries to appear relaxed in society, he remains a caged animal. When I think of him, I imagine him laying animal traps in a wood in the Yukon, fishing by the light of a full moon, walking to an isolated farmhouse in the middle of a blizzard and delivering a snivelling brat from a peasant woman's firm thighs.

We've done so much for you. That was what Mother always said whenever I complained about something. Are you sad? Yes, Mother. But we've done so much for you. Do you feel lonely? Yes, Mother. But we've done so much for you. Don't you like the way we furnished the house for you? No, Mother. Not even the art deco prints in the corridor? No, Mother. Not even the little pictures of dolls we put in the living room? No, Mother. What about the wall lights in the dining room? Don't you even like those? No, Mother. But they're art deco! I still don't like them, Mother. But we've done so much for you. And aren't you pleased that we bought you a computer? And a motorbike? And a car? And a house? No, Mother, I'm not pleased. But we've done so much for you. Yes, Mother. You've done so much for me. Perhaps too much.

Plants can also die of too much water, Mother.

New Year's Eve with a bang

O N BOARD THE FAMILY FLAGSHIP, polished specially for the occasion, I passed, for the first and last time as a free man, through the wrought-iron gate of the Aquatrade Resort that cold New Year's Eve …

We left our coats in a cloakroom that looked like the fitting area of a shop that rents costumes for fancy dress parties. In a corner was the cemetery of furs, where ermines, minks, arctic seals and white foxes battled ferociously for a centimetre of coat hanger. The ballroom was a dazzle of crystal and a parade of liveried waiters weaving between the guests. Solitary and curious, I swam through the hotel's reception rooms sparkling with Pompeian reds, sumptuous rooms of marble and stucco. I was like a fish out of water in an unknown aquarium, trying to keep my distance from the strange creatures populating the depths of the party. Every now and again, during the aperitif, they emerged from their lairs—greedy landowners sprang up from behind thick plants to plunder slices of bread spread with caviar from trays held by blameless waiters, unscrupulous surveyors scenting property speculation went out of their way to polish their grammar for their entrance into society, doddery old ladies held out their ringed hands to the few men daring enough to throw themselves into the ordeal of kissing them.

After a while, I approached a small group of people who seemed to be carrying on a conversation that was less dull than the others. In the centre of the group, impeccable in a blazer with gold buttons, I recognised Vanes Corallo, a playboy of mixed village and Roman origins, who had emigrated from the village as a little boy, worked in advertising and led the good life in Rome, "in the days when you only saw the gentry in the streets, not the louts you see today," as he said. He was a confirmed night bird, a great smoker of Marlboro, a prodigious imbiber of wines and spirits, and an inveterate patron of clubs and whores, only giving them up when the bill became "inconvenient".

"No, the place isn't the same, it's full of louts … "

Corales, like all genuine parvenus, was a hybrid who deep down despised both the poor and the gentry. But if he had to choose between the two, he was on the side of the gentry, modifying his scorn into adulation.

I started to eavesdrop, while pretending to write a message on my mobile phone.

"You know what's been the ruin of Rome, Contessa? The underground. The stations at Piazza di Spagna and Piazzale Flaminio. The louts started flocking in from the outskirts on Saturday afternoons, clogging up the centre and in a few years … Well, the result is there for all to see … "

"Ah, Vanes, how well you speak. I remember, before the war … "

"You don't need to tell me, Contessa, I lived through the war … "

"Ah, my dear man, it must have been terrible … "

"Indeed it was. These young people today aren't interested in anything … They're always glued to their mobile phones, or their Playstations … "

"How right you are, how right you are … "

"If it were up to me, Contessa, I'd wish a decent war on everyone. Every generation ought to experience a war.

Yesterday, I was watching those young Palestinians on the TV news … Handsome boys, slim, athletic, with a light in their eyes, bright faces, all that determination. They remind me so much of when we were young … "

I moved quietly away, and there, in front of a mustard-coloured circular sofa beneath a glittering crystal chandelier, I saw him. The Duce himself, Gattai, hand on hip, an extinguished cigar hanging from his lips, his shirt open on his patriotic chest, a massive Rolex on his wrist and that white hair with its marble sheen. He was talking to the Mayor, who was circling impatiently around him like a pilot fish. I couldn't hear what they were saying, but with them I saw a strange figure in a brown suit, a handsome man with an olive complexion, long black hair gathered into a ponytail, a thick black beard and two very intelligent Levantine eyes. There was something decidedly disquieting about him.

The guests were asked to take their seats at large circular tables on which were place cards. The seating arrangements were a masterpiece of diplomacy—Communists with Communists, bourgeois with bourgeois, Catholics with Catholics. The criteria taken into account were wealth, political allegiance, group affiliations, and family ties. Gattai's press office had done a meticulous PR job, taking months to draw up the shortlist of guests and their respective tables. My family and I had been placed with some distant relations who had come down in the world and were only tolerated by my grandmother because there could no longer be any competition for the inheritance.

"For instance," a cousin of my father's was saying, "it's not true that there's unemployment, it's just that people, especially the young, don't want to work … Just think, on my estate this summer, one of my workers left, just before the threshing started. A disaster. I let it be known that I was hiring a tractor driver and—"

"Lucky you," my grandmother cut in. "You can get by with a couple of workers. If you only knew the trouble we have on a big estate like ours, twenty specialised workers plus the casual labourers … "

"Oh, yes, I don't envy you there … What was I saying? Oh yes, this worker left and I let it be known in the village … Two young boys presented themselves … You know the first thing they asked me? The very first thing even before wanting to know what kind of work I was offering? Do you know? *How much do you pay a month?* they asked. Can you imagine? *How much do you pay a month?* Even before finding out what the work was. Insane," my father's cousin concluded solemnly, diving back into his truffle risotto.

"And then they say they can't find work," someone else said, I can't remember who. The rest of the table were nodding their heads slowly as if to say, it's a mad world.

By the ninth course we were still only at the beginning, someone was coming out with the tenth speech of the kind I've already reported, and my grandfather was on the verge of a glycaemic coma. I excused myself, saying I had to go to the toilet, and left the table.

Ten minutes later I was knocking back a bottle of champagne behind the kitchen, in the company of a Filipino waiter. Without a coat, it was freezing cold, but the champagne was starting to have an effect and the fauna inside gave me the courage to stay outside and resist the cold.

I loosened my tie, lit a cigarette and told the Filipino, who might in fact have been Sinhalese, not that it matters, that my grandfather used to whip the peasants. And that he would certainly have whipped him, too. God knows if he understood what I was saying. The Filipino was smiling with a glazed look on his face, the result of alcohol mixed with tiredness. I told him that if it had been true, my great-grandfather Terenzio would certainly have challenged that pig Gattai to a duel. He should have seen my great-grandfather, if only he'd seen him ... If only he'd seen him, he'd have understood immediately how things were. I told the Filipino that my great-grandfather had once invited a whole group of men to a fish dinner in Viareggio. His guests had eaten oysters, bream and dentex and drunk champagne to their heart's content. The waiter, seeing the bill rising astronomically, had dared to cast doubt on his customers' solubility.

"Tell me how much," my grandfather had said.

"So far, signore, two thousand five hundred lire."

"Not the bill. The restaurant. How much do you want for the restaurant?"

"Excuse me?"

"Perhaps I didn't make myself clear. I want to buy everything. Let me see the owner."

Those were good times. Before the family started drifting, a ship without a helmsman, no son with the makings of a leader, no one with the courage to stay on deck even in rough seas. If I had been born a few years earlier, I might have embarked on a whaling ship, or sold cattle in the Maremma, but in a real cattle market, not the one they hold these days for the tourists in the Parco dell'Uccellina.

Buoyed up by a false nostalgia, like old school companions, the Filipino and I downed another bottle. And then yet another. I stared into that perpetually smiling terracotta face and felt a little angry at his indifference to my words, his lack of involvement with the course of history, the thousands of years of evolution that had gone before us, moulding us and making us the people we were.

"Lucky you, for not understanding," I said to him finally.

He nodded and smiled, and it was only then that I realised that he really didn't understand, that he couldn't speak Italian and hadn't understood a single word I had said.

I lay down on a wicker bench hidden beneath a pile of coats that smelt of onions and age. From the back of the reception room came a tinkling of cutlery, my eyelids drooped over my lazy eyes, and my last image before I fell into an alcoholic stupor was a long shot of waiters gliding across the sidereal marble whirling trays that shone like Homeric shields. When I awoke, I realised from the desserts (tiramisu, profiteroles and crème brûlée) being sped from table to table that the banquet must be almost over. In the expectation that I would soon be hearing salvoes of sparkling wine corks saluting the New Year, I decided to go to the bathroom because the champagne had had an effect on my bladder. The door of the men's toilet was locked. The women's toilet was engaged. I waited for what I thought was a polite length of time, but no one came out. Then I heard whimpering coming from inside. I knocked.

Whimpering.

I knocked more loudly.

The whimpering grew louder.

"Who's there? What's happening? Is everything all right?"

No answer.

Then the door opened and a beautiful girl in a silvery evening dress came out. She had large hazel eyes, a flustered look on her face and smudged make-up. She looked at me in embarrassment and hurried away. I hesitated a moment in the doorway, and was just about to enter when Ottone Gattai's son Otello came out of the same toilet. He was in his shirtsleeves and his hair was dishevelled. Acting as if nothing had happened, he stuffed his shirt into his trousers as best he

155

could in front of the mirror, took out a pocket comb, held it under the tap, and smoothed his oily black hair. He took a cigarette from his pocket, stuck it in his mouth with a vulgar gesture, looked at me contemptuously, and set off along the corridor. I decided not to use that same toilet, and as soon as I got outside I found a secluded little fountain, believed to provide miraculous cures for conjunctivitis.

Then I was drawn back inside by a sudden silence, as if a chorus were observing a pause in a score. I returned to the main reception room of the hotel where, like a tribune, Gattai had climbed on to the pedestal of the Greco-Roman statue (a muscular torso without limbs or head discovered during the extension works for the Aquatrade Resort) and was tinkling the glass in his hand to ask for silence. The murmur in the hall ceased immediately. It was eleven forty-five according to the big clock.

"Ladies and gentlemen. Thank you for being here to celebrate the year which is just about to start, and thank you for appreciating this splendid dinner offered by Aquatrade. Before midnight, which is almost upon us"— here he stuck two fingers inside his shirt collar to loosen the pressure of his tie on that wrestler's neck of his—"we have a surprise for our guests. We'd like you to see the New Year in with a bang, which is why we've laid on a magnificent firework display. It won't be long now, so I advise you to put on your coats and follow me out into the square to enjoy the show."

Reluctantly, the guests slowly left the hall, made sluggish by the food and wine, and proceeded to the square in the grounds, watched over by the Medicean portico. It was bitterly cold.

The Aquatrade Resort's team of pyrotechnists had arranged two lines of luminous fountains beneath the portico, and various batteries and rocket launchers in a corona round the Christmas tree which stood in the middle of the square like the mast of a ship. Other firing units were spread around the surrounding meadow, aimed threateningly at the neutral, star-filled sky. A huge Catherine wheel had been placed at the top of a flower bed, right in the middle of the gravel square. Wrapped in a heavy black cloak, Unterwasser was directing operations, nervously checking his stopwatch, shooting off curt, precise orders, reviewing all the young waiters and employees who had been drafted into the firing squad for the occasion. Everyone was at their posts. I glanced at the triumphal arch that towered over the middle of the park, the solitary vestige of the baths' Fascist past. On the arch a powerful long-range rocket had been placed.

It was now very close to midnight. The guests gathered up by the waiters were all led into the square. A few more minutes were lost because there were some shirkers missing from the roll call, including an old couple who had clung to the radiators and were refusing to come outside. In the end, even the most quarrelsome were made to see reason, and the guests in their entirety assembled in front of the big Christmas tree. One minute to midnight. I looked at those bewildered people lined up under the portico, their faces white with cold, lost souls caught in the pincers of time between the year that had gone and the one that had not yet begun. They were waiting only for Gattai to do what he wished with their lives. He, the emperor, who had come out onto the balcony overlooking the portico, unconcerned by the wind, was waiting to give the signal for the celebration of his own greatness to begin.

Ten, nine, eight … The voice is coming from the balcony overlooking the portico. A butler with a megaphone, standing stiffly beside Gattai, is giving the countdown … Five, four, three—Gattai raises his arm in the air—two, one.

Gattai brings his arm down like a level crossing. Like creatures of the dark emerging from their lairs, little waiters run up to the fuses. They each know where to go, what to do, they swarm about, light their fires, and quickly withdraw. The square is alive with the hissing of fuses. The fireworks go up. WHEEEEEEEE, WHEEEEEEEE, BOOOOM, BOOOOM, SHHHHH, SHHHHHH, one after the other like a flight formation rising in the air. Now the fountains of light go off, green plumes glistening like dragon's scales, then bursts of red light like ships burning in a harbour, turning the night to day, the great luminous wheel turns, it turns and steams and spouts white and silvery light, softly at first, then ever louder, while the rockets explode in the sky. Gattai's voracious eyes reflect vermilion roses, cascades of gold dust that fade into the darkness. Orange stars, purple tracers and blue comets pierce the black sky. Ladies and gentlemen, all hail the New Year. Welcome to Year One of the thermal empire. The crowd are struck dumb by so much firepower. Only the grand finale is still to come. A waiter slips in between the explosions, dodging the bombardment, and makes his way through the smoke of the battlefield until he is at the foot of the arch with the inscription SALVS PER AQVAM. He lights the fuse and runs away. The fire moves up the fuse, climbing the wall like a gecko, approaching the lethal, powder-filled rocket. It is now directly under the missile. Everyone screws up their eyes, and some instinctively put their hands over their ears. But at the last moment, there comes only a dull plop, like a large cigarette extinguished in the snow. What's great about it is that nothing happens. There is a moment of embarrassment. In the air, there is something like a sense of applause dissipated. Gattai says nothing. He is grim-faced. From the terrace he goes back into the lit reception rooms, through the windows of which you can glimpse the splendour of the frescoed ceilings. The guests trickle back in, half frozen. In the air, the smell of wet powder, like the smell after a storm. People's breath mingles with the smoke from the burnt cardboard. Everyone goes back in. I don't. I remain alone on the white gravel square. With my hands in my pockets, looking fondly at that stillborn missile at the top of the arch, that rebellious device which has denied victory to its general. I have decided—for tonight, it will be my idol.

Suddenly, there's an unexpected glow, to which no one pays attention because they have all gone back inside. Lapilli are coming from the tail of the missile. The fuse starts moving again. Yes! The missile snorts, sizzles, swells and whistles, frees itself from the launch pad and goes off. Yes, it goes off. But it doesn't go up. No, it veers sideways. Like a shot that goes wide in a football match, it veers sideways. And heads directly for the terrace. The terrace where Gattai had been standing a minute earlier, like the Duce on the balcony of Palazzo Venezia. And with an ear-splitting whistle, it goes in through the large open window, behind which the chandeliers and frescoed ceilings of the reception rooms can be seen.

Very slowly, without an overcoat, I walk back along the gravel avenue which crunches like pack ice beneath the treacherous soles of my slip-ons. The first night of the year is also the last of the previous year, ice-cold and filled with stars, and in the air there is the acrid smell of battle.

Sheiks and gangsters

A LL I KNEW ABOUT ARABS was that they had once been philosophers and mathematicians, that they had occupied Sicily, that they were cultivated sultans and formidable horsemen, who more than once had led our Crusaders a merry dance, in other words, the little I had read in my school books. I imagined the caliphates a thousand miles away, beyond the *mare nostrum*, where the sun set over the minarets accompanied by the litanies of the muezzin.

It was about thirty years ago that we started to see the first Moroccans in our area. Some of them were Tunisians, but we called them all Moroccans. In any case, they were nothing like the Arabs depicted in my school books. True, they had dark complexions and many of them had moustaches, but they were neither sultans nor horsemen. They sold balloons at festivals and village fairs, and if you looked older than you were and you approached them in the right way they would open the trunks of their cars where they kept porn videos hidden under poor-quality pirated Madonna and Edoardo Bennato compilations. These Moroccan vendors all travelled in clapped-out diesel cars, or rather, I now remember, they almost all had white Fiat Regatas with PA registrations or blue 132s with VT registrations. At the time, I didn't know anything else about Arabs, nor could I, because globalisation of goods and people was all a long way away, a lot further than the minarets.

Many things had changed since those years, and I hadn't thought any more about Arabs, at least until the day when they were right there in front of me. I was in the square, sitting on the big wall minding my own business and hoping no one would come and start a conversation and disturb my thoughts, which, I remember, were coming along nicely that day, when I heard a rumble approaching from the main road. It sounded like the fire from anti-aircraft guns, ever closer, ever angrier. I leant over the wall to get a better look. In the distance, on the stretch of road that appeared between the broom and the bushes, I saw them. They were coming along the main road in serried ranks, speeding in a southerly direction. Mounted on those black steeds, their white cloaks rustled in the wind like the banners of a conquering army. They raced along the red-hot asphalt, and the steel of their harness and weapons shone with glory in the morning sun. Then they disappeared from view. So was this the fearful Numidian cavalry, the terror of the Roman legions, which we'd read about in our Latin translations? I strained my ears, trying to distinguish the direction of the sound. It was actually coming towards me. So the land had fallen to the Arabs without a fight. Before I could hatch an escape plan, the Arabs overran the square.

Dozens of motorbikes. Shiny black Harley Davidsons, driven by men without helmets. They were wearing white tunics, with massive chains, showy watches and gold-framed Ray-Bans, and their keffiyehs were held tight across their foreheads with strips of black material. The exhaust pipes glistened in the midday light, and sent up a deafening roar like a big engine with its pistons out of phase. Then I looked at them more closely. Their tunics were spotted with insects—flies, wasps, midges—like mosquito nets

161

that had seen better days. They parked their motorbikes where it was forbidden to park, piling them one beside the other, too close not to fall against each other as they got off. They got off awkwardly, like people who are not familiar with motorbikes. Then, en masse, they headed for the restaurant. As they walked away, there was a huge crash, like hundreds of pots being knocked over. One of the bikes had fallen down, taking another ten with it.

They weren't Numidian horsemen, but Arab sheiks staying at the Resort as part of a tour of Italy on hired Harleys. I learnt that from a woman friend who did the rooms at the hotel. After that day, I never saw them again. The people who did start to see them were the doctors in the orthopaedic department of the hospital in Siena. It was there that many of them spent the end of their grand tour, bruised and sore.

The Arabs on their bikes may have had only a clumsy walk-on part, but the Russians were a fixed presence. The thermal conventions which Gatti had sponsored from Moscow to Vladivostok were starting to bear fruit. They arrived in their Ferraris, Porsches, Maseratis, Bentleys, Rolls Royces and Aston Martins. They arrived with screeching tyres, and parked wherever they wanted, in defiance of any no parking signs. I would observe them, their white, freckled skins, their clear, wicked little eyes, their short hair that made them look like retired officers, the beautiful legs of the blondes coming through the ground-level doors of their custom-built cars—these were people who made no attempt to pass unnoticed. Compared with the Arabs' naively displayed wealth, the Russians were true professionals. Their philosophy was much subtler, because they didn't use money to buy goods and show them off. What interested them was neither the money nor the goods, nor the transaction, but the very nature of the relationship revealed in that transaction—an asymmetrical relationship of obedience and domination, a sado-masochistic, master-servant relationship, in which the person with a bulging wallet is the master and the person excited by that bulge is the servant. What mattered to the Russians was to humiliate the other party in the transaction with the asymmetrical power of their wealth. It doesn't matter *how much* you pay for something, what matters is *how much you're prepared* to pay for something. There needn't be a connection between the price and the goods, buy a custom-built car, a diamond or a mansion for an astronomical amount, those are all good things, you just have to have the money. What counts is not how much you're prepared to pay for a strawberry when strawberries are in season, but how much you're prepared to pay for it when strawberries are out of season. And then leave it on the plate. That's the whole game.

The trouble is, I was born here

I KNOW THESE PLACES WELL. If you're born in a place, the more you love it, the more you hate it. And the trouble is, I was born here. I know the landscape by heart, the outlines of the hills, the changing light, the colours of the seasons, the roads with all their bends, all their ups and downs.

The Cassia, which descends towards Siena, for example. I could draw it for you with my eyes closed, like a blind man. After bending over the Ponte del Paglia like a hunchback, it stretches out full-length as far as the tunnel through Mount Amiata. Then it emerges from the tunnel as quick as a bullet, crosses the forty-eighth parallel and begins a sullen spiral towards San Quirico. From there it draws breath, goes into neutral and rolls for kilometres along those viaducts set down on the grey, undulating ridges, the muddy bed of a primordial sea in which whales once swam. They even found a whale once in a field they were ploughing, a whole whale, with all its bones intact from head to tail. They reassembled it just as it had been in the cloister of the Academy of Sciences in Siena.

And along the road, stop at that lay-by from where you can photograph a clump of cypresses standing close together in the middle of a field. It's on all the postcards, that image. But true cypresses stand alone and emaciated at the top of some fallow land or face each other in rows along the avenues that lead to the cemetery or to some parish or villa old enough to have seen them being planted. As solitary as a cypress, that's how I feel some days.

Today is one of those days. And on days like this, I like
to think that somewhere, beyond the rotted leaves in this
wood, beyond the clearing where we've made our camp,
beyond this thick fog you wish you could shovel away like
snow, the village is still there. My village.

I feel as though I can see it and hear it, beyond the fog,
down there in the valley. I hear Corinto's bar echoing to
the billiard balls going click, click, then whishing across
the green baize. I see the cone of light falling lopsidedly
from the hanging lamp over the billiard table. Behind the
bar counter is Corinto, and behind Corinto the coloured
bottles of Vov cream liqueur and China Martini, and on
the shelf above the counter I see the white vase of Amarena
Fabbri cherries with the blue decorations, and next to the
cash register the bowl of sweets—the Rossanas with their
cream centres, the mint-flavoured Sperlaris, the lemon-
flavoured ones with the striped wrappers, the little sugar
balls and the loose chocolates, with their coloured wrappers
swimming in the bowl like little tropical fish, each colour a
taste—green and gold for milk chocolate, black and gold
for fondant, red and gold for amaretto, and if you dig deep
in the bottom of the bowl you might also find a banana-
flavoured Perugina, let's hope Dad remembers to bring me
back a couple when he comes home from his billiard game
and gives me a goodnight kiss and as I kiss him he smells of
smoke and the leather of his jacket, the kind of things dads
smell of when they come home from bars, in fact. I wish
the bar in my village still had ashtrays overflowing with
cigarette ends, the filters squashed like bugs, and dense
smoke the colour of aniseed clinging to the place even
when the shutter has been lowered and the bar is closed,
because the smoke lives in that bar like a lodger, and you
can't evict it even when the door is open, and in fact if you

open the door there's always someone who tells you to close it. I don't know why, right now, instead of these branches, I have in front of my eyes the black and white bricks of Corinto's bar, so blackened you can no longer tell the black from the white, and I feel nostalgic for the voice of De Zan doing the commentary on the Giro d'Italia on the TV and saying that Saronni has broken away and is gaining a few minutes on his followers, that's the way he puts it, and that Moser is in trouble on the Pordoi pass ... and some people in the room are looking grim because they would have preferred it if Saronni hadn't broken away at all.

I wish Gino, the antiquarian, was still in the village, old Gino who used to shoot pellets at the furniture to obtain a worm-eaten effect, and whose shop was full of grandfather clocks that all struck at the same time and when they did that Cosetta the madwoman would appear in the doorway and say, "Clocks, clocks, clocks, it's time we don't have enough of, time, time, time!"

And whatever happened to Battista's general store? With the cheap cigarettes, the rhubarb-and-honey-flavoured sweets, the lined sheets of foolscap paper for classroom use which you bought first thing in the morning, when it was still dark, with the street lamps still lit, on those December days as short as a match. I wish the Tecla bakery were still open and I had a thousand lire in my pocket to spend on a focaccia with oil and rosemary straight from the oven. What about the other shops, Azolino the shoemaker and Primo the barber and Ilio the carpenter whose cock was the length of seven wax matches? I wish the wooden goalposts made by the carpenter's grandfather were still standing in the open space at the entrance to the village, and the net we'd pooled our money to buy from the knitwear factory, and I wish the ball were still bouncing

sullenly off that background full of holes. And I wish I
could close my eyes for a moment and try to imagine
the square by the bridge as it used to be, full of the cries
and innocent curses of the Saturday afternoon football
match, when we got off the school bus at half past two
and didn't even go home to put away our satchels but
launched ourselves in pursuit of the ball on the asphalt,
and the bigger and better ones never, ever let you get
near it. Unless you volunteered to go and recover the ball
from a patch of nettles—when you have time, go and
see Agesilao (the village blacksmith) and he'll straighten
those feet for you, a voice would shout from the field.

If I close my eyes, I can make the cool water flow from
the Piscinello spring, I can make the shade fall over my
flushed face, I can make the smell of wet earth rise around
the spring, I can make that gush of icy water go down
in one gulp, deep down into my dry throat. I can drink
that water, I just have to try and ignore the jokes of my
thirsty friends who make me laugh as I'm drinking so the
water goes up my nose. I wish that nothing had changed,
that there was still a living village beyond the hill, with
the fires blazing and the bitter smell of firewood rising in
the brown air of winter, not this village of second homes
with its square all spruced up with little street lamps and
the ghetto of the spa with its spiky aluminium railings and
neon and barbed wire.

Stop clinging to memories like a shipwreck survivor
clinging to a lifeboat. That's what Lea would tell me if
I told her my thoughts. And anyway you sometimes pass
off other people's memories as your own, and sometimes
you speak as if you'd lived for a thousand years, you're a
vampire of memories, a parasite of remembrance, and
I just don't understand you any more. That's what she

would say, too. But you know. You know that rather than live in this prototype of an inhabitable present, this plan for a world on a scale of 1:1, drawn in the image of a surveyor, this dream of a future as reassuring as an election poster, I prefer to die fighting. And anyway I'm sorry, is it my fault—I would tell her—if the past is the one thing in which I recognise myself, if it's only in looking back that I can find the courage to look forward?

"What are you thinking about?" Lea asks me.

"Nothing."

Sadat Mawazini

THE INDIVIDUAL I had noticed at the New Year's Eve celebration was becoming an increasingly familiar sight. He would come into the square, his mouth covered with his moustache so that it was difficult to read his lips. More and more often I would see the Mayor, Gattai and Mawazini walking around the square in an indecipherable manner, gesticulating, arguing animatedly, covering spaces and distances with the pace of a site supervisor, as if their eyes were seeing something that wasn't yet there. The municipal surveyor was with them, which tended to put paid to any visionary hypotheses but rather to guarantee a certain realism in any construction plans.

When something happens in the village, people soon know about it. The fact that he was always in Gattai's company and constantly going in and out of the town hall certainly didn't pass unnoticed. In no time at all he had become very chummy with the Mayor, who, like all ignorant people, suffered terribly from a complex about art. He had bought a tumbledown farmhouse, which he was refurbishing. His name was Sadat Mawazini, and it's only now, when I've seen his name written in a catalogue, that I feel confident enough to write it without making any mistakes. He was a modern artist. Or what they call modern. A painter and sculptor, according to the critics. He was from Arabia and nobody's quite sure how exactly he had ended up in our area. Sante, who was always well-informed but refused to reveal his sources, said that his father was an emir—one of the worst exploiters of the Arab people, and I quote—who had sent his children to study in the West.

"How do you know? Who told you?"

"Are you kidding? Just mark my words."

And I did. What I was wondering was—What on earth was Gattai up to? What was he doing with an Arab artist? He had approval from the municipality, capital from the Russians, goodwill from the banks, and political protection from the Party, so why did he need an Arab artist? He might be ignorant, but he was intelligent. He wasn't like the Mayor. There was no way he would suffer from the widespread cultural complex that affected almost everyone in local government, a mixture of deference, hate and admiration which those lacking in culture feel towards scholars, men of letters, intellectuals and critics. There had to be something behind it. I would simply have to wait, and time would provide the answer.

Mawazini's first act was to organise a happening by conceptual artists in the streets of the village. They were all rich kids who didn't want to study and certainly didn't want to work, kids who'd failed in every other field except art, where it takes a whole lifetime before you're finally deemed a failure and you can always conceal your failure with the excuse that people don't understand you. For a week, the young artists, more young than artists, carefully dressed down in line with their assumed air of scruffy Communist intellectuals, busied themselves with their installations. They went to and from the paint shop, emerging with screws and nails wrapped in newspaper, hammers stuck into their dirty jeans like revolvers.

On the Saturday of the exhibition the village was full of people. There was an installation in every quarter. I walked

around, just to have a look. In front of the shoemaker's in
the little square with the well, there was a queue of people
trying to get into the Church of the Conception to see the
exhibit by a young American artist. The floor was covered
with sand, there was a sandcastle in the middle and a
bucket and spade in a corner.

The other exhibits were more or less of the same ilk:
bubbles of blown glass stuck to a wall, a festoon made
with toilet paper, a stepladder in a garage. Mawazini's own
exhibit in the parish church I had left for last. I entered the
silent nave, with the metaphysical light through the rose
window lightening all the forms, making me feel as if I
was bodiless. The wooden altarpiece from the school of
Simone Martini had disappeared, the golden one with the
Byzantine-style Madonna in the blue drapery suffused with
gold, the baby Jesus clinging to her neck, and a moving,
pitiful look in her eyes as if to say, I know how much I
have suffered. In its place, high in the apse behind the altar,
there was a large black eye, a searching eye. It was the eye
of God, the priest explained, and it was looking straight at
you, wretched sinner.

"I'm sorry, Father," I said, "but what's happened to the
altarpiece?"

"Oh yes, it needed restoring, it was all worm-eaten.
Signor Sadat is taking care of it, what a dear man ... "

After so many priests embittered by exile, celibacy and
ignorance, their own and that of the parishioners, we now
had a highly educated, distinguished old priest, who was
extremely thin and in poor health. When the weather was
bad, he did not even come to services for fear of catching
a cold. And as the gas heaters were almost always switched
off because they consumed too much, what with the price
of gas nowadays, on the few occasions when he officiated

in winter he would say Mass wearing gloves and a skullcap and with the stole in front of his mouth. As his voice was naturally thin anyway, you couldn't understand a word he said.

A few days later, I realised that the doors of the church—a pair of quite decent seventeenth-century doors of solid cherry wood—were shinier than usual, too shiny not to be suspicious ... I went closer, but couldn't find any trace of roughness in the wood, any marks of time. The wood gave off an intoxicating smell of paint. It wasn't the usual stale restoration smell, the smell of stain or resin of some kind. No, the doors were brand new. They were copies. What had happened to the old ones? They had been replaced with a pair of similar doors, still of cherrywood, but lighter, varnished and machine carved, approximate copies of the originals.

I asked the sacristan for information.

"They were all worm-eaten," he said. "Have you seen how beautiful the new ones are?"

On the way back home I caught sight of Mawazini in the doorway of the shop Once upon a Time. He was talking to the antique dealer, Carrai. The two of them shook hands and parted before I was close enough to overhear any words. But I could imagine.

We are working for ourselves

WE WERE USED to the historic compromise. Seeing a priest arm in arm with a Communist made my blood neither boil nor freeze, and how many times had I seen Party leaders, fiery orators, fiercely anti-clerical partisans and Garibaldians waiting impatiently at mass to suck the host and take Communion.

The only true hardliner was Professor Oronzo Giancane, a Bakunian anarchist whom everyone avoided like the plague, his beret pulled down over his head, entrenched behind his problematic black beard. He would celebrate Lent in his own way, and every Good Friday would bring from home a foil-wrapped pork roll, sit down on the steps of the church, and start eating it with exasperating slowness.

But seeing the octogenarian priest, the Communist mayor, and the Arab artist sitting at the same table in the restaurant in the square, elbow to elbow like apostles in a fresco of the Last Supper, huddled around their master Ottone Gattai, who was holding court in the centre of the composition, was a truly extraordinary sight.

After this vision I had another, an even more alarming one if possible—the municipal surveyor measuring the length and width of the square with a tape. Surveyor Colzi was infamous in the area for having desecrated a number of places of ineffable beauty. Among his works was the criminal restoration of the main square of Cetona, which had been entirely repaved in blinding white marble so that it looked like something halfway between a ski slope and a salt pit and was unbearable in the summer without powerful sunglasses. He was also responsible—and this was something he was especially proud of—for the small trees and the *anti-view hedges*, so called because placed just a metre in front of the benches, a stroke of genius which meant that anyone who sat there found his view blocked by a shapeless mass of evergreen bushes. His, too, was the idea for the campsite and the parking place for campers in the park adjacent to the castle, fortunately thwarted at the last moment by a rare, timely intervention from the Academy of Fine Arts. In short, Colzi was a true phenomenon in his field. Apart from a kind of fetish for asphalt and concrete, he also had an undeclared perversion involving traffic lights and roundabouts, and for years had been pursuing a personal crusade on the need to put a roundabout at the entrance to the village, just in front of the monument to the unknown soldier. To improve the road system, he said. Accidents recorded at that junction since the invention of the wheel—none. Jams—an unknown occurrence.

We were coming up to elections, and the Mayor was anxious to be re-elected. Although sponsored by both the Party and the thermal lobby, he was making cautious overtures to the centre and going through hoops to reach an understanding with the right-wing worthies, because, he thought, if you have the priests and the bourgeois against you, not even Gattai can help you. So, a few months before dissolving the council and temporarily leaving office, the Mayor had decided to mark his departure with a little gift. The great giveaway at the end of his mandate, the star attraction, like the firework display at the spa.

One Monday morning, having woken up late out of laziness, I stood at the parapet in the castle's garden, a terraced garden which looked out on the village square—

from this parapet my grandfather, in the days when he was still in good health, would watch the advance of the harvester through his binoculars, ready to contact the estate manager by radio in case the machine hesitated, slowed down or caused unfortunate delays—and was stunned by the vision that met my eyes. A dozen workers in orange overalls, armed with sledgehammers and pickaxes, and a powerful Fiat-New Holland excavator (if it broke down, who was responsible? Fiat or New Holland?) which was effortlessly tearing up the old paving on the square. The age-old surface of flat stones of irregular size and cut, worn smooth by time and the heavy steps of the villagers, was coming away like a crumbly crust beneath the steel claws of the excavator. I rushed to the scene of the misdeed.

"What are you doing?"

"Can't you read?" one of the workers replied.

UPGRADING AND REPAVING OF THE SQUARE, A PROJECT OF THE DELLA PECORA GROUP ON BEHALF OF SICUL-TOSC LTD. WORKS DIRECTOR— ENGINEER LEPANTO. SITE SUPERVISOR— SURVEYOR COLZI. WORK TO BE CARRIED OUT AS PRESCRIBED BY LAW.

The next day I paid a visit to the town hall, because I needed to get a better idea of what was going on. The Mayor was not there, he was in Russia with Gattai and would not be back until the following week, I was told by one of those rather slow-witted ushers town halls are forced to hire because of a famous law. So I approached the technical office. Surveyor Colzi made no attempt to conceal his annoyance at my legitimate requests as a citizen, and was sparing with his answers. The few times he deigned to reply, he did so without even looking me in the eyes while pretending to look for important papers in that untidy office. I was standing there, unsure what to do next, when I was informed by a trainee not yet accustomed to the municipal employee's code of silence that, without any consultation, a radical plan to upgrade (as they say these days) the square had been approved. The trainee showed me the Della Pecora plans, officially belonging to Sicul-Tosc Ltd but actually the property of Ottone Gattai's son, Otello. And while the trainee was incautiously unrolling the plans and pointing out the magnificence of the project, a telephone rang in the other room. He went to answer it, and I seized my chance—I grabbed the plans and hotfooted it out of there.

Once I was home, I studied the plans at my leisure. Apart from the repaving, and the placing of ergonomic street furniture such as benches that faced two ways, hanging lamps, and cubic marble road humps to demarcate the parking area, the project also involved the indiscriminate cutting down of the old acacias that gave shade to the square. Why such a passion for deforestation? Why did those age-old trees have to pay the price for local politicians' infinitely frustrated ambitions? There was a reason. On the plan I saw something I would have hoped I'd never see. In the upper corner of the square was the most beautiful tree, our favourite since we had been children. It was the oldest of the acacias, the one whose leafy branches had so often sheltered us from the prying eyes of the square, making us feel like adults as we opened our mouths for the first kiss or the first cigarette. Even now that we were, so to speak, grown up, we still read the newspaper in its shade. There, amid the dense spider's web of lines and points on the plan, precisely where the acacia should be, was a geometric scribble that was supposed to be a statue. An imposing statue on a pedestal. An accident of forms that left no doubt as to the figure depicted—the clawed serpent, symbol of Aquatrade.

They're cutting down the trees

"THEY'RE CUTTING DOWN THE TREES," I said.

"I'm having lunch on my own today, and I don't know what to eat," Conti said, lounging at the table outside the bar. "I may make myself a salad with tinned meat—"

"Are you crazy?" Sante interrupted him, trying to light a cigarette with wax matches inside the lapel of his jacket to protect the light from the sirocco that had risen, spoiling the weather and everyone's mood.

"Why? What's wrong with that?"

"It's all dog."

"What do you mean, dog?"

"When I was doing my military service, we saw a meat lorry overturn once at Roncobilaccio. Our convoy stopped to lend support. The doors of the cold store had broken open … "

Everyone grew quiet to hear the end of the story.

"Skinned dogs."

"Get away," Conti said, smiling unconvincingly. "I don't believe you."

"It's no laughing matter. I tell you, it was all skinned dog."

"Forget about skinned dogs," I said. "Did you hear what I said? They're cutting down the trees!"

"Is that possible?" someone said.

"They've torn up the paving, taken away the travertine benches and the old iron lamp-posts, and now they're cutting down the trees."

"What are you talking about?"

"Even this one you're leaning on now!" I said, beating with my hand on the trunk of the acacia which was giving us shade. "Yes, snip, snip, and even this one will be gone. And in its place, they're going to put a statue."

"What do you mean, a statue? How did you hear that?"

"You should attend a few council meetings instead of playing cards."

"Hey, how about a game of cards tonight?"

"No, guys, let's be serious for once, we can't let this thing pass. We have to do something, otherwise they'll spoil everything.'

And I looked spellbound at the soft valley stretching before our eyes.

The square enjoyed a wonderful view. On the right were the last hills of the Val d'Orcia. On the left, the inaccessible woods of the Rufeno. Straight ahead, the reclining head of the Civitella and the broken-off peak of the Amiata, which rose solidly into the sky of the Maremma, swelling with blue on clear summer evenings.

The square was built on a terrace built soon after the unification of Italy. On one side the buildings, on the other a stretch of stone which fell away precipitously for a dozen metres. That architect was a bright fellow. The wall had been erected in 1888, according to the inscription on the stone in the centre. The old people used to tell the story of this half-mad guy, who later opened a farm breeding earthworms I don't know where, probably near Montevarchi, not that it matters, anyway, this guy when he was a boy used to ride his bicycle along the top of the wall. He would do the whole cornice on a woman's bike with

179

Graziella-type wheels. Ahead of him the undulating ridges as far as the eye could see, and below him thirty metres of nothing. Every time I leant over, I thought of the danger of that act, the control of movement, the concentration, the determination not to look down, the precision of the pedalling, and that small bicycle wheel advancing unsteadily to the end of the cornice.

The acacias were close to the wall. Trees are never planted by chance. No peasant ever planted an apple tree or a pear tree at the top of a hill thinking that a hundred years later a Japanese tourist might take a splendid photo of it with his digital camera, or that there might be an *Under the Tuscan Sun* calendar with its cover showing that solitary pear tree at the top of a hill.

No, he thought of the shade it would give when the temperature was especially high, he thought of where he would put his bottle of wine to protect it from the sun, and the white pulp of the pear he had just enjoyed beneath the tree. Acacias are trees with deep roots, roots that intertwine and join together, trapping the earth. They're planted on escarpments and cliffs, along the banks of ditches, where the earth falls away, where it yields, where people are afraid it might spoil. The reason they had planted those acacias there was because they didn't want the embankment of the square to move, putting pressure on the wall that contained it.

"What do you mean, they're cutting down the trees?" Conti asked, coming back from wherever he'd been. "Have they gone mad?"

"That's what they're saying," Sante said.

"What if they plant those horrible Arizona cypresses? We have to do something."

"I'll tell you what we're going to do," I said. "We're going to start a citizens' committee."

"No way!" Garrone said.

"If I say we will, we will!"

"OK, guys, do it," Sante said. "But I'm going to lunch, I'm really hungry."

The company had broken up, everyone anxious to get home and put his feet under the table. Then Conti changed direction, and stopped Garrone.

"Do you really believe that story about skinned dogs?"

"No, I don't, what about you?"

"Me neither."

"What time is it? God, it's late. I'm having lunch with the in-laws, I'd invite you, my mother-in-law has made a roast with peppers, but it could be a bit heavy for lunch. Anyway, see you later."

The whine of the chainsaws

I WAS WOKEN by the whine of the chainsaws. By nine in the morning, the clearance operation had begun and the trunk of the first acacia was lying motionless on the square. The first to fall had been "our" acacia, which had served us so well over the years. I protested once again to the workers, who told me the trees were all sick and that I should mind my own business. I stood on that battlefield, watching in a state of angry powerlessness as all the acacias on the square fell one after another. The chainsaws attacked the tender wood like a cancer, spitting out air and sawdust.

Conti, Sante, Garrone, Tito and a few others arrived later. They didn't say a word. They stood in line, their hands behind their backs, as if at a funeral. We looked in silence at the rough trunk of the largest acacia, defenceless in the middle of the square, swarming with a myriad of little black insects escaping from the earth that had been moved from the base of the trunk. In the thickest part of the foliage was a nest of turtle doves, like pollen caught in someone's hair.

A bleak, dusty plateau. That was how the square looked when the workers had finished. It was a break with the past, a clean break, just spread everything with salt and usher in a new era under the banner of Ottone Gattai's illegitimate kingdom.

The serpent

THE SQUARE WAS REPAVED with ordinary machine-cut stones. The old travertine benches, masterfully hand-carved by local stonecutters, were removed and replaced by modern wood-and-iron benches. Benches that faced two ways, one looking towards the square, and the other the valley, in such a way that the people sitting on them would turn their backs on each other. Flowerbeds were laid, making the square one big toilet for dogs. The wrought-iron lamp-posts ended up in the back of a lorry, and powerful halogen lamps were placed on the roofs and walls of the houses, like floodlights in a maximum-security prison. At the far end of the square and along the avenue they also planted hothouse lime trees, so thin and shabby they made it look as though the village had just come through a period of famine. Only when all that remained of the old square was the name did they move on to the final solution—the placing of the statue.

Sadat Mawazini supervised the operation. Dressed in an impeccable beige linen suit, he waved his arms like an overzealous parking attendant and called out in his approximate but effective Italian, "Come come come. Stop. Down down, a little more, slow. Slow! Like that … " directing the delicate manoeuvres of the crane. Slowly the arm of the crane descended, bringing a long narrow parallelepiped to rest inside a base in square sections. Once the white stone pedestal had been put in place, the sculpture, hidden beneath a sheet, was laid down on top

183

of it. Sadat was stroking his beard and smoking contentedly. Then he crushed his cigarette like a scorpion beneath the heel of his slip-ons and started giving orders to the team of workers. One very short worker took a stepladder and climbed onto the pedestal. He disappeared beneath the sheet like a child beneath the blankets, and hammered and screwed until the mysterious sculpture was firmly fixed to its base.

People were following the scene with a degree of mistrust despite the Party's directive to support the operation in every way and give unconditional praise to the generous restoration of the square.

And yet everyone was pretending to be normal, while in fact showing signs of apprehension. The pensioners were talking about this and that, shielding their inscrutable faces beneath the brims of their hats, every now and again turning nervously towards the gap left by the cut-down trees, and constantly moving about, searching for a patch of shade in the deforested square. The housewives went in and out of the shops as usual, but threw alarmed glances at the installation that now dominated the centre of the square. The workers started fiddling with pipes at the base of the pedestal, and gradually unrolled a strange kind of siphon all the way to the corner of the square, where they fastened it to a cistern just under the ground which looked like a water heater or something of the kind. What the hell did a hydraulic contraption like that have to do with the statue? I really would have liked to know more, but Sadat Mawazini's broad sculptor's shoulders and his legion of workers standing in testudo formation around the statue blocked my view. But at last, Sadat Mawazini ordered them to fall out. The workers got their tools together and took their leave. Sadat Mawazini remained standing there with his hands on his hips, his legs slightly apart, like a father admiring his beloved creation.

"Have you finished?" I asked.

"God willing," the worker said. "The unveiling is tomorrow."

The following day, the square was packed with people. They were jammed in around the base of the statue, the top of which was covered by a sheet with a large ribbon. A sinister trio stood beneath the pedestal—the Mayor and Sadat Mawazini on either side—the former, in his ill-matched grey suit, his white shirt, his trousers belted under his belly, his regulation tricolour sash, a pair of pruning shears to cut the ribbon, and an unprecedented knot in his tie, as ungainly as the latter was impeccable, with his curly beard turned to the sky and his pony tail descending over the back of the cream suit—and Ottone Gattai in the middle, with his deep tan, his porcelain-white hair, his charismatic temples, his bather's chest under a shirt with a superb starched collar and the top two buttons undone. All at once, the hum of voices faded into silence.

"Citizens!" the Mayor declaimed, his chest swelling like a toad's. "May I have your attention for a moment? Allow me to make a brief introduction. As the value of a territory, in every sector—leaving aside a certain discourse—is ultimately the result of a blend of entrepreneurial elements and historical, cultural, social and political aspects, in short, the fruit not only of individual abilities but also of the contamination and development of local society, which simultaneously influences and by which those who produce and work are inevitably contaminated, any discourse on an awareness of the difference that exists between one territory and another similar to it—equal but different—is part of another discourse which is linked to the typicalness of the territory, which is certainly also a character of the territory itself. Now, if the territory in question is, with all the more reason, rich in history, and as you know better than I, in culture and in social and historical and, why not, also cultural dynamics and issues, if, as I was saying, in the past this type of discourse had the wrong emphasis, then there are many people who must make a mea culpa. Wishing to simplify the discourse by implementing it—"

At this point, Gattai delivered a blow to the Mayor's ribs with his elbow.

"But I won't expand any further," the Mayor said. "Let me take this opportunity to thank Signor Gattai, managing director of Aquatrade, the president of the savings bank, the various businesses, institutions and agencies involved, and of course all the people who have believed in this project from the start and have financed it. Last but not least, a special thank you to Mawazini, the artist who produced the statue. At last we too will have in our beautiful square a prestigious work by a foreign artist. Not before time. The people deserved something like this from us, and you know the people are—"

Gattai snatched the microphone from the Mayor's hand. "Enough chatter. Now, thanks to me, your village too has a fine monument it can be proud of. Let the celebrations begin!"

And with a brisk motion, he tugged on a thick rope. The sheet covering the statue fell at his feet like a bathrobe and the statue was revealed, as naked as a beautiful woman. Or rather, an ugly woman.

They called it 'the intestine', 'the tapir', 'the melted ice cream'. It wasn't easy to find the right epiphet for Sadat

Mawazini's creation. There were those who, off the tops of their heads, launched into poetic comparisons, and those who like me—like us—were struck speechless.

Atop the white base—"Authentic Turkish stone!" the Mayor said, rapping it with his knuckles before the stunned onlookers—was a crouching copper-coloured figure. It was a bronze cast coiled around itself like a pipe or a siphon. Or perhaps it was a pipe wrapped around a bronze cast. In other words, no one could figure out what it was. A critic had been brought along to explain the meaning of that hunchbacked bronze canker:

"The manifest reasons for the emergence of the Modern Style are still too woolly and random to be summed up in some wretched heuristics of common sense. Something similar could be said of its latent reasons—and here the attentive observer will forgive me my interpretative zeal … "

"What did he say?" an old man asked.

"Shut up and let me listen!" his wife silenced him.

" … which is why any determination of the phenomen-ological causes, as well as any repeated attempt at historical decoding, comes up against, not only the given-ness of the world, but also the ontological nature of the object/work of art, above all because of that consubstantial and contradictory feeling of fierce creative individualism which eludes any mystique of representation but which is intrinsic to the genesis of art or any other act of creation. It is pointless to try and trace Mawazini's art back to the marginal though courageous current of reptilism. The snake, a sacred animal in the Zoroastrian religion, and in other syncretic cults of Asia Minor in which Sadat Mawazini has shown a consistent interest … "

"Is he going to tell us what it is?" a man asked.

"He hasn't said yet," another replied, "but he's going to now."

" ... pointless to recall that the snake makes a powerful appearance in the Bible. And here we find the major age-old interpretative error of the commentators, who see the snake as an evil animal, a tempter, an emissary of Satan conspiring against divine harmony. What exegetic blindness! How can we not see in the reptile the primo-genial principle, the demiurgic force that triggers the principle of the fall (the fall understood as reascent)? Fortunately, Freud comes to our rescue here, tracing the snake back to a clear phallic symbol of sexual potency, although a touch flaccid, but if need be capable of growing hard immediately. If we take the cycle of Gilgamesh ... "

"The filthy bastard," a woman said. "What's he talking about?"

" ... it is no coincidence that Laocoön, son of Priam and Hecuba, or of Antenor according to other versions, is crushed together with his children by two sea serpents expressly sent by Poseidon, which connects to the serpent in Nietzsche, bitten in its turn by the courageous shepherd, thus exorcising the horror of the eternal return ... "

"A committee," I said. "We need a committee."

"It's a bit late now," Garrone said.

"I know a cultural under-secretary," I said. "Let's collect signatures and take them to him."

"We can try," Sante said.

" ... and let us not forget Minos, who, as Dante reminds us, makes judgements with his snake-like tail ... "

"You and Minos can both go to hell!" a voice called from the back of the crowd.

The critic's explanations notwithstanding, we understood well enough. In fact, we understood only too well. The work, entitled *Serpent Emerging from Hot Water*, represented the clawed serpent, the cursed logo of Aquatrade, in the act of squeezing in its coils a pipe from which hot water gushed. In the bottom part of the sculpture, the serpent's tail merged into the pipe itself. At the top, on the other hand, the reptile was opening its jaws wide and sticking out its forked tongue. A truly horrible spectacle. What, unfortunately, was still missing was the finishing touch. Gattai pressed a button hidden inside the statue and a little cloud of water and steam started to spout from the snake's mouth. The water turned into a fine drizzle that fell on the white base, slid down the bare sides of the stone, and then flowed into the little drainage channel at the foot of the statue. From there, through a series of smaller, invisible pipes, it was recovered and pumped back up to the top. And so on. So, apart from the horror of seeing that abortion of a statue in a medieval square, we had to swallow this ridiculous joke. The water of the statue/ fountain could not be thermal, for the simple reason that the nearest spring was some kilometres away, and after pumping it from such a distance the temperature would be so low as to render it barely lukewarm. That was the purpose of the water heater they had installed underground during the installation. The statue, which celebrated the triumph of the spa with steaming water oozing from the serpent's jaws, was quite simply a piece of rubbish. Far from being a thermal wonder, it was a common-or-garden domestic appliance. And God knows how much electricity that contraption consumed, all of it obviously at the taxpayers' expense.

The villagers' faces—now that's something I'll never be able to describe. When Gattai unveiled the statue, there was no gasp of astonishment. Instead there was silence. A solemn silence. No one understood. No one committed himself. With their hands behind their backs and their freshly ironed collars, the villagers leant forward, like turkeys scratching around a barn, moved circumspectly around the statue, and every now and again looked up, as if expecting a handful of feed from the sky. Gattai didn't really know what to do. The Mayor was looking at him with a completely neutral expression, waiting to see what expression Gattai assumed in order to copy it.

"Let's have a big hand for Sadat Mawazini's masterpiece. An artist who is capable of producing something more modern in a day than any other artistic movement in a decade!"

The applause was truly lukewarm.

"What do you think?" a few brave people said, in low voices.

"Well, yes, of course, I suppose so. How about you?"

"Me, too."

"Do you like it?"

"I don't really understand it."

They had all lost their heads. The mistake was that they had confused the modern with the ugly. The more ugly a thing was, the more modern. Anyone taking the trouble to go round the villages in the area since tourism lapped at their gates like a miraculous wave would find one eyesore after another, all put up in the name of that very same blessing known as tourism. The mayors, the administrators, the landowners, the shopkeepers, the artisans, the masses, everyone, but everyone, succumbed to the pernicious charm of modern art.

What was happening? Villages preserved for centuries in their virgin state—and this, I admit, we owe to the Party's wait-and-see policy during the Cold War—after having been almost completely depopulated were now being converted into villages full of second homes, rich, cultured people, intellectuals escaping from the city, managers who'd retired with golden handshakes, actors and VIPs in search of nature and silence. Confronted with this unforeseen exodus, the generation in the middle, the children of the baby boom and compulsory education, people who had illiterate fathers and graduate children, have suddenly found themselves in the middle of that cultural transformation. The old didn't care if such and such was a painter, writer, actor or journalist. They judged him on the basis of a few, ever-valid human criteria— Did he behave well when he was in the village? Was he a respectable person? Did he say hello to people? Did he expect credit in the shops? Did he annoy his neighbours? No? Then the person in question was a good man.

The generation in the middle, on the other hand, felt uncomfortable. They were ashamed of the backwardness of the village, the coarseness of its customs, the ignorance of the villagers. They had not grasped that the only reason so-called VIPs were ready to pay handsomely for run-down farmhouses in the middle of the countryside was the unspoilt nature of the landscape and the bluntness of the inhabitants, as yet unaffected by the disaster of reverse cultural adaptation. Hence the offensive against spontaneity, simplicity, and everything that survived of the past and refused to become folklore. Everywhere they tried to wipe out the traces of time, almost as if they were shameful—a damaged wall was immediately repaired, an old lamp-post replaced with a neon light, rough cobbles with paved streets. From village to village they applied this absurd cosmetic surgery, which soon turned into a real competition as to who was more cultured. Oh, so that village has organised a festival of multimedia theatre? Wait till you see our summer *tableau vivant* staged by a Lithuanian director! That was how the Mayors reasoned. Ugliness reigned but no one had the courage to denounce it. It wasn't that the emperor had no clothes—he was wearing a suit over his big belly.

As citizens who love and respect

To the Mayor,

Petition against the statue/fountain in the square.

As citizens who love and respect the harmony and beauty of our surroundings we protest strongly against the way in which changes have been made to the square.

We believe that the recent placing of the fountain known as The Serpent *in the middle of the square is particularly unfortunate, given that, in size, shape and colour, it clashes noticeably with its spatial and architectural context.*

We therefore demand that it be removed to another location still to be decided, provided that it is outside the historic centre.

The committee sponsoring this petition:
Federico Cremona
Ludovico Conti
Garrone Briganti
Sante Terrosi
Tito Dei

Apart from being sponsors of the petition, then, we were also its signatories. We had also written it, duplicated it and put it up in the bar and in the few shops owned by shopkeepers on the right or those on the left who could not read. The only one of us not to sign was Lea, who was against petitions as a concept. In her opinion, they were an example of the weakness of the referendum form, in which there is no negotiation but only winners and losers. She preferred direct action in the style of Greenpeace. To the rest of us, who still believed in democracy and its institutions at that time, a citizens' petition seemed the most reasonable thing.

The signatures accumulated, growing into a formidable list. We were the first to be surprised by those who signed up to our cause. The old signed because they didn't like the statue at all, the young signed because they were young and more rebellious. But strangers also signed, intellectuals who saw the statue as an insult to their aesthetic sense. We also managed to get the signatures of Rafaello Costa, the actor, who had been coming to our village for years for his holidays, Professor Pino Tovalieri, the eminent jurist, Gaia Severini, the television presenter, and others too numerous to mention.

It took some time for the Party to become aware of the scale of our initiative and to take serious countermeasures. We had reached more than six hundred signatures, many of which carried weight, when something happened that made me realise the counteroffensive had begun. The daughter of a local mechanic—well known as a true Party militant—had been eager to support our initiative by signing the petition.

But that same evening, her father, a large, forbidding, weather-beaten character, came to see me at home—and I hadn't even made her pregnant.

"What did you make my daughter sign?"

"Nobody made anyone sign anything. She signed of her own free will.

"Give me that list."

"I wouldn't dream of it."

"Give me the list or I'll make you."

"Listen, calm down, I'm not giving you the list. If there's any problem, send me your daughter."

And I closed the door in his face.

A few minutes later, the daughter appeared, accompanied by her father. She was silent, with her head down and her hands held in front of her lap.

"It's about today, my signature ... "

"What's wrong with it?"

"Nothing, it's just that I hadn't read it properly. I hadn't really understood it."

"Well, *I* understand perfectly well ... Wait, I'll go and fetch the list."

I handed it to her. With a mixture of hatred and concentration, the mechanic looked through the pages covered with illegible handwriting, picking out the names of the other traitors to the Party. His daughter lowered her eyes to the list, and drew a line through her name. She did not look up again. Her father looked at me with a smug expression that felt like a challenge. The comrades' fightback had begun—the signatories were reprimanded, household by household, and asked, more or less cordially, to retract. After the mechanic's daughter, others came. The haemorrhage appeared unstoppable.

To put together a concerted strategy, we met at the house of Professor Tovalieri, lecturer in Roman law at La Sapienza University in Rome, who had been the first signatory of the petition, apart from the sponsors, of course. Professor Tovalieri always dressed in white and got up early in the morning. Soon after dawn, you would find him in the square, where the one newsstand in the village was situated. He would buy all the newspapers, of every creed and political orientation. Then he would take that bundle of printed paper, sit down at a table in the bar, order a croissant and a cappuccino, and look through the papers to see if his latest article had been published and in which paper. When he found it, he would light a foul-smelling cigar, which would go out a hundred times an hour. If the article had suffered cuts, the professor would leave without touching his breakfast. If, on the other hand, it had been published intact, he would devour his breakfast in one mouthful. When the sun beat down on the square, the professor would languidly pull his panama hat down over his bald pate, which made him look like the character in *Death in Venice*.

Professor Tovalieri greeted us and led us into a light-filled drawing room surrounded by tall wooden bookcases crammed with books. Conti and I sat down on the sofa, Garrone in one of the immaculate white armchairs, Tito on a pouffe, and Sante, who had come directly from work and hadn't changed, on a low stool.

Professor Tovalieri, who had a tan that verged on the Creole, was wearing a white linen suit and a pair of leather shoes that made him seem like a satrap from some distant province of the Ottoman Empire. With economical gestures, he explained the greatness of classical art—from *classis classis*, third conjugation, the Roman fleet which, although less glorious than the illustrious legions, defeated the Phoenician ships, establishing Rome's domination of the seas—compared with the narrowness of modern art. We listened with rapt attention. The professor was holding a shoehorn with an ivory handle as he examined our situation from the point of view of Roman law.

"*Probatio rei spectat qui adfirma et non qui negat* ... And there's the rub! Isn't that right, dear boy?" he asked, seeking the approval of Sante, who had reached the third year of high school.

"Perhaps ... " Sante said.

"Listen, Professor," I insisted, otherwise we would have been there until late at night. "Don't forget that we're here because we need your support with the newspapers. Are you in a position to organise a press campaign on the destruction of the square?"

"Oh yes, of course, have no fear, my *cives* … "

In the end, Sante fell asleep in an armchair, and the rest of us crept out as Tovalieri was holding forth about the Codex Iustinianum.

To make as large a stir as possible in the newspapers, I also tried to enlist the help of Leone Azzati, an elderly, highly-respected ex-partisan, now well-known as a Vaticanist, who had retired to our village some years earlier. When I had finished explaining our stand on the issue of the statue, he told me that he was in total agreement with us and supported our actions. But when I handed him the petition, and the pen to sign it with, he shook his head and said no. I looked at him incredulously.

"Young man," he said, "when I was a little boy my mother taught me that guests shouldn't interfere in their hosts' business. And besides, I don't feel I'm fully informed of the facts."

I objected that he was not a guest—after all, he'd bought his house and regularly paid the local property tax—and I insisted that he did know the facts, because I'd just explained them to him, and if he wanted I would explain them again from the beginning. But there was nothing to be done. His mother was still his mother, he said. And he didn't sign.

Fortunately, Professor Tovalieri managed to get his article in an influential national newspaper. And the article did indeed cause a stir. In its wake, the local press began to show an interest, attracted by the thought of scandals and juicy gossip with which to fill their news pages.

A provincial newspaper carried an interview with Mawazini, who accused us of being ignorant vandals incapable of understanding his art. But the involvement in our initiative of a star like Rafaello Costa—even though his popularity was in decline—and the affection shown for our village by Gaia Severini, the TV presenter, soon led the television networks to take an interest in the case. We released an interview in which we were calm but firm, holding up the newspaper headlines that demonstrated the verbal aggression to which a peaceful citizens' committee was being subjected. The report made a great splash and even the regional heritage board was forced to open an inquiry into the case. The miracle of television! It was also thanks to TV, I can't deny, that we managed to slow down the haemorrhage of villagers' names—almost all of them changed their minds—and gain further support from strangers and holidaymakers.

Strengthened by this media endorsement, we proceeded to the town hall to deliver the signatures. In solemn silence, we climbed the stone staircase in the municipal foyer, with the booty of six hundred signatures sleeping in a leather briefcase held tightly under my arm. On the landing, we came across Rudi, Gattai's dog, peeing on a plant pot. The Mayor received us sitting entrenched behind his desk. We stood there tensely, close together, like a five-a-side football team posing for a photograph. Without saying a word, I placed the bundle of signatures on the desk. The Mayor examined the folder.

"You're against progress," he said, pointing his finger at me.
"Of course."
"How can that be?"
"Who told you that progress is a positive thing?"
"That's a good one. You're talking nonsense."

"Maybe so. But you know what doctors say when a sick person gets worse?"

"What do they say?"

"They say that the illness is in progress. Yes, they say, the tumour is progressing. So you see, progress, in itself, isn't always a good thing."

"We're all healthy here, it's only you who are sick. All of you. How can it be, I ask myself, how can it be that you don't understand? We replace old, sick acacias with splendid lime trees, we put new paving in the square, we remove the loose old paving stones, the hard benches, the dim lighting, we make everything brand new, we bring you the work of an internationally famous artist ... And you ... you ... "—the Mayor was becoming heated—" ... don't like any of it!"

"The acacias, as everyone knows, weren't sick. A few of the stones needed fixing and everything would have been fine. The dim lighting, as you call it, came from art nouveau lamps dating from the late nineteenth century—the neon you've put in gives more light than floodlights in a sports field and now you need sunglasses to cross the square at night. The benches were the work of local stonecutters, some of whom are still alive, so you can ask them. The statue in question is the worst thing seen in this area since the German retreat. As for Sadat Mawazini, apart from a small circle of critics who go out to dinner with him, I don't know if he's internationally famous, he seems to me more like an international con man. Here are the signatures. Six hundred and eighty-three of them."

"To me, your signatures are worth precisely zero. Zero multiplied by six hundred and eighty-six."

"Eighty-three—"

"Whatever. Don't waste any more of my time."

"So you have no intention of removing the serpent?"

"The serpent stays, you're the ones who are going."

When the snake dies, its poison dies with it

W HEN THE SNAKE DIES, says a proverb, its poison dies with it. Maybe so. But our hideous serpent was still very much alive, even if motionless, curled up in the middle of the square, and Ottone Gattai's spa was prospering as never before. The controversy about *The Serpent* had held the stage all summer. What with all the interviews, corrections, articles, TV reports, statements and denials, we had reached September. The last holidaymakers had left and the thin shadows of the lime trees were lengthening on the square. The time for polemics was over, along with the scorching summer. The last after-effects would wear off soon. Beneath the light dew of October, the village would be empty and dark, ready to greet the first cold and the short November days. Life, after that peaceful act of protest—the first in living memory—against the Party, would resume its bland everyday course. When you came down to it, all that publicity had simply benefited Aquatrade. The media exposure, as they call it these days, the opinions of experts and politicians—even a minister had become fascinated by the case and promised to look into it, then had forgotten all about it—in the end had given Gattai a lot of free publicity. As long as it's talked about, right? And it was certainly talked about. Tourist parties came, pensioners, journalists, critics, young couples, nosey parkers, all anxious to see the cause of all the trouble in a small Tuscan village where the age-old animosity between the Guelfs and the Ghibellines had been rekindled, all because of a stupid statue. And everyone who saw it had to have their say. That sculpture, just like the serpent in the Holy Scriptures, seemed to have no purpose other than to sow discord among men.

But like all human affairs, even this one had a beginning, a middle and an end. And the end was near. The controversy was on the wane, the game appeared to have ended with the indisputable victory of the Mayor and the defeat of the citizens' committee, both confirmed by the continuing presence of the statue in the middle of the square. It was then that alarm bells started ringing in Gattai's nimble brain. He didn't like the fact that people's attention had wandered away—he had to make the affair newsworthy again. And to counter this decline in interest, the hot-water magnate had what I must admit was a truly brilliant idea—a literary competition.

Announcing the first edition of the short story competition, Serpents's Tales

The stories may be based on fact or works of pure imagination.

They must be set in our village and must have as their protagonist The Serpent, *the beloved mascot of the thermal revival.*

Manuscripts—no shorter than three or longer than ten typewritten pages—must be submitted in triplicate, with the name and address of the author together with a waiver of copyright and a photocopy of a Party membership card.

The competition is open to all.

Please send in a sealed envelope to Serpent's Tales

Postal box 70B11 53100 Siena

The jury consists of:
Ottone Gattai, thermal entrepreneur
Gaia Severini, television presenter
Raffaello Costa, actor

Leone Azzati, journalist
Pino Tovalieri, noted academic
Rossana Cremona, writer

The prize is a miniature, made entirely of oxidised copper and limestone, of Sadat Mawazini's celebrated work The Serpent, *now in the square.*

The competition has been made possible by a grant from Aquatrade.

I hadn't thought him capable of anything like that, I didn't know his lively but coarse mind concealed such Machiavellian subtlety. By launching a competition, Gattai had managed in one fell swoop to legitimise that controversial work of art and to lure to his side the very people we poor fools had thought of as the thoroughbreds who would win the Derby for us. In the municipality and the spa, it had taken very little to make his former detractors change horses in midstream—an amnesty for infringement of building regulations, a substantial refund of expenses, a season ticket for treatments and massages, the promise of a grant from the Cultural Department, and the game had been won. Our intellectuals, our front-line troops, had turned out be a bunch of turncoats more concerned with popularity than principle.

Rossana Cremona. I was walking, depressed and aimless, that name on the poster still fixed on my retina and burning up my insides like a cough. My own grandmother was on the jury. Another betrayal. How could she? Even though my whole family, as was their wont, had been against my initiative, and had taken care not to sign the petition, distancing themselves from their degenerate grandson both publicly and privately, I had never imagined they would do anything like that. It was one thing to disapprove, another to collaborate.

Writer. Well, she did write—melodramatic romantic novels, overflowing with fine sentiments set down in naive, bland prose, which nevertheless seemed to make their female readers forget the kettle on the stove. An expert short-story writer and indefatigable novelist, my grandmother was not the only one to write. In my family everyone wrote. It was a kind of curse, some kind of taint in the blood perhaps, like haemophilia in the Tsars or favism in Sardinians, I don't know. Long poems, short poems, long short stories or short novels (which come to the same thing), long novels, very long novels, *con fabula* or *sin fabula*, essays, satires, pamphlets, sonnets, madrigals, fairy tales, almanacs, invoices, checks, ledger books, anything involving marks left by a pen on a paper. Not surprising, then, that I had indulged my own literary urges from an early age, urges I had soon abandoned. If you let on that you were writing something, the competition became fierce. At table, between one course and the next, it took very little for the fight to start:

"The other night, I was tossing and turning in bed and couldn't get to sleep, and I had an idea for a story. Tell me what you think. There's this man who—"

"Last night I had this idea for a trilogy about a detective," my father would cut in. "In the first of the three books—"

"My novel comes out on Saturday," my grandmother would slip into the conversation. "As you see, once again I've been quicker than all of you."

That's why I wasn't unduly shocked when during Sunday lunch my grandmother had the impudence to ask me, "By the way, why don't you take part?"

"Come on, Grandma, let's drop the subject."

"Your father has already submitted a wonderful story."

I looked at my father, who looked down at his pasta *au gratin* and said nothing.

Et tu, Father. I was alone. As solitary as a cypress in my battle.

"It's an old thing I wrote many years ago … You know I don't really care about prizes."

"But how can you take part in a competition where your mother's on the jury?"

"That's irrelevant," my grandmother said. "I'll be completely impartial, as if he weren't my son."

"Mother!" my father said.

Now my father

NOW MY FATHER IS GOING UP to receive his prize. With a somewhat affected nonchalance and a stunned smile, he tries to pass along the tightly packed row of legs separating him from the platform. There are so many people, the theatre is a small one, my father's a large man, it's no joke getting up there.

"Gentlemen, we have our winner, the village doctor," the TV presenter says. "Let's give him a big hand, shall we?"

"Be careful, the lead's short, the microphone won't reach, no, maybe if … Look, it's better if he goes around … No, this way, on the other side … No, not like that, there, yes, yes, like that, perfect. Be careful on the steps … "

My father advances towards the platform. He trips on the top step of the little wooden flight of steps leading on to the platform and it's a miracle that he doesn't fall to the ground. He'd like to swear, I know him. Somewhere inside him, at this moment, one of those innocent oaths, blasted something, nothing vulgar, blasted something, is stillborn. My father climbs onto the platform. He's wearing his fustian jacket with the martingale. I have the same one, but of velvet, fustian doesn't suit me. The presenter has nothing to offer him except her universal smile. There is a moment of embarrassment because no one knows who ought to speak first, the prize-giver or the prize-winner. It's the former who breaks the ice. That's what they pay her for.

"Well, now, Doctor, perhaps you'd like to tell us something about your story, which is entitled … "—

she searches for the title on the small sheet of paper she clutches between her painted nails—"*The Passing of the Grey Partridges?*"

"I'll talk about it in a moment. But first, if you'll allow me, I'd like to say a few words."

The presenter hesitates for a moment, her face furrows with worry at this unscheduled addition to the programme.

"Of course!"

And she hands the microphone to my father.

He hesitates, embarrassed. He's not used to microphones. He takes a deep breath into his capacious lungs. In a moment, his voice, that voice so similar to mine that we're often mistaken for each other on the telephone, that voice I acquired when I became a man, that virile but hoarse voice, will fill the hall. My father holds the microphone like a torch. And I know what my father will say. I always know what he's going to say. I know what jokes he'll tell over a meal in a restaurant, I know what comments he'll make on a particular politician's statements on television, I know why he won't like a particular film but will like a particular book, I know at what bend he'll change gear, I know when he'll phone me, I know how long it'll take him to become impatient with the waiter, that he'll buy himself a yellow sweater identical to one he already has, that he'll ask a passer-by for a light. I know all that. And the reason I know isn't because my father is predictable, because he's an open book, or because he's taken for granted. I know because I am also him. I am him and I am me, I am him while still being me, I am me while still being him. I am Terenzio, I am Fede, I am Vanni and then Fede again. *Da capo.* I am all of them. I am all the Terenzios, Vannis and Federicos in the Cremona family and in history, I am all the fathers and children and families who have generated the families of the fathers and children and families that existed before mine, before that curious creature descended from the tree to see the sun rising over the horizon of a new territory, before the whales swam in the vineyards where today we collect shells. I am what I am because of the ancient helix that drives life, because of the torch of humanity passing from hand to hand, from womb to womb. I am what I am because of the law, written in dust, to which all creatures belong. I am what I am because of that lamb's bone trapped in the sixth step on the stairs of the castle. That's why I know what my father is about to say.

Before talking about his hunting story, which has ripened in a drawer for God knows how many years, a story which like all stories brings the dead back to life, before saying that the inspiration came from a true story, that it was inspired by an episode that really happened, that it's an affectionate memory of my grandfather, before citing Turgenev's *Sportsman's Sketches*, he'll say what he really thinks.

He'll say that after working all his life, after treating public patients and private patients for half-a-century, after tending to the bodies of men and women, old people and babies, but especially old people, after touching them, listening to their chests, supporting their smells, analysing their moods, breathing their breaths and tolerating their complaints, he, the first salaried worker of our entire breed, the broken ring in the chain, will say that he was born in this village, that he knows the life, death and miracles of the living and the dead, he'll say that he's never had anything from the village and its people. Anything. Only insults in return for favours, hatred and malevolence as small change to a man who paid with the coin of humility and constant readiness to help. And he'll say that after more than half-a-century of serving the public, he's finally reached a simple, unchallengeable judgment on the human race—people don't deserve anything. That's what he thinks. It's what he says every time he comes home tired from work, takes off his shoes and throws himself down on the sofa. Go on, Father, go on, say it. Tell them that the daily trading in venom has poisoned you, tell them you've had enough and can't wait to retire, so that you can turn off your mobile phone, take your dog out early in the morning, go hunting for woodcock. And while you're about it, say thank you but really I can't, it was a weakness, a sin of vanity, that you took part in the competition only because my grandmother insisted, that the son in you wanted to take part and the father has never won out over the son, tell them that you did it because it was winter and you were bored the way you always are in winter, and perhaps you also felt a bit lonely. Tell them, thank you from the bottom of your heart, but you, or rather we, tell them, "I'm very grateful, but I really don't know what to do with this prize. Our house is full of knick knacks, there's so much stuff that very soon there won't be any more room for us, and so, even though I'd like to take it I really don't know where we'd put it." And while you're about it, tell them the statue's already ugly life-size, so imagine it in miniature—ugliness can't be shrunk, only enlarged.

Go on, Father, go on. Tell them. Now.

My father is holding the microphone like a torch. He opens his mouth.

"I wanted to say one thing. I was born in this village … "

Go on, Father, tell them.

"I was born here a good many years ago. I won't go into details. And for thirty years, yes, thirty years, I've been the doctor here. For thirty years I've been helping the public.

And I've formed an opinion of this village and its people, who I've always tried to serve as best I can, with respect, and humility. I think they're all … "

Go on, Father, tell them.

"All of them, from first to last … "

Go on, Father. Tell them. Give it to them.

"Good people."

Good people, my father said. Good people, those are the words he used.

"And I'd like to consider this prize you're conferring on me, in this splendid setting, as in some way … in some way a prize for my whole career. A demonstration of your esteem and of the affection you've shown me throughout the years."

The people applaud. Father's eyes are watery.

"No, it's the truth. I'm sorry, the emotion's too much for me. That's why I'm taking this opportunity to recall another citizen who loved these places and these people, my grandfather, the protagonist of the story."

Your grandfather. My great-grandfather. The man who whipped the peasants.

"This prize is for him, too. And I'd like to thank everyone, in the first place the jury … "

My father looks at my grandmother, wrapped in her fur coat in the front row. My grandmother makes a small gesture of approval.

" … then the public, the inhabitants of the village, Signor Gattai, Sadat Mawazini … "

I have to leave. It's hot in here. Impossible to breathe.

" … and of course the Mayor, the Savings Bank, the Mountain Territorial Association … "

I climb the stairs of the theatre two-by-two. They aren't stairs, they're the hold of a submarine …

" ... the Voluntary Ambulance Brigade, the village band ... "

I look down. Straight ahead of me. I'm not the one climbing. Just my feet.

" ... the pastry shop which provided the catering, the cellar which offered ... "

The applause follows me to the door. Air.

Air. The sky is my friend. Too many houses around me. Too many front doors. Someone might come out of one of them. Someone I've been saying hello to since I was little and no longer have any desire to say hello to.

Tell them, Father. Tell them what you won't tell them.

I see the swollen bellies of the chub

I SEE THE SWOLLEN BELLIES OF THE CHUB. I see them floating on the water like lifeless white water lilies. The prehistoric head of a goby entangled in seaweed, the spotted livery of a barbel abandoned to the current.

Death has passed. Today, death has passed this way.

And to think that just yesterday life flowed. It flowed slowly past the banks of the stream. In May, the green backs of the dace would dart about, ready to spawn, in August the fish would spend all day in their lairs, then leap out nervous with hunger, snap a dragonfly and immediately shoot into the safe shade of the roots. In September, the chub would throw themselves on the blackberries that had dropped in the heat, and in winter the barbels would swim lazily back upstream in search of warmer water. Everything was alive along the stream. I would be coming back from school and would choke at the thought of being part of all that life. I would get on my cross-country moped with the red mud guards and the blue saddle, the bag with the rods over my shoulder, my jacket with fur pockets stuffed with corks, plums and floats which made a noise like a maracas with every jolt on the rough ground. A rapid glance at the water to decide which line to use—a round float if the current was strong, a thin line if the water was transparent. Then I would go to the dunghill on Pietro's farm, to flush out some earthworms. The spade would sink into the dunghill, and there they were, shining at the bottom, red and fat, affronted by the sunlight. When the summers were hot and dry and the earth was like burnt sawdust, the worms would bury themselves as deep as possible to find a little humidity. Then it would take several blows with the spade to dig them out, but in the end, however far an animal goes, man will always find it. You had to be quick to grab them with your fingers before they dived back into the darkness of the earth. The stream with its summer langours and autumn gusts, its abrupt bends and calm sweeps, its nervous twists and sensible pools. The stream which disappeared and reappeared in the middle of the thorn bushes or between the rows of poplars which cut across the fields, the stream which murmured in the heat or rushed breathlessly towards the lake. The stream with its spring light embroidering the shadows between the elders, the stream with the pollen caught in the spiders' webs like dead butterflies, the stream with the frogs, the dragonflies on the surface of the water, the stream with the fish tails held straight against the current, the stream where you fished with your hands if you had the courage to put them right inside the lairs, the stream with the water snakes and the little green and yellow pike, the stream with those legendary eels, never seen, never fished, only mentioned by old fishermen, who, if you asked them when it was that they had fished for eels, would look into the distance and say, Before you were born. Before they built the weir downstream. Making you feel guilty for being so young.

I still see the swollen bellies of the chub turning round and round. And the spotted liveries of the barbels abandoned to the current. And the heads of the lifeless gobies, and the white ribs of the frogs opened like nutcrackers. An intolerable spectacle.

The person who had done this had to pay, whoever it was. And I had a good idea who it had been.

211

People shoot themselves in the foot

I HEARD THIS STORY from an estate agent. You can take it as true. A middle-aged man who's in financial difficulty decides to sell his house. He isn't very old, but there's no need to make him younger than he is.

Yet something strange happens. When the estate agency phones to tell him that a customer who's interested in the house is coming to see it, he prepares himself conscientiously for the encounter. But instead of making himself look down at heel, which he is, he dyes his hair black, dresses in sporty youthful clothes, and finds unexpected reserves of energy. It's not hard to imagine that the customers are alarmed by this unexpected burst of youth and the deal duly falls through.

This is a good example of how people sometimes shoot themselves in the foot. And I did something similar the day when I went to the *carabinieri* barracks in the village to lodge a complaint against persons unknown for causing an environmental catastrophe. I knew from an acquaintance who worked as a pool attendant that on the very days when the fish blight had occurred, the Olympic pool at the resort had been drained and cleaned. The drainage pipes led directly into the stream. That mass of hot water mixed with chlorine could well have affected the stream's delicate ecosystem. Unfortunately I had no evidence to back up my theory. The only thing I could do was attach to my statement a photographic record of the disaster—dead and dying fish, frogs and grass snakes. As he put the photographs back into the envelope, the marshal made light of the situation, saying that there was "no point making a drama" out of the deaths of a few fish, it might be a spontaneous blight, perhaps a parasite, a pandemic. Yes, marshal, of course, a case of collective suicide! I had collected a sample and taken it to a private lab for analysis. In the water of the stream there turned out to be clear traces of chlorine, and an unwarranted increase in sulphur, manganese and iron, all minerals present in the water of the baths. The marshal transmitted my complaint to the prosecutor's department, because he had no choice, and the prosecutor's department opened and closed in record time a ridiculous investigation which concluded with this case of environmental damage being dismissed as the work of persons unknown. But, in return, these persons unknown, after denying any responsibility for the affair, did not take long in making themselves known.

The expropriation

Having identified malfeasance in the improper use of public hot waters for private ends, notice is hereby given that all waters present in the holding known as La Torre, the property of Rossana Cremona and sons, be immediately handed over for intubation and pumping to the Aquatrade thermal resort opened by Ottone Gattai. If said operation has not been carried out within two weeks, said waters will be sequestered and the taps sealed.

Yours faithfully
Andrea Chechi (lawyer)

I had always known it might end like this. I put the telegram back down on the desk and looked at my father, who was looking at me sternly.

"Why did you do it?"

"Because it was the only thing to do."

"There's never only one thing to do, even when it seems that way, there are always at least two … "

"But they expropriated our olive grove, they cut down the trees, they stripped the square, poisoned the moat. When you're under siege, you don't serve tea and pastries to the barbarians camping outside the walls."

"What a poet! Do you realise that, in trying to save the fish, you've ruined a family? Do you realise they've called off the deal for the transfer of the other property? Do you realise that thanks to your playing the Pericles of the Val di Chiana we're being sued? Do you realise how much your act of bravado will cost us? Well, do you or don't you?"

"Yes, I do."

"And despite all that, you're still convinced that you did the right thing?"

"Do you remember when I was going to school and I was always worried by the Saturday maths test, always afraid of Signora Cannoli who would hit us on the head if we made a mistake? Do you remember what you used to say? Do what you have to do, whatever happens, you used to say. Well, I did what I had to do, whatever happens."

What happened was that they took everything from us. Everything, down to the last farm. My grandmother made a scene, said that I wasn't blood of her blood, then fainted and had to be put to bed. My uncle burst into tears, refused to come out of the hot-water swimming pool until the *carabinieri* sealed up the springs. Then he sat there naked in the dried-up tub like dead coral. My family all stopped talking to me. More out of shame than necessity, the whole family moved north, to stay with distant relatives. Only my mother would send me affectionate letters from time to time asking me how I was and admonishing me not to catch cold and to always read the use-by date on tinned food.

Now that I was finally free, there was only one thing left to do—go underground.

Not a line

THE STRANGEST THING is that although our war, our guerrilla conflict, claimed its dead and wounded, no one ever said a word about it. Not a line in the papers, not a single report on TV. Despite the rigid censorship of the media, some news filtered through all the same. Some people knew, or found out, and in some pensioners' bars or cultural associations it was talked about sotto voce, and the validity of our reasons was discussed, the opportunity to take up arms in support of our cause and follow the path of resistance against thermal globalisation. Some followed our example and formed little partisan bands, launching a military campaign in enemy-occupied thermal territories. Unfortunately, from the beginning there was a lack of liaison between the groups, and bottlenecks in the chain of command. All of which gave the enemy time to regroup, take the appropriate countermeasures and, above all, keep the conflict going in the medium and long term, to the point where guerrilla tactics lose their impetus and it becomes a wearying war of attrition. Which is already a defeat, like a movement becoming a political party.

They were days of fierce clashes
and uncertain outcomes

THEY WERE DAYS of fierce clashes and uncertain outcomes. At the beginning, the revolt, like all revolts from below, was swept along on a wave of enthusiasm. Our first action was heroic. We lay in wait on the Cassia and hijacked a bus carrying Russian tourists from Fiumicino to the resort. I remember it was summer and scorching hot, we were all sweating and I remember that as we waited for the bus, which had been signalled by the lookouts, my pants were riding up inside my buttocks. Garrone was peeing himself, but the orders were imperative. It was forbidden to move away from our positions—we couldn't run the risk of jeopardising the ambush just because someone wanted to pee. Tito was standing in the middle of the road as a decoy, behind a stall full of shoes, belts and bags with designer labels at half price (all fakes bought as a job lot from a Chinaman in Prato). We hoped this bait would attract the attention of the tourists but we weren't sure. Fortunately, the coach driver slammed on the brakes at the sight of the stall, and the Russians got out brandishing big wallets stuffed with euros. We came out into the open, armed to the teeth. It was child's play to neutralise the driver and hijack the party.

For several days, we kept the hostages in a shelter we had prepared inside an abandoned sheep fold. Except that keeping the hostages, as the history of kidnapping teaches, turned out to be more difficult than taking them. We were not to know that the group hadn't come straight from

Fiumicino, but had spent a couple of days by the sea, on the beaches of Circeo, where their milky skins had all been scalded by the Mediterranean sun. At night the hostages moaned like lepers and the sheepfold was like a lazaret. We were forced to buy quintals of aftershave lotion to lessen those moans, which might have given us away.

We claimed responsibility for the kidnapping in an anonymous communiqué addressed to the Aquatrade Resort, in which we announced our firm decision to move on to armed struggle after realising the futility of civil protest. We explained that our act was intended as a protest against the capitalistic and violently anti-proletarian reorganisation of the thermal apparatus. More generally, we talked about the profit motive pursued by Ottone Gattai and his thermal imperialism, the concentration of water resources and the pluto-Masonic cartels which were forming around his spas. We threatened to kill the hostages if Aquatrade refused to negotiate. They replied a couple of days later, leaving a terse note in the dustbin of a service area at Kilometre 66 on the main road, as instructed. The note read as follows:

We politely request that you keep the hostages for a few days longer, at the moment the hotel is full.

Thank you

The management

I watch you sleeping

I WATCH YOU SLEEPING. Curled up on one side, your knees drawn up. You look like a child. Who would ever have thought it? I'd assumed that that night on the island of Giglio would be the first and last time I'd be in a tent with you. Instead of which, we've now spent so many nights under this grey oilcloth. Your knees are pulled up towards your chest and your little body coiled like a shell, and I feel almost as if I could hold you in the palm of one hand, like a little bird. In the identical position as that night in the tent on the island of Giglio, you are sleeping.

It was you who led me to that campsite on Giglio, or rather my love for you. You, the woman who for me is all women.

The fact that you had bought the tent with a former boyfriend who was a fanatical camper was something I found hard to swallow, because of that indefensible reflex of retroactive jealousy we always feel towards the situations the people we love have lived through or the objects they have possessed before us, or without us. It isn't easy to wage war with just a degree under your belt—at university they filled my head with structuralism and didn't teach me how to clean a breechblock—but even camping is no joke. On the island of Giglio we had a couple from Genoa as neighbours—a little older than us, the man tidy and sporty, the woman pedantic and polite, as a couple close and soppy. They told us that at the far end of the rundown little beach, the one where we all went, there was a path that climbed the promontory and continued beyond it, where there were lots of quiet little bays and inlets, sheltered from the ravenous onslaught of the tourists who flocked to the beach.

After making our way through a jungle of tattoos, eczema, sunburn, cleavage, stretch marks, flaccid breasts, oiled bellies, biceps and triceps, we came to a spur of rock some fifty metres high.

From there, a narrow lane like a mule track climbed up the jagged wall of rock, a thin tongue that disappeared amid the myrtle and broom to then reappear some twenty metres further on, amid bushes white with dust. We started climbing. The path was steep, but we were young and had good legs. Not that we're old now, for Heaven's sake, but … We felt young, there, that's what I meant. I could feel Lea behind me, highly focused, a tough cookie. On the journey I had started to get to know her better, knew she was alert, confident, an invaluable navigator, a loyal companion. With her at my side, we were a real team. Even though every now and again on our travels, Lea would disappear inside a bubble of silence. She would stop talking to me, answering me, looking at me, she would become invisible, impenetrable. Her eyes staring into infinity, her lips tight. And her silences were like stone quarries I had to cross barefoot. I felt like a wayfarer in a desert of silence. Then, suddenly, her voice, like an oasis. And everything would go back to the way it was before.

I turned towards her, not out of anxiety, just for the pleasure of looking at her.

I saw her trudging, her muscular thighs swelling with the effort inside her khaki shorts, her sinews stretched like steel cables, I felt her breath coming faster, so I slowed down, stopped completely and let her go ahead of me, so that she could set the pace for the climb. No, it's not true, not completely anyway. There's another reason why I sent her ahead—it was also, and above all, so that I could look at her arse. Her beautiful female arse climbing obediently up the hill, her buttocks tightening in the more difficult stretches, and relaxing when the road started to level off. I was the snake and you the charmer, and in this way we reached the top. All at once, between the holm oaks, a blue window. The sea, smooth and glittering, there in front of our eyes. We descended the steep path to the point where we could proceed. The road petered out in front of a ruin buried in vegetation. Beneath us, at the bottom of a sheer wall of rock, a blue dizziness. A small deserted creek, with little waves breaking as white foam on the pebbled beach.

"Shall we try?" you said, you who are now asleep.

"Wait here," I said, I who am now watching you sleep.

Watching out for vipers and thorns, I ventured around the crumbling walls, looking for a gap through which we could get down to the sea. The dusty shrubs gave off a strong, bitter smell, a burnt summer smell. Twenty metres below me, I saw a goat standing on a big rock, and had the strange impression that it was looking at me. There was a way. Between the rocks, like one of those puzzles where you join the dots, there were traces of a path that led down to the sea. I went back to Lea.

"There may be a way."

"Let's go, then."

"I don't know if it's possible, we'll need our hands and legs to get down."

"Well, I brought those."

There was no discouraging Lea. We started to climb down. I took the bag with the water and the fruit and put it over my shoulder. At first the descent was quite pleasant, for stretches of it you only had to grab hold of the roots or the bushes. Then it got more difficult and you could only let yourself down once you'd found the next foothold. Lea took off her slippers and I saw her little feet searching for the right foothold on the red-hot rocks, her muscles contracting and her back arching. As stubborn as a goat, she leapt from rock to rock, ever closer to the motionless sea. We descended without speaking, beneath a harsh sun that had risen very high in the sky as if standing in judgement over us. It was more than half-an-hour before our feet came to rest on something flat. The beach was red-hot and the sea green. I kissed her on her forehead and felt the salty taste of her sweat.

We took each other by the hand and dived into the ice-cold, transparent water. We swam naked and free in the sea. Then we came out of the water, put our costumes back on and sheltered from the sun beneath a large jutting rock. We washed away the salt from our lips by eating the fruit. We kissed. We drank the small amount of water we had brought with us as if, with every sip, we were drinking life.

Perhaps we were the chosen ones, perhaps someone was giving us a second chance, the chance to start afresh, to give birth to a new line of men who would be less coarse and vulgar than those who had colonised the world so far. But we weren't the chosen ones. And no one was granting us a second chance. Because, totally undeserved, there suddenly arrived a dinghy full of vulgar, noisy Florentines with their wives and children, who started lighting cigarettes, speaking in loud voices, unwrapping ice creams, throwing balls and doing other things that told us our day was over. We collected our things and, like goats, just as we had arrived, we vanished between the rocks.

And of everything that happened that day, it is your flushed face surrounded by the scent of myrtle and the frantic music of the cicadas that has stayed with me like salt on the skin.

And that's what I'm thinking about as I watch you sleeping. All at once you wake with a start.

I'm sorry, darling, I woke you, I'm sorry, I know, my thoughts make too much noise. You look at me, and something stirs deep in your eyes. Affection, love, tenderness, I don't know what it is, because it's already gone.

There's just Lea and me

THERE'S JUST LEA AND ME. We are descending those steep erosion furrows with our hearts in our mouths. No stars tonight. The torch searches hysterically in the darkness. Lea is a few steps ahead of me, her Garand over her shoulder. We go through a cane thicket and now we start to hear the roar of the water. The spring is there. A few metres from us. We crouch and smell the rough smell of the earth, a sickly smell of mildew and mud, a cemetery smell. Lea has lain down on her stomach on the ground like a lioness. I am a few metres further down than her. There are only two sentries guarding the spring, two sentries motionless beneath a neon floodlight's cold umbrella of light. They are standing bolt upright in front of the wire fence that protects the spring. One is smoking, the other is silent. They don't even want to talk now, they're just waiting for dawn, when they'll be relieved. It's cold tonight, my fingers are stiff on the trigger, and the barrel of the rifle is a frozen pipe. Beneath the floodlight, the sentries, cold and sleepy, are no longer men but targets. Lea looks at me, shoulders her rifle, concentrates, takes aim and presses the trigger. No shot. Only a metallic click. The Garand has jammed.

"You shoot!" she hisses at me.

I have to be really quick, because the click of the trigger was heard in the lugubrious silence of the night. "Did you hear that?" one of the sentries said to the other.

I cock the rifle. I aim. Through the sight, I see one of the sentries adjusting his beret. If I fired now, he would fall like a pine cone. But I don't fire.

"Do you love me?"

"What?"

"I'm asking if you love me."

"Shoot."

"Do you love me?"

"Do you want to get us killed?"

"Tell me if you love me."

"Shoot, idiot, shoot!"

"DO YOU LOVE ME, LEA?"

The sentries have heard us. One is coming towards us.

Pow! Pow! Pow! Three sharp shots. Earth and dust rain down on us. The sentry has seen us and is firing blindly into the cane thicket. Blue flames emerge from the barrel of his weapon. The bullets whistle through the dried canes, which crumble like papyrus.

I escape, I fly up the path, amid the branches and leaves. Hands, feet, like a monkey I try to get away, trudging up that steep area. The trees are all over me, the thorns scratch my face, I can't turn, I can only run. I don't see you, Lea, I don't hear you, you're not behind me, I've lost you. I'm aware only of my heart exploding inside my lungs and the shots and the voices and the barking of the dogs following me. The darkness is a big spider's web clinging to my face. You are somewhere below me, and like me you are trying to save yourself, and yet I haven't stopped, I haven't thought about you, I've thought about me. Only me. Like a madman I clamber up the ridge, where the dogs can't follow me, where no one can follow me, only a goat, like that day on the island of Giglio, do you remember, Lea? Only this time there's no time, there's no way, I can't help you, I can't—or maybe I won't?—hold out my hand to you in the most difficult stretches, I can't point out the right foothold, the right edge. I clamber up randomly, angrily.

No one can stop me. I scratch my hands and break my nails on these rocks but no one can stop me. I can't even stop myself, I feel hunted, I'm scared, I don't know what of, but I'm scared, more scared than I've ever been, down there there aren't only men and dogs following me, down there there's everything I don't want to be, everything I hate about myself. But up there, there may be the possibility of starting afresh, just like in that little cove on Giglio, do you remember, Lea? Up there is the dawn of a new day, up there is the man I'd like to be. It's not far to the top, not far to salvation. I'm almost there. Almost there. My back is killing me, my nails are broken, my muscles ache, but I'm safe. Safe. The night is dark and no longer throbs with the voices of men and the barking of dogs. It is a night without moon or stars, a night without heroes, a night like the nights before man appeared on the earth. I lie down on a big rock. I grasp this thousand-year-old stone womb like an orphan of time, and wait. I wait for death, I wait for life, something will come. But nothing comes. And I feel as though my body is no longer mine, because I can't move even a finger. The sweat is freezing on me and my thoughts are becoming as heavy as rods. Thoughts that say I've lost you, Lea. I've lost you, I've lost your respect, and I've lost my own self-respect. I am an admiral abandoning his ship, a husband leaving his family, I am a king setting sail from Brindisi while his people are adrift. I am a coward. A weary coward. I stay here, motionless on this rock, looking at the black immensity of the sky. And I wait. And I pray. For a predatory sleep, a sleep without dreams and without sleep, to come and take me away from you, from me, from all this. Forgive me, Lea, forgive me if you can.

You haven't looked me in the eyes since that night

YOU HAVEN'T LOOKED ME IN THE EYES since that night. In the morning, in the camp, you stride resolutely into the tent, and the boys, who had seen me come back alone, didn't say a word because there wasn't a word to say. Since then, we haven't spoken about that night. But things that aren't said don't die but live like spores inside us and sooner or later germinate, you can be sure of that. In your blue eyes that avoid me, in your hips that evade me, in your replies that needle me, I seem to feel all the fear of that night, the discomfort of the sweat freezing on my body. We've pretended that nothing happened and have kept going. But at night, in the darkness of the tent, in the promiscuous warmth of the sleeping bag, you've made me feel like a refugee in search of intimacy. Even in front of my men you're cold and standoffish. Sometimes, in the morning, I've tried to make it look as if we made love during the night, but I don't think anyone takes any notice. Antoine gave up on love some time ago, when he found another man's shirt among his shirts, and since then he's been waiting to receive the death certificate of his ex-wife, a belly dancer he met in a night club in Pigalle, or a letter from his lawyer on the windy coast of Normandy telling him that the matter is closed for ever. The others have wives and children at home, and on moonlit nights they weep and whine about their distant love, and sing sad songs about embraces in railway stations and husbands who didn't come back from the front. I'm the only one with a woman in tow. But since that fateful night, you haven't wanted me any more. Since that time, you've consistently rejected me. After a while, I even stopped trying. That's why this evening when you said, "Come!" and you said it in a tone that wouldn't allow any objection, I didn't believe you. Then when you took me by the hand and led me here, to the middle of the wood, to this place I love, my hopes started to build.

A place which, whatever the land registry says now, used to be mine, or rather, not exactly mine, but my family's. It's a little out-of-the-way spring, which wasn't included in the grounds of the resort, being too far from the hotel and having too little water. It isn't marked on the maps, and few people know of its existence. It wasn't requisitioned, because they looked into it and realised that from such a distance there was no point even pumping the water, because by the time it arrived, it would be, if not actually cold, then certainly lukewarm. Gattai's scouts, who scour the territory in search of hot water, must have classified it as a secondary spring, and did not connect it to the heating conduit which joins all the springs in the area and channels them into the large central reservoir.

It's a small, square travertine tank, two meters by two, with sides as smooth as a stone on a riverbed and a flat bottom. And below the tank, a few metres further down, there's a small waterfall, the water of which disperses, steaming, through the fields. The number of times, sweating and happy, we went to bathe there after football games. The spring has a wall around it, but there are no guards. Climbing the electrified fence was child's play, we cut off the current a long time ago, and nobody has bothered to switch it back on.

Your clothes are there

Your CLOTHES ARE THERE, together with mine, on the ground, at the foot of the tank. We are naked in the tank. We are floating together, as light as twins in the womb. What's happening tonight? Why did you wake up with a start and suddenly desire me? Why specifically tonight and not all the other nights when I desired you so much that I felt ill and you always rejected me? Since the war began, I haven't had you, yes, now it can be told, all those mornings in the camp, when I waited after you left the tent, let a reasonable amount of time pass, then left the tent and showed myself to the men, in the sharp morning air, with a happy, triumphant look on my face like someone who's had what he wanted, it was all play-acting. I did it for them, because I didn't want them to see that they were being led by a defeated man. Actually, that isn't true, I did it for me, in order not to think about your rejection, and what it meant, I preferred that deception just so as not to feel hurt. Now you're here with me, in my arms, searching for my mouth in the darkness, and I feel as though I have a ghost in my arms. It's a ghost I'm clasping, the ghost of a painting, this nude woman in hot water. The emotion is so strong, I've dreamt so much of this moment through these long months of war, that I think I'll die, or rather, I'm sure I'll die, at the very instant I enter you, I'll cease to exist, just like the first time we made love, the first time I felt you. I died then. I died because afterwards I was a different man, because you wiped out the me before you, you wiped him out and replaced him with a man who was neither better

229

nor worse, just different. My life is before and after you, and there are two lives, you are the nativity and I am the years, before and after Lea, that's the way my memories should be dated. I feel your hands searching for me, and I'm excited, too excited, it's as if this is all new to me. I hope I can see it through, because as it is right now it's not enough, oh God, how tense I am, give me a moment, Lea, only a moment, so that I can take a deep breath, so that I can concentrate, because I know the things we want too much always disappoint, and I don't want to disappoint you. I hear drops coming off your hair and raining on the surface of the water, falling one by one, like the beads of a rosary falling to the floor, they make a deafening noise, like the blood beating in a person's veins, the flow of my own blood tonight seems like traffic on a distant highway, like a train in a tunnel, and my muscles feel hard and cold, my body heavy and complicated, while yours is easy and light, very light, you are a kite and I'm afraid to let go of you because I'm certain you would fly off into the sky. You'd fly up to the stars and I wouldn't see you again, but I don't let go of you, oh no, I don't let go of you, I hug you as tight as I can. And now you hug me, too, you hug me where only you have hugged me since I've known you, and you kiss me gently behind my ear. You part your legs and move until you're on top of me. My back is out of the water, I'm cold, I feel as if I'm going down, rushing to the bottom like a wreck, I want to get out. But it's too late, and you're guiding me towards you, gently, and I can't move, you've paralysed me. I feel like a piece of meat taken out of the freezer, wait, Lea, maybe I'm not ready, I'm afraid I won't be able to come inside you, my love. You look at me with those beautiful, pitiless eyes, and you continue. And I feel an opening, a warm little opening. It is the way that will admit me to the miracle of your body, but I'm too excited and can't manage it. I desire you too much, you must give me a moment, just a moment and I'll be with you. But you don't wait, you insist, resolute and impatient, and the hole is a narrow one and I don't know where to go, until something opens, there, I feel something opening gently, like the bud of a rose opening in the morning, suddenly the whole world becomes warm and damp, like being in water, but more than in water, and I'm there. I'm inside you.

I've slipped inside like a cat under a door. I have to stay calm, I have to stay calm. I have to be careful not to come out, not to find myself out again because I wasn't ready, perhaps I'm still not ready, no, I wasn't ready, not yet I say, if only I'd waited a bit, not too long, just a bit, everything would be easier for me. Slowly, slowly, you move on top of me, and it's you who are moving, it's you who are turning around me, I am a planet and you are a satellite around me. And now at last I summon a bit of courage, the blood swelling my veins beats faster, flows through my body, swells the tissues, my heart, too, beats faster, my breathing becomes more resolute, yes yes, it must be like this, I'm doing it—*I'm making love with you again.*

I wasn't ready, but I'm doing it all the same, and it keeps getting better, I heard a moan, yes, I can't have been mistaken, it really was a moan, your moan, like the moan of a hungry cat, it's unmistakable, I'd recognise it even in a harem with a thousand women moaning, and it means that I'm readier now than I was before, I summon my courage, my body is becoming stronger now, my sinews are tightening, my muscles becoming more supple. Now you're moving quickly on top of me, and you cling to my neck, you move your hand over my face like a blind woman, I throw my head back and abandon myself to you. I'm yours, Lea, take me.

Little waves overflow from the tank—the volume our bodies occupy as they make love. We could find a formula that expresses us, you and I making love are equivalent to the quantity of water in the tank minus what overflows. Yes, you and I making love are the equivalent of this material, we are the water overflowing, and the water overflowing is the equivalent of you and me making love. This water sustains us and drives us, from top to bottom it's equal to the weight of the water displaced. I don't know if it has anything to do with Archimedes, in my opinion it's more to do with you, Lea. It's more to do with you, and with me, too. And now your body is breathing inside me, there, it seems to me that I've stopped thinking, it seems to me rather that I'm swimming effortlessly in the hot water that has given birth to your beauty. I throw my head back and rest it against the travertine edge of the tank and you gasp and sigh on top of me, there are no stars on this night of love, no moon, no fireflies, there is only you.

But something's wrong.

I feel something.

At the back of my throat.

Oh God, there's something at the back of my throat.

Wait, Lea, wait, there's something. Stop a second. Let me see.

I recognise the taste, like rust … I feel as though I have a red-hot poker down my throat.

It's blood. Blood.

Only blood. All blood. Blood running down from my nose into my throat, flowing down and filling my mouth, and my stomach, so much blood I can't swallow it. And you are moving ever more quickly on top of me. And the water is overflowing from the tank.

Stop, Lea. Stop. I may be dying, I'm dying inside you. Apart from when I had to change the flowers with my grandmother in the family chapel and I read my name on the tombstone, I never died before now. I'm dying like Fede that summer's day, the circle of life is closing, Lea, the wheel of time is winding down, the ring of the chain no longer holds, it's breaking, I'm dying, Lea, and with me my story also ends and with it all the stories that have gone before me.

"Stop, Lea, I'm dying."

"What?"

"I'm dying."

"Me, too, don't stop, I'm nearly there … "

"Stop, Lea, I beg you. Stop."

"What do you mean?"

"Stop."

I can't swallow my blood, there's too much of it, I feel like vomiting, my stomach is full of blood. It's a hot bitter froth, like the gall that's boiling in my throat. I feel as if I'm choking. I'll choke to death if you don't stop.

I pull my head up and now the blood starts to come out of my nose. And it doesn't come out like the way it used to when I was a schoolboy and the sun reappeared in March. It comes out with a rage that seems like the revenge of a jealous god. A god who is jealous of you. It comes out with incredible pressure, it gushes in the darkness and turns the water red, even though there's little light and I can't see clearly, with the eyes of my soul I know that the water is turning red, like the Trasimeno and the Arbia, it's turning this little tank red after the battle of our bodies. I'm soiling your face and hair and lips with blood. It's horrible to see your angelic face spattered with blood, my blood, it's like seeing the Madonna spattered with mud, it's an outrage, it's the last thing I'd want to see. The haemorrhage doesn't stop, and neither do you.

"Keep going, I'm nearly there."

You gasp, still on top of me.

I feel as if I'm going. I don't have any strength. I can't even breathe, I have to do something, I have to decide if I want to live or make love with you.

I have to choose—me or you.

With my last ounce of strength, I take you by the shoulders and push you away.

Now we are looking at each other in silence, panting in the corners of the tank, like two exhausted boxers in the corners of the ring. I hear your heavy breathing. I get my breath back. Time passes. I don't know how long we stay there like that. The haemorrhage slows down. The blood has almost stopped running. There, it's stopped completely.

I'll go

"I'LL GO," she says.

We're all sitting round the fire and she is trying to revive the embers with a little stick from the tent. I see the flames dancing in the corners of her eyes.

"I'll go," she says again.

No one says anything. Because they all know that when Lea says something, that's it.

"Go where?" Conti asks.

"Into the hole," Lea replies. "I'll go."

The flames of the fire light their dark faces.

"You could barely fit a dog in there," Sante says.

"If Beelzebub went in," Lea says, "so can I." And she says it slowly, as if talking to the insane.

"That's just a story, Lea," I say. "I don't even know if it's true."

"You always told me the story, didn't you? And that's enough for me," and she makes a little pause in the middle, as if, between one sentence and the next, she has swallowed a hazelnut she had in her mouth. "I'll avenge poor Beelzebub," she goes on, her eyes still fixed on the flames.

"Beelzebub was your grandfather's dog, right?" Palombo asks.

"My grandfather's twin brother," I say, "but I'd rather not talk about it."

"*Bien*," Antoine says, "*nous savons que le tunnel conduit sous la station thermale. Mais nous ne savons pas où. Comment tu veux*

235

le faire?" He's already accepted the fact that Lea's decision is final.

"Do you have a plan?" Tito asks.

"I'll go down into the hole and carry on until I'm right underneath. If there's a way in, there must be a way out. And I'll find it. I'll turn off that damned tap once and for all. I'll take with me the charge we stole from the warehouse in the travertine quarry. I'll put it in the underground cellars, in the spa's central pump. And boom! With the pressure that's under there, the water will sweep everything away. Gattai, his damned spa and this absurd war."

"I can't let you go," I say. "If anything happened to you, I'd never forgive myself." I sound like a character in a film.

"We have to try," Garrone says. "We've lost the war, there's no getting around that."

"*À la guerre comme à la guerre,*" Antoine says, taking a solid swig from his flask of brandy.

"What if we surrendered?" Palombo says. "We put up a good fight. That's all that counts, isn't it?"

"We're not going to surrender," Garrone says. "Let her try."

I look at Lea, sitting in silence, waiting for a reaction from me. Not approval or permission, what she wants at this moment is freedom.

We're almost there

W E'RE ALMOST THERE. Lea is about to go down into the hole. She is walking a few metres ahead of me across the bleak clearing. It's a mild night, with a full moon that falls on the earth like marble dust. There is so much light that the olive trees provide shade. A timid hare runs across the white clearing. She is walking ahead of me, walking like years ago, when we were young lovers camping on the island of Giglio and I watched her climbing like a doe between the myrtles and the broom. Except that, compared to then, this time I'm not the one who lets her go in front of me to enjoy the sight of her lovely arse. No, this time she's the one who goes in front, and that's it. She's the one who doesn't wait for me, who has stronger lungs and legs than me. She's the one who decided who goes in front and who behind. She's the only one. It's a bitter pill to swallow. We've been walking since one in the morning. Without exchanging a single word. All I can hear is her steps rustling lightly on the ground. Her boots crushing the dried branches. And my heavy legs and head, crammed with dark thoughts. The moon is high in the sky and down in the valley the pale ridges shine like the crests of waves breaking offshore. We've already left the ruined kiln behind us, and now we're crossing the field filled with large stones that look like meteorites. In a while, we will enter the wood and reach *the pit*, the hole, the target, the origin and end of all things. The hole which a psychoanalyst would say symbolises my mother, and with her all the vaginas in the world, the hole that could swallow Lea and our mission, the hole that could mean victory or defeat.

The undergrowth bars our way, slowing us down, but Lea keeps going regardless. She overdoes it, angrily pushing aside the branches and fronds, oblivious to the fact that as they spring back they hit me in the face and I have to cover myself with the back of my hand in order not to lose an eye. Here is the dry bank of the stream, here is the large beech tree opening its arms in the middle of the clearing. No witches dancing naked, only the open eyes of a screech owl glowing in the darkness. I feel as if we're in a documentary film with no plot or characters.

Don't go, Lea, don't go. You still have time. Do you remember when you told me you liked my teeth? And that August bank holiday when we quarrelled and then made up and ate fish on the shores of the lake, do you remember? And that photograph I took of you leaning against a wall near the large painted wheel of a cart? Do you remember? I'd like to shout it out with all the breath I still have in my lungs. But not a sound emerges from my mouth.

And Lea is there, on the threshold of the hole. The cone of light from the torch illumines the edge of the pit. Lea turns. She looks at me with those eyes that send shivers down my spine. Her slender legs, the belt with the steel snap hook round her waist. The acetylene torch, the knife tied to her calf, the rucksack with the explosive—the equipment is all ready. Lea ties the rope to a solid oak branch with a bowline knot. She snaps the steel hook shut. Then she pulls hard, to make sure the knot and the rope will hold—it would support an ox.

She looks at me the way a mother looks at a child about to go off to summer camp. She comes softly towards me and plants a little kiss next to my ear. She runs her hand through my hair, gently, without passion. I'd like to tell her a whole lot of things, things that don't come to me at the moment, things I didn't say when it *was* the moment. Things it's too late to say now. So this goodbye of ours passes in silence, with all the gravity of a farewell. There's barely time for a last, irrevocable look. Lea plunges into the hole, the light of the torch is swallowed by the darkness, loose mould rushes into the void, the rope goes taut under the weight of her slender body. And she is no longer there.

It isn't true that machines are digital and life analogue, not always. Discrete states, on and off, zero-one, that's how machines function. Yet human beings also function that way. A minute earlier, Lea was with me, a moment later she's no longer there, if you make love to a girl, a moment earlier you're a son, a moment later, a father. Son-father, healthy-sick, alive-dead. Even life works in binary terms.

Seeing Lea go down into that hole isn't like seeing a wife go into the kitchen to make dinner, or a diver throw herself off the springboard and vanish in a cylindrical splash, and nor is it like seeing a pretty girl vanish round the corner. Dinner will soon be on the table, the diver will come back up in a moment, you'll see the girl again somewhere else.

Lea, though, has gone down below, she's gone down and that's it. She's disappeared in the most horrible way. As soon as she disappeared into that hole, I felt more alone than I've ever felt in my life, not even when I was five years old and lost my mother at the supermarket did I feel so alone. I'm not scared, I don't feel pain, or sorrow. I feel alone. Alone. A solitude so great that it swallows everything else. I've been caught in a blizzard of solitude on the edge of that hole, it descends over the world and covers everything, my thoughts, my heartbeats, the hills, the woods and even the moon.

I lean over the edge of the hole, but there's only darkness and silence, and nothing else.

"LEA! LEAAAAA! LEAAAAAAAAAAAA!"

There, the cry I had stifled in my lungs comes back up again. So it really was me who came with you to this place, who saw you disappear down below. Because for a moment I'd been afraid that the sad young man walking across the clearing two steps behind that beautiful girl wasn't me. The young man who was walking with his eyes lowered and his arms dangling, who should have held himself straighter. I swear that when I saw him reflected in the pool at the foot of the beech tree I wondered who the young man with you actually was.

So that young man was me, yes, now I'm sure of it, it was really me, even if sometimes I have difficulty recognising myself. But yes, it's mine, this voice weeping in the night. This voice which has come after having abandoned me, which comes back and rends the darkness, makes the moon tremble, makes the birds fly away and the leaves fall.

My voice cries out your name.

But you have gone, my Lea has gone, like a star swallowed up by a black hole.

The reasons for the defeat

THE REASONS FOR THE DEFEAT were many and varied. Usually when you win you win for one reason only, when you lose, on the other hand, you lose always for more than one reason. It was above all a question of gross errors of judgment, scarcity of material, poor fighting skills, naivety about strategy, perfunctory reading of Sun Tzu, lack of staying power in the medium to long term, motivational crises, plus, let's admit it, my weak leadership abilities, but above all, general and widespread human failings. Perhaps, when you come down to it, the way of revolution is simpler than it seems—shoot all those in uniform and then, only then, those wearing hats. That was Sante's plan at the beginning, and although I found it a bit rough and ready at the time, I'd totally reinstate it today.

Peace is a home match, war an away game. You fight outside your comfort zone. And being outside your comfort zone creates fear. Because beyond that barrier, you won't meet only the enemy, you will also meet yourself. And it might be an ugly encounter. Going to war with someone is a bit like going on holiday, I mean, it's for sure that you'll have a chance to get to know people. And it's only now that we have fought and lost the war that I can say I really got to know my friends. And myself, too, unfortunately.

I'm not saying that everything we did was wrong, no, what we did is in the history books, the kind that don't get written. And this is even more to our credit. If, on rainy days, our children and grandchildren are patient enough, and compassionate enough, to listen to us we'll tell them all about it. Perhaps historical perspective will make everything clearer and it will be possible to speak of this guerrilla war as a social seedbed, a human experiment, a piece of avant-garde situationist theatre, or whatever. Of course, it depends on whether you're judging the man or the work, but let's leave these tricky questions to retired soldiers, doctors propping up the bar and other scientists of history, who have the deluded idea that they can treat the past as an exact science, forgetting that there was a day in which the past was the present, and as such, impossible to see clearly. In any case, it was absurd to think that a gang of student partisans could prevail over the bureaucracy of thermal capitalism. It was absurd to think that a partisan war could defeat Nazism without the militaristic swagger of the Allies. Especially if we take into account our total lack of awareness. We thought we were fighting a local war, without realising that it was global, we still believed in the plots of the old Westerns, the good guys on one side and the bad guys on the other, Indians against the Seventh Cavalry, rich against poor, servants against masters, the just against the wicked … We were under the impression that we were fighting a thermal guerrilla war, but we hadn't understood. None of us had understood that before you wage a war, you have to understand it, to study it. The old categories by which we fought were unfit for purpose, patriotism and heroism as unusable as rusty muskets. We needed to grasp the new criteria of war, rewrite Sun Tzu and his stratagems, revise the rules of engagement and overcome the old outdated conventions. In the era of elite standardisation, symbolised by the phrase 'exclusive for everyone', it wasn't possible to separate the civilians from the military, you couldn't export democracy, all you could do was import dictatorship. We had committed the sin of shortsightedness—none of us had seen straight. The one winning strategy with which to fight and win a true *glocal* war like ours was not to contain the centrifugal thrust of the global within the centripetal thrust of the local. Desistance was the winning strategy. Desist desist desist. There is no other way. Desist from the fight in order to win the war. Unfortunately I realised it too late, only taking stock of the situation when it was already all over. It wasn't Sun Tzu we should have looked at, but Mahatma Gandhi, he was the keystone. Desistance is the one practicable path to revolution. Only by practising desistance can we really bring the capitalist enemy to his knees. Because while we desist, the war continues by itself, just as the day continues while you're downloading a film from the Internet. Outwardly mild desistance doesn't arouse suspicions, but is a thousand times more effective than any terrorist act. You just have to desist from desisting, that's the concept. Surrender to consumerism, conformism, tourism, celebrity culture, soft-centred liberalism, bipartisanship, the high cost of living, expensive petrol, inflation, globalisation, privatisation, centralisation, payment by instalments, surrender to everything. Surrendering will lead you to ultimate victory, I'm certain of that. You just have to consume as much as possible, stop recycling, throw an object away even if you could mend it, take your car even for short distances, and when possible, even more than one car per person, leave the lights on and the heating and the air conditioning, perhaps with the windows open out of contempt for the Carnot cycle, start the dishwasher without waiting for it to be fully loaded, take a bath instead of a shower, never drink water from the tap but only expensive mineral water, possibly from a fjord, and other acts of that nature.

Apparently innocuous acts, which seem to be on the common agenda, but actually undermine the system and hasten the end. Erode society from within, dismantle the great Meccano by putting one screw in your pocket at a time, waste resources and devastate the planet without seeming to, produce wealth in the short term and poverty in the long term, gather today in order to sow tomorrow. It's the hen I want, or rather, the chicken, roasted, I really don't know what to do with the egg. Only in this way will we pave the way to disaster and lay the foundation for a future rebirth.

It is the tame consumer who is the true prototype of the revolutionary, the average man is Superman, the common citizen the suicide bomber of society, and how. There's really no need to blow yourself up in a supermarket, just go to the supermarket, take your wife to IKEA, your children to Euro Disney, take out a subscription to Sky, take a trip to Mediaworld at Christmastime. And sooner or later, all this will end. It's just a matter of time.

Dead dinosaurs

D EAD DINOSAURS. And rotted plants. That's what burns in our engines, that's why people are at each other's throats, that's what rules the world, that's what has saved and ruined nations. Oil, black gold, it's what we all believe in. But when you get down to it, there's nothing noble about it, it's just dying matter, the result of patient entropy—decomposed brachiosauruses, soaked horsetails, reeds and water lilies that have gone off. It just takes time, a lot of time and they're all good for something. Give me the time that nature has and I'll show you what I get out, apart from oil. A brontosaurus is barely enough to take a bus on an excursion to San Marino and back, a little Jurassic rodent moves a pick-up truck from the farm to the village fête, with a triceratops any idiot can waltz around in his Golf GT, that's how things go. We're talking about sacrificing the dead for the living, of obscure procedures to tame an even more obscure power which lies in the depths of the earth and moves the machinery of the world's engine. Oil is the bad conscience of mankind, the id of civilisation, black sludge made up of nothing but instinct and impulse. In the name of oil, the most terrible crimes can be committed and nobody has to feel guilty. Maybe that's why oil is black, because it gathers together all the sewage of souls, all the bad feelings, all the evil of the world, which then fills the tanks of happy families on the roads over the August bank holiday, the hot sin that rains on our heads from the metal rings of the shower, the vice that heats our apartments and lights our hospitals. But just as those big animals that grazed placidly in the marshes of the Cretaceous period are dead, so too oil will die. Or rather, it is life that is born from death, and to death it will return, as long as thermodynamics are still worth anything. Nothing is created, everything is destroyed. And then? That's where the genius of Gattai comes in, instinctively grasping something that others cannot grasp rationally, a prophet of money, a dog who sniffs the earthquake in the air before it happens and has an intuition, as simple and brilliant as all intuitions.

Water

W E HADN'T REALISED what was involved, what was really at stake.

Behind Gattai's thermal rise, there was something quite different. The bastard was light years ahead of us ignorant soldiers. In the long run, the spa was a dummy activity, a diversion, a cover. The stakes of that battle were much, much higher than we knew at the time.

Water, simple water. H_2O, *eau*, *Wasser*, *agua*. And there's so much of it in our village, we're nothing short of a thermal power, right behind Baden Baden, Vichy and Luha ovice. This village, no bigger than a nutshell, lies over an underground sea of water.

That was Ottone Gattai's idea, to get to those deposits of water. The fact that it was also hot was a mere detail, a dirty job carried out in the belly of the earth for third parties—some of whom you didn't even have to pay—an inconvenience to be put to work and exploited while waiting for the tedious civilisation of oil to fade in order to be converted into the civilisation of water.

You just have to watch a bit of television and read the newspapers. Only yesterday, there was an interview with Van Rubinstein, chairman of H_2O Chemical Water Solutions, one of the twenty richest men in the world, who says that there are populations currently enjoying an economic and demographic boom. That means millions of hands holding out their glasses, millions of people with thirsts to be quenched. For some time now, the profits made from water have surpassed those made from oil, but at the time, who could have predicted it? That crafty devil Van Rubinstein, a few Wall Street financiers, a few analysts from Palo Alto, and Ottone Gattai, son of a ragman from Pistoia and now magnate of Aquatrade Water, *the water that makes you pee like a king*, as the radio jingle says. Many water experts estimate that the value of equipment and services relating to the sector globally is a trifling $400 billion. Dora McDry, who follows numerous water companies for Goldman Sachs, is convinced, insofar as it's possible to predict these things, that in future water will be a driving force in the world economy. Just one year ago, Liquid Financial Services announced the first in a series of investments in the sector, a plant for purifying waste water in Mexico City—a deal worth $280 million. The directors of General Water have, in the last few years, bought four companies interested in water: Drink&Dry, Osmotics, Ionics and Rain Environmental Systems. Thus the portfolio of the water sector covers the entire range of technologies which industries, the Chinese government, the Indian government, and the water authorities in New York or Rome may need one day. One day which is already today. And that's without mentioning the Germans. Look at the activities of Waterbank—three years ago they acquired Deutsche Filter for almost $1 billion, as well as six smaller companies.

"There is no platform for treatment or phase of the process for which our company does not produce the right technology."

I'm not the one saying that, but Otto Unterwasser, Gattai's old police chief, now at the head of the group—a combined profit of $75.4 billion, two billion simply in mineral water alone. The World Ratings Agency, which correctly predicted the extinction of the monk seal, the sour orange and pinball machines, predicts that in ten years' time, out of a world population of seven point nine billion people, five billion will live in regions where there is little or no drinkable water. According to the World Bank, the Middle East, where five per cent of the world population already live, is very rich in oil, or rather, was, but does not have even one percent of the world's water resources. And you just have to turn the periscope east to see the kind of dead end we're heading for. Industrialised China is increasingly thirsty, not just for water but for companies who can efficiently administer the scarce water resources. Russia—rivers, ice, and lakes. Russia is the United Arab Emirates of water, it is the real undisputed water power with which we have to come to terms if we don't want air coming out of our showers. And what is Gattai's role in all this? He has restructured everything, the spa has become a secondary source of income, most of the hot water he cools and purifies of its mineral residue, and then into the great lung it goes, to be pumped everywhere. Tanker lorries with the Aquatrade serpent logo set off to distribute water to thirsty cities and towns. Now, with water rationing, swimming pools are forbidden by law, they're only permitted at Gattai's spa. He says that, thanks to the technology at his disposal at the spa, half of which has been converted into an enormous purification plant, not a single drop needs to be wasted, because the water in which we swim, the water we use to wash ourselves, the water we pee, in the end, whether we like it or not, once it's been passed through kilometres of filters and coils, softeners and purifiers, in the end we drink it down again.

The smell of hay

I REMEMBER THE SMELL OF HAY at the Certosa di Pontignano. And I also remember Nada's raucous voice echoing in the air, and the concert platform and the people who were there, and her red cheeks and her warm hands searching for mine and taking me away from there through the olives and the high grass.

And then I remember making love on a carpet of grass, with the fireflies rather than the stars looking down at us. I seem almost to see myself afterwards, lying exhausted, drained, half senseless on the hard earth, like a wayfarer knocked down by a coach and robbed by brigands. Of that magical night I remember flashes of distant fires exploding in the name of unknown patron saints, a green corolla opening high in the sky, and my heart like a bird that has escaped from a cage and flown away. And I remember strange things, absurd things, like her knickers that had gone missing. Swallowed by the darkness. And a lingering fantasy about a fox escaping into the depths of the wood clutching that sinful male trophy of a woman in its mouth. That's what I remember of that night. And it certainly isn't the last memory I have of her, of Lea I mean, no, on the contrary, it's one of the first. Now it's the only one. It is a memory as sharp as a thorn that's been driven into my heart and won't come out. All the other memories I've managed to eradicate but this one really won't be driven out. Who knows where, and when, memories are formed, who knows the moment when the flow of reality is crystallised, takes shape and life, and becomes memory. In general it snows between minus two and plus two degrees celsius, it mustn't be either too cold or too warm. It is precisely within that margin, like the gap between the two blades of a pair of scissors, that the molecules of water in suspension in the clouds become crystals of ice and form into mysterious geometric shapes which mathematicians call fractals. In my opinion, the same thing happens with memories, there must surely exist a margin within which reality becomes crystallised as memory. I couldn't say how long or sharp the blades of this pair of scissors are, or what hands are guiding it. All I know is that sometimes trivial events are cut out of the fabric of our lives, sometimes crucial events, sometimes painful ones, sometimes happy ones. Without rhyme or reason, making an absurd garment to wear throughout one's life.

And the memory of our bodies in the middle of the hay, that's all I have left of you. Lea.

I waited so long for you

I WAITED SO LONG FOR YOU. I waited for you at the entrance to the tent, on the ford across the river, in front of the fire, at the top of the hill. But you didn't come. As soon as I had time I climbed up there and watched over that hole like a mother watching over her son's body. I looked inside that pitch-black hole. But there was no sound, no light, just a smell like the smell of hell, rising like an invisible column. Every evening, at sunset, after another day without you, I would look through my binoculars at the pink monster of the resort, and feel like some emigrant's wife waiting at the door of her house for her husband to return from abroad. I imagined you in the belly of the building, chained up in some Orwellian room at the mercy of pitiless torturers, a thought as heartbreaking as it was unbearable. Then night would fall, as oppressive as the turn of a key in a lock.

The boys didn't say anything to me. After the anxiety of the first few days, they had gradually stopped asking questions or indulging in speculation, until they almost stopped speaking to me. The war was lost, we had all realised that, even if we didn't have the courage to say it. The resort was an invincible Moloch which vomited money into Gattai's coffers. Unterwasser had hired other policemen and it was becoming ever more difficult to score a bull's eye with any particular act, even a purely demonstrative one. The army was breaking up, they were all waiting for a sign from me, they were all impatient to go home. But from certain unfinished sentences, from

252

certain embarrassed looks among my men, I realised that something had happened, something I ought to have known about but they weren't telling me. Then one day, coming back from a patrol, while I was looking at the pink monster and sighing, with grief I think, Garrone approached me and put a hand on my shoulder, paternally. This from a guy who's usually quite curt in his manner and hates any kind of mawkishness.

"What is it?"

For a moment he looked at the others. Antoine nodded gravely. Conti pretended that nothing was happening, but it was clear that he, too, was in agreement. Tito was staring at me as if from behind a window.

Garrone took a dirty, crumpled piece of paper from his shirt pocket and handed it to me. "Don't take it too hard, old man," he said. "These things happen."

And if I hadn't found out, I might still be there waiting.

The young woman was Lea

THERE WAS A HEADLINE, a photograph and an article. The headline said something like '*VIP WEDDING*'. In the photograph were a young man and a young woman, a young woman I knew and a young man who looked familiar.

The young woman was Lea, and she was beautiful, very beautiful. She was standing in front of a majestic wooden door in a stone frame, at the top of a flight of steps outside a church, or perhaps a cathedral, with a white facade, as blinding as salt, flooded with very clear transparent light typical of early summer. She was wearing a long white dress, her hair was pulled back like a renaissance Madonna, and she had a thin veil over her face, although it had been raised, and she was smiling, clearly moved, revealing her very white teeth, because teeth are important, and should always be cared for. Her eyes were half-closed, and she was slightly lifting one hand, in which she held a bouquet, while with the other she was shielding her eyes, because of that natural reflex you have when people are throwing something at you, like rice. Ordinary grains of rice. Although the photographer had miscalculated the exposure time, making them look little scratches, or a shower of little chalk marks scrawled on the blackness beyond the open door of the cathedral.

Next to Lea there was a young man with dark hair plastered with gel, and the kind of face that had features so regular, you could see them a hundred times and they still wouldn't stay with you. Glowing with pride at his catch, he was giving himself to the photographers and the crowd, safe in his impeccable morning suit, which—even admitting that I'm prejudiced—didn't really suit him. Not because it didn't fit him or was badly cut, no, the cut was just right, it was the man inside who wasn't right. At least to me—to him, I suppose, everything was fine and dandy.

It's just that not everyone can wear everything. Some clothes you have to know how to wear, and Ottone Gattai's son Otello, the hot water heir, really didn't know how to wear a morning suit. On him it looked, as they say where I come from, like a tie on a pig.

What an idiot you are

AND YET THERE MUST HAVE BEEN A POINT, an indefinite point in the sheaf of straight lines of our love, among all the things that might have happened but didn't, there must have been a point when you stopped loving me. I've often wondered about this because, in my opinion, dropping someone the way you did was something you must have decided a long time earlier. All love stories have an ending, and all endings have a beginning, even those that seem to end suddenly are simply explosions where the fuse was lit much earlier. Which is why I wonder—When, when did all this begin? What was the exact point when everything changed, what was the exact moment when I became nothing to you? I know it's difficult to say, "Here, now, *it's now*." Where, where was it that you stopped believing in me? That you stopped smiling at me? Loving me. I want to know.

And perhaps I do know. Because I have dug up another memory, a memory I didn't know I had, I thought the one in the hay was the only one, but another one had survived, and it seems to me this is the very one I'm looking for. It's a memory from peacetime, before the war, when Gattai was only a name to me. It's the memory of an evening, a little episode that I had repressed.

We're having dinner at the house of friends. Everything's fine. We've finished dinner and are chatting, drinking, smoking. I go to the kitchen to wash my hands. You appear in the doorway with your glass in your hand. You move your head slowly and wave the glass in front of me, you make a circular gesture with your arm, as if drawing a magic circle with your glass. And you look at me.

"What an idiot you are."

If I had an electronic microscope, I would put your mind under it, and photograph *your* brain at *that* moment. If it were possible, I'd like to witness the entire chemical reaction, I'd like to translate it into a formula, I'd like to section your synapses, I'd like to open and determine that it was *that* evening, during *that* dinner, at *that* moment, in *that* kitchen, in *that* house, that you decided I was an idiot.

I'd like to see the nerve ends guiding your mouth, and, at that precise moment, ordering your lips to retract a little and let me glimpse your snow-white teeth. I'd like to measure the intensity of the electrical stimuli from your brain that order your voice to assume that tone, to form that sinusoid, that and no other, I'd like to know how many neurons commanded your vocal chords to articulate that sound which comes up from your lungs and through your throat and fills the warm, moist riverbed of your mouth and comes out like this:

"What an idiot you are."

So I heard you correctly. It sounds just like that. While you slowly move your head and make a half-moon with the glass of wine in your hand.

Why? Why do you say that to me? Because you think it. And do you know why it hurts me? Because I wasn't expecting it. Because I didn't deserve it. Not that evening, others maybe, but not that evening when—now I remember it well—I wasn't an idiot at all.

This isn't NASA

I T WAS AFTER Lea left that I started having a few problems. I would wake up every morning without an erection. No desire, no dreams, no fantasies. Nothing. I took a blood test. Everything was fine. They told me I should take a sperm test. I went to the lab. They gave me a test tube and pointed me towards a little room. In the bare little room, which smelt of disinfectant, there was a small TV set combined with a DVD player. On the TV, they were showing a porn film. There was a blonde woman with a tattoo in the form of a dolphin on her back, and a man taking her from behind. The room where this was happening contained an oval glass table, a white sofa with black-and-white imitation cowhide cushions, and an empty bookcase. It looked like the house of a sad person, and I didn't think I would ever like to live in the house where they shot that film. I watched the film for a while. Then a guy with a shaved head arrived, and a black woman with abnormally large lips. The woman started giving the man an interminable blow job. And I got the feeling he, too, was having trouble having an erection. But in the end he got it up and fucked her strenuously but without much enthusiasm, as if he had to finish an exercise at the gym. I watched the film for a while longer. But I couldn't get an erection, I felt as if I was squeezing a dead fish in my hands. So I closed my eyes and thought about the last time I made love with Lea. It almost seemed to me as if I could smell the gamy smell of her pussy, feel the weight of her hair on my face, the grace of her neck and that secret little indentation behind her neck that reminded me of the smooth bottom of a shell, and something moved. I tried to stick with that thought, like a tightrope walker I remained suspended on that fragile, desperate fantasy. The wire held and I got to the end. I managed my little task, the test tube swarming with life, a swarm of identical little creatures that don't seem particularly threatening, even though it may be their fault that everything went wrong, and with every day that passes I become ever more convinced that those spermatozoa, the recipients of my genetic inheritance, are fine just where they are, frozen in a test tube buried inside the fridge of an aseptic laboratory, rather than in the comfortable abysses of my body. The sperm tests said that everything was fine. Sugar, choice proteins, albumen and a respectable colony of sperm, which don't determine destinies, but simply swim in the sea of life, as the doctor says. Sperm like anyone else's, in other words.

I asked the andrologist for further tests but he told me there was no need. I asked him if he could map my DNA, but he replied, this isn't NASA, and it'll be twenty years before you'll be able to get that kind of thing on the national health service.

Time has passed

T IME HAS PASSED. How much, I can't say. Apparently, they're going to build an international airport with a hovercraft shuttle service after all. They have exhumed the old scale model they had in the town hall, the one by Lepanto and Della Pecora. Obviously, they will have to make certain modifications, they will have to take account of the fact that the world has changed since nine-eleven, not to mention health-and-safety regulations, environmental factors, emergency exits, access for the handicapped. But the municipal surveyor says that, overall, the project was a good one and still holds up. They finally abandoned for good the idea of district heating, because even the most visionary have realised that heating hot water was a nonsense. Even the Mayor has realised that, he now has more time to walk his dog because he's no longer the Mayor, just one of the many accountants in the Party, which seems just the same to me even though they've held a lot of congresses and done a lot of voting and say they are more democratic now than they used to be. We shall see. Whichever way you look at it, Ottone Gattai is still the one in charge. Who, apart from filling our swimming pools, has now also started bottling water. He sells it around the world, with self-congratulatory labels that promise health and wellbeing to any idiot willing to believe it.

As far as health and wellbeing are concerned, they said on TV that sleeping on your side is bad for you. It puts pressure on the heart. In addition to which, drinking is bad for you, smoking is bad for you, eating is bad for you, sport is bad for you (my calf got swollen when I went running), and making love is bad for you, oh yes, that's definitely bad for you. In short, everything is bad for you. There's only one thing you can do. Walk. So I walk, *lento pede*, one foot behind the other, I let my shoes carry me and set off for a stroll. I walk slowly, like a bridesmaid in the old days. I see places and people, and as I walk it occurs to me that nothing ties me to these places and these people except these places, these people. Sometimes I walk as far as the square, where that statue by Sadat Mawazini—who since then has had an exhibition at the Museum of Modern Art in New York—the statue that was the reason for the forming of the Committee, is still there in the middle, getting all rusty like a decommissioned boat. I think it's there to stay. Every now and again, the villagers look at it and walk straight on, without going too close. Only the dogs go closer, to pee on it, and the kids, to play where the dogs have just peed. I have to say it's not a beautiful sight, definitely not, but I pay less and less attention to it, even supposing I even glance at it. One thing I have noticed, though, is that those benches that face both ways, which at the time seemed quite pointless to me, do now serve a purpose, because the villagers sit down on one side and strangers on the other. They turn their backs on each other like duellists, and don't mix, rich and poor, like oil and water, so no one has any complaints.

The war is over

THE WAR IS OVER, and no one talks about it any more, as if it had never been fought. Antoine didn't go and live in Sweden—even though the temperature there is constantly rising due to global warming—nor did he leave for some remote region of the world to fight for another lost cause. Instead of putting his expertise in guerrilla war at the disposal of his fellow man, he preferred to put his expertise in wine at Gattai's disposal and become head wine waiter of the restaurant in the resort. He says that red wine has no future and that sooner or later we'll have sparkling wine here, too, it's only a matter of time. According to him, by September next year at the latest, in the village bars, people will be drinking only Crémant d'Alsace. That may be so, but in the meantime red, although overvalued, will remain, and I still like to keep a nice bottle of Chianti for winter days when the chimney is drawing and the north wind is blowing under the door, or for when I decide to try that Sienese ham which is maturing down in the cellar. And anyway, the village bars are always empty, or rather, when I look closely, I realise the old bars aren't even there any more, only crappy wine shops and souvenir places.

Tito left his job at the Pensione Bardassi and now he's working as a lift operator at the resort. He doesn't look at all bad in his uniform, although the hat comes down a bit too low over his forehead, and with the tips he gets he almost manages to pay his month's rent.

After years of hesitating and putting it off, Garrone married his girlfriend—she would have left him if he hadn't—and moved to the city. He lives with his family (her family), because seeing the prices of property—which never seem to stop rising—he gave up the idea of buying a house. Living together is not always a bed of roses, but he's done well for himself because her parents are decent people, she's a nice girl, he's a nice guy, and together they make a really nice couple. He opened a car rental firm, he picks up tourists from the airport, Russians, Chinese, Americans, it's all the same to him, he picks them up and takes them to a few outlets where they get ripped off buying belts and handbags, with designer labels obviously, then off for a quick tour of the sights—*On your right you can see the Duomo, on your left* … before he gets them back on board their planes.

Palombo, the one who came from the sea, was one of the last to arrive and one of the first to leave. I heard from a fisherman who was passing through that he went back to his village, and is watching over the yachts in Cala Galera. Who knows? Among all those yachts, he might even end up watching over Paul Newman's.

Sante, after the resistance, or rather the desistance, because at this point I really think we can call it that, went back to his old job as a road-mender. Every morning, he gets up at dawn, puts on his orange uniform and sets off in his pick-up truck, up and down the roads of the province. As the rumour has spread that he's an anarchist and a revolutionary, because of that idea of his of putting everyone with uniforms and hats up against the wall, the authorities in Siena have taken him away from his old team and have given only a few little-used secondary roads. That may be why he's turned gloomy and taciturn. He doesn't go out any more, flees the company of friends and when he isn't at work he's always at home with his wife and children.

And I'm sorry because I know that we disappointed him, and I'm sure it's because he doesn't want to have to think again about the defeat that when we meet on the street he avoids looking me in the eyes, we wave to each other perfunctorily and carry on walking.

Conti is still the same, he now works as an assistant in a local designer outlet. He's always clean-shaven and smartly dressed, with bright silk ties and impeccable pastel-coloured suits. His sense of style is innate, because there are some things no one can teach, like for example socks matching the lining of his raincoat—he's the only person I've ever seen do that. He's really a designer *manqué*, who even allows himself the quirk of being heterosexual. Every now and again, I go to see him in his shop, he makes a big fuss of me and even offers me half-price on last year's collection. You sure you don't want to see it? he says. Really, thank you, I don't need anything. Then wait for me, I knock off very soon. We can go and have a cocktail, an *americano*, there's a place round the corner where they do it properly, with a slice of cucumber and angostura ... I taught it to them, and he nudges me with his elbow. As if I'd already agreed. No, Luca, I'm really sorry, I'm in a bit of a hurry this evening, maybe another time?

I haven't married, and I know my grandmother isn't happy about that, but I am living with someone. Do you remember that girl who said *Please, please go*, that evening when we almost got run over? Do you remember I had the impression she was looking at me from behind the window? It wasn't an impression.

Her name is Irina, she's blonde, she's Russian, or rather Belorussian, and woe betide you if you confuse the two.

Irina isn't actually from Minsk, she's from Katyn, near Minsk. And I have to be careful because she's so beautiful, every man would like to sleep with her and I get scared that if I turn my back they might succeed. She's stopped working as an escort, one reason being that those rich semi-mafiosi get tired of a girl after a while and take up with another, younger one. I don't judge her for her past. She says she loves me and that's enough for me. If only you could see how beautiful she is. Maybe she does drink a bit too much, but for them vodka is like wine for us, and they even have a proverb which says one glass of vodka is not enough, two are too many, and three are not enough. Unfortunately she doesn't know how to play chess, these new Russians really don't know how to play chess. I've even tried with some millionaire guests of the hotel, but to no avail.

Шахматы (Chess?) I've occasionally asked men sitting on their own, half asleep, in the lobby of the Resort.

Водку (Vodka?) they replied.

Шахматы (Chess?)

Водку (Vodka?)

Goodnight Charlie! (Goodnight Charlie.)

And it's a real pity because I'd even dusted off an old opening I used to use a long time ago, the Scotch—1 e4, e5; 2 Nf3, Nc6, 3 d4, after which the most famous follow up is 3 e:d4, which is an unfashionable variant these days because moving a pawn into d4 on the white is considered premature. And yet I'm still convinced of the validity of this move, because very often the opponent is tempted by the votive offer of that pawn and if he moves finds himself with a knight fork and one castle less. He loses the knight but gains the castle, and with the cost of property these days that seems to me a good investment. All the more so if he's really lost a castle, the way we have. Yes, because we met more or less the same fate as the Barbetti Martorellis, who today live all together in an ugly detached house on the Amiata.

Most of my family have moved to stay with some distant relatives in Piacenza, and spend their afternoons in a fog-shrouded farmhouse sipping tea and evoking times past. The case I brought against Gattai for causing an environmental catastrophe ended in my being sentenced for slander and my grandmother (everything was in her name) for illicit exploitation of the thermal springs for private pleasure. For all intents and purposes, they ruined us. To pay the legal costs, the remission and various sanctions, we had to sell everything, the estate, the farms (my uncle didn't want to leave the dried-up swimming pool and it took two bailiffs to pull him out by force). My grandmother negotiated, and now that we've lost everything and don't have a cent, we have to be content to play Monopoly like everybody else, 'Park of Victory', 'Short Lane', 'Narrow Lane', 'Largo Magellano', and so on. Even our castle went to Signor Ottone Gattai, who hoisted the hated symbol of the clawed serpent on the tower and converted the manor house into an extremely chic Relais Château, a kind of ten-star annex of the thermal resort used for weddings, christenings, conventions, and things like that. God knows what my grandfather Terenzio, the one who whipped the peasants, would say if he knew that Filipino waiters were sliding around on the marble floors of the drawing rooms in their slip-ons and the ballroom was being used for PowerPoint presentations.

After that story which won him the prize, my father gave up his profession and devoted himself to writing full time. He writes genre novels, producing at least one a year, and apparently they're acclaimed, as they say, by public and critics alike. I don't read them because it's always unpleasant to read things by people you know, especially when the people are people you respect and love, but if he's happy then I'm happy, because perhaps he was more cut out to be a writer than a doctor.

About my grandfather Terenzio, I say grandfather but he was actually my great-grandfather, I have formed an opinion—he didn't whip the peasants enough. But these are unpopular ideas and I keep them to myself. As for the twin, the one who had the same name as me, and who like me wanted to change things, I've thought it over and concluded that we aren't really alike, and perhaps it's better that way. I buttonholed a world-famous geneticist who was on holiday in the resort, having the full treatment, and told him about my theory of dominant destinies and recessive destinies. He patiently explained that although it's quite possible to speak about recessive and dominant characteristics, these are limited to the colour of the eyes, the shade of the hair, hereditary illnesses, as for destinies …
No, he assured me that these really cannot be transmitted. So I'd made a real blunder in believing that poor Federico Cremona might be alive again in me. Even the theories of Professor Voinea of the University of Bucharest now appear to be completely outdated, if not totally lacking in any serious scientific foundation … Apparently, his assistant was actually expelled from the university after being caught manipulating the experimental data. The latest studies on the subject demonstrate that the divergences between an ancestor and its descendant involve about four point one million DNA sequences out of three billion, and we're not even talking about peas. It has been scientifically demonstrated that the differences between one man and another are five to seven times greater than were once believed. So in the end, my DNA and that of my great

uncle Fede are only remotely connected, and if we met we would barely recognise each other.

Since Lea left, I have even started smoking again, I go to the tobacconist's and ask for a packet of Marlboro Reds. "Have you come for your vice?" he asks. "Yes," I say. I pay and he takes the packet from the shelf and passes it to me. On it are the words SMOKING CAUSES IMPOTENCE. I turn it over. On the other side are the words SMOKING KILLS. That's better already. I light one.

I'm now working, or rather I *too* am now working, for the father of the man who cuckolded me. In the end, Signor Gattai was quite understanding, and offered me a contract to clean the swimming pools. I drain them all once a month, and even if a few chub die when all that hot water ends up in the stream, never mind. Anyway they don't die, because there are no more fish in the stream. I drain the swimming pool and start scraping the seaweed from the bottom, and every time I wonder how it manages to reform so quickly. Seaweed doesn't disgust me, it's just a bit slimy but it doesn't disgust me, to tell the truth almost nothing disgusts me. Actually, if I was someone who easily got disgusted, I wouldn't be able to do this job at all. You have no idea the kind of things that can be found at the bottom of swimming pools—hair, sanitary towels, sticking plasters, condoms, earrings, mobile phones, bracelets, wedding rings, chains and once I even found a pair of gold dentures. I put up an announcement in the swimming pool but nobody came forward. So after a while I threw them away. I throw everything away. And keep scraping. Every now and again, when my back hurts, I stop for a moment to catch my breath and my eye falls on the large notice on the wall of the swimming pool.

IT IS STRICTLY FORBIDDEN TO USE BOATS IN THE POOL. PLEASE DO NOT DISTURB THE PEACE AND QUIET OF THE BATHERS WITH SPLASHING, LOUD NOISE AND DIVING (WHETHER JACKKNIFE OR FIGURATIVE, SUCH AS CANDLE OR BOMB). IT IS ALSO FORBIDDEN TO UPROOT OR TRAMPLE ANY VEGETATION AT THE BOTTOM OF THE POOL. USE OF THE POOL IS FORBIDDEN TO ALCOHOLICS AND SUFFERERS FROM AEROPHAGY. GUESTS ARE KINDLY REQUESTED TO TAKE A SHOWER BEFORE USING THE POOL.

THANK YOU

THE MANAGEMENT

I've come to the conclusion that, in the world we live in, most things are forbidden these days. It would be good if thinking about Lea was also forbidden, it's difficult not to think about her. Lea has been on her honeymoon for years. It has been one of the most gossiped-about marriages of the century. "WHO IS THE MYSTERY GIRL WHO MADE THE PRINCE OF THE SPAS LOSE HIS HEAD?" was the headline in a weekly scandal sheet. Below it was a snapshot of the couple on the deck of a yacht. "Our photograph shows Otello Gattai under the spell of the mystery girl," said the caption. Every now and again, I read a short item in the gossip columns. The last one said that they were coming to the end of their third consecutive round-the-world trip. According to the journalist, Signora Gattai, that was what they called her, had declared in a press conference that she was planning to celebrate the New Year in the islands of Fiji, and then jump on a jet and travel towards the sun at supersonic speed to celebrate the New Year several times. Signora Gattai said she was sure she would break the unproven record for toasting the New Year. As far as I'm concerned I've seen enough years pass by already, so I'm damned if I'm going to welcome the new ones with open arms.

Last year, I spent New Year's Eve alone at home, in my slippers, watching TV with Irina. At midnight we took out a bottle of sparkling wine from Lidl, maybe bubbly will take over, as Antoine says, but it gives me a touch of acidity. As for Irina, it's obvious they go to her head because she intimated to me rather explicitly that there was the possibility of carnal intercourse. I didn't even want it, but I don't find saying no easy either, and in the end I yielded, as usual. Go and get ready, I'll be right there, I said. And I went out on the terrace. The air wasn't even especially cold, that kind of cold is a thing of the past now. I remember that the resort was lit up like day and looked like a cruise ship sailing through the night. From the building came a kind of euphoria of voices and music, then great flowers of fire rose high in the sky, green, red, blue and gold. But this time there were no problems, no fires or human torches, this time everything was done by the book. I thought again of when I made love with Lea in the middle of the hay and we saw those distant fires shining for us. Then the grand finale, a rocket climbed very high in the sky, and a kind of huge crystal glass shattered into a thousand pieces with a deafening boom that rang through the valley, and as a silver shower descended from the sky, a great silence fell.

Tonight, I'm on the little terrace again and outside there's a great silence, the rifles that made the revolution are silent, the distant fires are silent, the frescoed drawing rooms of the hotels are silent. The only sound is the dull rumble of the cascade filling the pool. If I think of all the water—all the water that has flowed since this story started, all the water that has flowed since the birth of man and perhaps even earlier, and all the water that will still flow when we are no longer here—I start to feel a little melancholy.

I'm coming, Irina, I'm coming. Yes, I have to go. Women always make you wait but should never be kept waiting.

It's certain that the sky is still vast tonight, and the stars are still shining. I wonder if Lea is looking at the same sky with different eyes, or a different sky with the same eyes. But none of that matters any more because, when you get down to it, all the water that has flowed is water under the bridge.

ONE LAST THING.

Vanni was sitting alone on the steps of the castle. Relatives, friends, everyone had left. His exhausted mother had withdrawn to her rooms, his father had gone to earth in the darkness of his study. The sun, the tears, the kisses, the embraces, the funeral, his tie as narrow as his shoes, but Vanni was not tired. His temples were throbbing and his eyes burning, but he was not tired.

He would spend the rest of his life there, on those stairs, like a stone on the banks of the river, he thought. It was getting dark, and Vanni was watching the birds crossing the soft blue fifth of the sky. From the depths of the garden rose the exhausted scent of jasmine mixed with the bitter scent of bay. The stone lions on the columns at the top of the staircase stood guard over that silence.

In his sermon, the priest had said that God moves in mysterious ways and that if we cannot find a reason for death it is because in our smallness we cannot see the greatness of the Lord. Vanni didn't care about the grand design, it was the line he saw, only the line. And the line was short and broken.

Vanni did not hear the door of the castle open and close. Filippo, a thin curly-haired boy wearing ample short trousers over his thin legs and a crumpled vest, slowly descended the staircase and sat down next to Vanni. Filippo was the wet nurse's youngest son, they said he was a bit cracked, backward, because of the fact that he almost never spoke. They said that Rosa was old when she had had him. Too old, that was why he had come out like that.

The boy sat down on the stairs, put his arms tight around his scraped knees, and let his head sink onto his rickety little chest. He was like a baby pigeon that hasn't yet learnt how to fly. Vanni looked at him with hatred, almost as if everything was his fault.

"Hello."

Vanni did not reply.

"Mother says that once when she gave you a bath, she took off the bracelets with your names on. And when she put them on again she wasn't sure which of them was yours and which of them was Fede's."

Vanni did not move, his eyes looking beyond the sky.

"Do you think it's possible you died and your brother is still alive?"

Vanni was silent. Then he stood up.

"It's possible," he said.

Then he ran his hand through the boy's hair, stroked him, and headed towards the door. Thinking that perhaps it was Vanni lying in that marble bed, and Fede who was climbing the stairs of the castle. And imagining his own death seemed to him less painful than accepting his brother's death.